PRAIRIE ALLIGATORS

PRAIRIE ALLIGATORS

A Nick Spivak Mystery

Henry Polz

iUniverse, Inc.

New York Lincoln Shanghai

Prairie Alligators
A Nick Spivak Mystery

iUniverse, Inc.

For information address:
iUniverse, Inc.
2021 Pine Lake Road, Suite 100
Lincoln, NE 68512
www.iuniverse.com

Chicago is the main character of this story. Chicago has produced a distinctive
group of good guys, bad guys, scams, dreams, and a landscape of neighborhoods,
industry, ethnicities, and bungalows. The characters and places in *Prairie Alligators*
are fictitious for the most part, but draw upon this Chicago lore. A few real places
are named because they serve good food and evoke the mood of Chicago.

ISBN: 0-595-31476-7

Printed in the United States of America

Most of our problems can be solved. Some
require commitment. But all will have to
be wrestled with like alligators in a swamp.

—*Mayor Harold Washington, May 1983*

Mayor Washington,
Takes more than sewers to drain this swamp.
You're a very fine man.
You're an alligator man.

—*Lew Kreinberg, May 1983*

In this sense, Chicago was just the site of
a country fair, albeit the grandest, most
spectacular fair the world had ever seen.

—*William Cronin, Nature's Metropolis, 1991*

FOREWORD

A man with greasy blond hair tied into a stubby ponytail hunched over in the front seat of a beat-up panel truck across the street from the new Chicago public library. Above him, several mammoth gargoyle owls stared down from atop the library, ambiguously representing wisdom and death.

Unaware of being watched, he prepared two thin lines of white powder on the cracked plastic dashboard with a single-edged razor blade, compulsively dicing and dividing the granular powder. Giggling to himself, he considered blasting off solo without the drag of his partner, who was pumping ten dollars of unleaded regular into the old truck.

"Naw. Can't do it," he mumbled.

The image of Tom Woods' body slumped in the back of the truck suddenly flashed through his mind like a migraine headache, an inexcusable twist of fate that he still couldn't comprehend. Downtown had ordered them to drive Woods around town with the other guy and then take them to the Brewery tunnel. Woods wouldn't talk.

He shuddered at the recollection of what had happened next, the cold, damp feeling of impending doom climbing his body like a frightened rat, clawing at his throat until he couldn't breath.

Bending closer to the dashboard, he hungrily inhaled one line of cocaine through the tightly rolled dollar bill as if it was his lifeline to the future, any future away from dead bodies.

Satisfied, he leaned back with closed eyes, feeling the warmth, the energy. He was on top of it; this was his city. He opened his eyes slowly, bursting with the joy of control, until he spied a huge menacing owl with gigantic claws and devil-ish red eyes perched on top of the building next to the gas station, ready to swoop. He gasped for breath: it wanted him bad. His heart pulsed in his mouth. Fear tasted like shit.

"What the fuck is that?" he screamed at his partner, who was launching himself through the driver's door.

"That's a dead bird, shit for brains," the driver growled, grabbing hold of the other's jacket and jerking him against the door. His bloodshot eyes fixed on the single remaining line of coke.

"Motherfucker! I'm going to dump you with the Rev. It'd serve you right. We're sitting in the South Loop with cops all around us. And you're snorting dust with a dead man in the back of this piece of shit truck.

"Shit for brains!"

"I didn't kill him."

"Fuck you, asshole! You dropped the bag," the driver spat, jamming the truck into gear and steering out onto the near-empty Congress Expressway.

"Let's finish this business. I've been up all night and I'm crashing bad."

The driver suddenly pulled off the expressway at Wells Street, less than two blocks after he had gotten on. The truck stopped, spewing exhaust and steam into the air.

"That's my line," he barked, grabbing the rolled dollar bill from the ashtray and inhaling the white powder that had begun to scatter out of its neatly demarcated line. Priorities had to be attended to.

"Where to, smart guy?" he asked, squeezing his nose between his fingers one last time for good measure.

"West on Van Buren."

The blue truck was the only vehicle on Van Buren at 6 AM. The compulsive dicer gingerly climbed into the back of the truck and pulled the body towards the double rear doors.

"Stop before Halsted," he yelled, struggling with the deadweight arms and legs of the Reverend Tom Woods.

Suddenly the truck skidded, bumping over a curb before abruptly stopping. The dead body flapped onto ponytail's lap and pinned him against the doors.

"Dump that motherfucker, you dumb shit," erupted from the front seat. "Van Buren's one-way and you almost got us nailed by a Gonnella bread truck! Shit for brains!"

The man with the ponytail wrapped his arms around the body, his face only inches from that of Tom Woods, and lifted. Dead weight. He screamed as Woods' left eyelid jerked open and a green eyeball fixed on him.

The back doors banged open and Woods' body tumbled out, arms and legs in a twisted heap, as the panel truck lurched forward, skidding east.

The doors slapped like broken wings against the sides of the accelerating truck, producing a loud, repetitive clapping. Ponytail somehow pulled the doors shut, and stumbled back to the front seat, grabbing for anything as the truck lurched over the curb and onto the street. No cars in sight. He twisted his way through the narrow space that divided the two front seats and the crazed driver, tumbling into a sitting position. Relief! He looked up at the driver who glanced at him with coke-mad eyes and gave him the thumbs up and what was left of a boyish grin. He got no reply.

The man with the ponytail threw up onto the dashboard.

On Saturday afternoon, October 19, 1991, photographer Harold Raymond was explaining to a homicide dick named Sergeant Edward Radachek at the Monroe Street Station on Chicago's West Side that he couldn't tell whether a homeless person was dead or alive when sprawled on the sidewalk, squeezed under a bench, or huddled in a building cranny.

"They all look the same dead, passed out, or asleep," he confessed. Raymond did not earn his living as a photographer; he worked at a branch library in the Irving Park neighborhood of Chicago. But photography was his passion: his first exhibition of homeless photos had opened the previous spring at a small gallery on West Randolph Street with scant notice.

"Most people just walk by the homeless on the streets and don't recognize they're alive. One more body. They stink. Even the cops don't pay attention."

Raymond caught his breath and sighed.

"That's what happened with the dead man on Van Buren," he continued, his thin white fingers intertwined on the table in front of him. Raymond's rumpled clothes hid a body that had gone to seed. Now it had that comfortable look of defeat.

"Only when I turned back and photographed him did I see the blood."

This was Raymond's fifth rendition of how he had found the body. Frayed nerves produced anxious nodding as everyone clutched empty coffee cups. In contrast to the homicide dick and a sleepy stenographer, Raymond seemed to gain strength with every retelling of the story. He liked his role as witness, and each time dredged up new information about the weather, food smells, and traffic conditions.

"The number 8 bus was running late."

"Okay. You snap pictures of drunks on your days off from stacking books," the sergeant sneered, his diction marking him as over fifty and from a southside Slavic enclave. "Why Van Buren Street on a Saturday morning? Why not Grant Park?"

"I'm a reference librarian, Sergeant."

"I'm very sorry," Radachek replied.

"Everyone has an address," Raymond responded, ignoring the sergeant's venom.

"Where we set down roots—if even for a season or weekend. Even the mentally ill have a homing instinct. My photographs record what home means for homeless people—under highways, in cardboard boxes, out in the parks."

The cop reared back in his chair and threw Raymond a blank, skeptical look.

"I was on Van Buren Street because, until a few months ago, a colony of homeless lived in the thicket of bushes and weeds that covered the expressway embankments around the Circle. That's the name for the spaghetti bowl of highways that meet below the embankments."

"Tell me about it," said the dick.

"It was a rabbit run, full of passageways connecting to small clearings, islands of warmth and a bit of protection against the elements and roving predators, most often human."

"Last year the highway department cut back the bushes—the first time in twenty-five years—and destroyed their home. One less place to hide. I wanted to capture this act of good government for posterity."

"And how do you know so much about the homeless, rabbit runs, and human predators?" the cop laughed. "Maybe you're not telling the whole story."

"I am telling the truth…officer!"

"I don't think so," Radachek replied. "We've talked to a few store owners in Greektown and they swear you've been hanging around that corner every Saturday. And stomping in the bushes as well! What gives, Raymond?"

Harold Raymond didn't answer right away.

The cop got up and walked the room. Then he sat down again and fired. "Well?"

Raymond hesitated and spilled his story.

"I'm looking for my brother if you really want to know," he said. "He was in a half-way house in Uptown and disappeared in August. We found him in those bushes the last time, about a year ago. I was sure he would return to familiar territory."

The homicide dick and Raymond stared at each other for a moment until Raymond dropped his eyes, a gesture of defeat or perhaps accommodation.

"So you were on Van Buren Street at 10 o'clock Saturday morning," the cop started again, "And you were so concerned for the so-called homeless that you failed to stop and check for signs of life as you stepped over the body. Is that your story?"

"No! I didn't stop! Just like you wouldn't stop, I'm sure, unless Joe Citizen from Winnetka raised a stink," Raymond retorted, his body now erect in its crumpled, brown corduroy.

"Something about the man on the sidewalk made me look back. Maybe the clothes. Haircut. The awkward position of the arms and legs on the ground. I don't know!" Raymond muttered. "He didn't fit the pattern. That's why I looked back. And, of course, I also turned because of the panhandler."

The phrase hung in the air.

"What panhandler? You've told us this story four times without the panhandler. And now its come back to you," the cop bellowed.

Radachek stormed out of his chair and knocked over a half-empty styrofoam cup of cold coffee as the table rattled. He paced the room, shaking his head in disbelief. All the commotion woke up the stenographer who looked about expectantly, poised to record the endgame of the interrogation. Coffee dripped onto the speckled tile floor.

"Well, I didn't really see anyone," Raymond said, his head hung low over the army-green conference table in the interrogation room. "It was just a voice…. someone whispering, 'Quarter for some coffee.'"

"When I turned I saw no one. Just a sprawled man on the broken sidewalk. I looked through the camera to frame the shot and that's when I saw the blood. I ran to the man and felt for a pulse; he was dead. As I touched him, I realized that this man was different. His clothes fit; the haircut wasn't institutional. The dead man didn't belong here. This wasn't his home."

The big green sightseeing bus with the extra-tall windows nearly flattened the bundle of rags and scarves slowly advancing down 18th Street pushing a shopping cart filled with aluminum cans, copper pipe, and long pieces of gutter. It was a bright, blue Saturday afternoon on the near south side of Chicago. Large banners draped on the sides of the bus read: ***VOTE YES FOR CASINOS.***

The bus swerved to avoid the cart, causing the passengers to grab the seats in front of them and to slide awkwardly against their seatmates. A silver-haired man who stood in the front of the bus stumbled but avoided falling by grabbing onto the stainless steel pole behind the driver's seat. The microphone attached to a five-foot tangle of cord fell from his hands and bounced off the floor, sending an ear-splitting screech throughout the bus.

"Vote 'yes' and no more of that garbage will walk on our downtown streets," he managed to say once he had recovered, an uneasy, toothy smile breaking out on his tanned face. The bus returned to its languid rubberneck pace, oblivious of the inconvenience it had caused other vehicles.

After all, the City of Chicago was the sponsor of the tour. And the silver-haired man was Alderman Edward Devereaux, head of the City Council's Finance Committee and a third-generation pol from Chicago's southwest side. Persistent charges of nepotism, conflict of interest, and backroom deals had plagued his career, but Devereaux's unquestioned love for Chicago and history of public service confused, and frequently silenced, the most rabid of his critics.

Starting with a brunch in the renovated Dearborn Station at the northernmost end of Dearborn Park, the new-town-in-town of 10,000 affluent voters, the tour was supposed to acquaint state legislators, business lobbyists, and the press about the Mayor's legislative proposal for casinos and gambling in Chicago, which would soon be floated in the rump legislative session in Springfield. Similar bills had failed to pass twice in previous sessions because of voter concern about mobsters and government featherbedding. Chicago pols hoped that this time around a groundbreaking *quid pro quo* could be crafted that would lead to not only gambling, but also a new regional airport, and enormous bond issues for capital improvements.

Over a lunch of grilled chicken breasts and pasta salad, Alfred Neese, the octogenarian architect-philosopher of Chicago, and the originator of the city's cereal-box architecture, reminded everyone that Chicago's future was anchored in its past.

"Not its central location in the prairie midlands! Not its lake and river access! Not its boiling pot of ethnicities! None of these!" he annunciated in his cultivated, private-school voice. "The past that matters for Chicago's tomorrow is its history as the railroad capital of the United States, starting in 1848. Six passenger stations and dozens or railroads graced Chicago's muddy plain by World War II. Only three of the stations remain open today, high-rises towering above two of them, and many of the railroads have consolidated. Chicago remains the rail freight capital of the world, loading over 35,000 boxcars a day on its 8,000 miles of track and switching yards.

"What the golden era of the passenger railroad bequeathed to Chicago," Neese emphasized with great flourish, "are abandoned train yards on all sides of Chicago's downtown. Over 1,500 acres in the 1960s. Abandoned, full of weeds, and serving as a habitat for wild animals, this empty, developable prairie became Chicago's ticket to unrivaled downtown revitalization and to status as a global city in the past twenty years."

He concluded with a grand swooping gesture of his long arms that beckoned the audience to look outside Dearborn Station and embrace the magic of Chicago's transformation.

Most of the audience ignored Alfred Neese; they had experienced his sprawling narration about Chicago's future many times before. And Neese's mannered tone was about as convincing as the grilled chicken.

After lunch, they noisily loaded onto the big green bus for a tour of the near south side, from Dearborn Park to Chinatown, and from the lakefront to the low-income Mexican-American neighborhood of Pilsen and the half-abandoned Schoenhofen Brewery. As the bus tour moved along, several passengers had dozed off. A few others clutched their stomachs in reaction to the bus's near demolition of the homeless entrepreneur.

Now it was open mike time as the bus headed north on Canal Street past the Brewery.

"What happens if the Casino bill doesn't pass, Alderman Devereaux?"

Devereaux stood up again. "We hope that won't happen," he nodded reassuringly, speaking with an intimacy usually reserved for close friends. "I promise you that the Mayor and City Council have already taken steps to make sure that this underutilized land is developed for public purposes whether the Casino Bill passes Springfield or not. It is that important for Chicago's future. As you may know, the larger Tax Development District already contains the proposed Casino Development Corridor and allows developers to use future property tax payments to pay for development costs. We have approximately $3 billion of development on the drawing boards. And that's just the beginning!"

"So why the casino?" another asked from the back of the bus.

Devereaux's body straightened as he replied with patriotic fervor. "We're in a life or death struggle to save this great city, my friends. We cannot afford to cede any economic advantage to another city, county, or state. It's that simple! It's that important for our future!"

CHAPTER 1

▼

The honking cab brought me back to the present and my impending flight to Chicago. I had been worrying, still half-asleep at 8 AM after a rough night. I stood in the vestibule of the Chesapeake Apartments at St. Paul and University Parkway in Baltimore—modest transitional housing for old people, students, the newly-divorced, and other miscreants in search of a short-term home. That was me.

I was conjuring up an image of Tom Woods, itinerant pastor, community activist, and friend. His face refused to come into focus, much like his personality. I saw his thinning, wispy white hair, and heard his southern hills' accent and crazy laugh.

The phone call that had come two days before on Saturday evening had interrupted my work on a report explaining why a Philadelphia non-profit organization named Housing For People was falling apart. Incomplete projects, a bad audit report, and disenchanted donors. In this case it wasn't cocaine or incompetence but the problems that success brings, like too much money, too many opportunities, and endless distractions. They took their eyes off the ball.

That's what I've done for many years, looking at organizations and neighborhoods and giving advice. Usually the organizations have a public purpose and the neighborhoods are low and moderate income. Along the way I've picked up other odd jobs. Sometimes I get paid. I would have to say that my work as a non-profit consultant is what's left of a calling that rose up and rolled over me during the late 1960s. My aspirations for big changes have given way to the satisfaction of making small things work better.

"Mr Spivak, Mr. Nick Spivak?" the voice had asked on that Saturday call. "Sergeant Radachek of the Chicago Police Department."

"Yeah, this is Spivak," I replied, enveloped by the sinking feeling of loss that always lurks as one grows older. Who was it this time? My stomach muscles tightened.

"Mr. Spivak, do you know a Reverend Thomas Woods of Altoona, Pennsylvania, formerly of Baltimore? He's about five feet ten, 190 pounds, fifty-five years old, with white hair."

"Yes I do. He's a friend," I said in a voice barely above a whisper. A sinking feeling engulfed me. I sat down in the Victorian desk chair I kept by the phone, in part because it didn't fit in with my other furniture.

"Why don't you just tell me what's going on," I urged, wondering why bad news required so many preliminaries. "What's happened to Tom? Tell me!"

"Slow down, Mr. Spivak," the restrained voice of the civil servant replied with a tone of practiced with people in distress. "I have to establish a few facts first. This is a murder investigation. Your friend, Reverend Woods, was found stabbed to death this morning on the West Side of Chicago. Your business card was in his wallet. We are trying to locate his next of kin, and find out why he was in Chicago at Halsted and Van Buren streets."

We talked for a few minutes more about Tom's lack of relatives, that I was probably the closest person to him, and that I would notify his ex-wife if I could find her in New York. I said I would fly to Chicago on Monday to make arrangements and to answer any additional questions.

He hung up before I could ask who had killed Tom.

"Hey! Mr. Spivak, wake up! Is that your cab out there?" a squeaky voice called from the front desk, my favorite old lady in the Chesapeake Apartments. "He's waiting on you!"

I plunged through the front door into the mist and fog, tossing my beaten suitcase and raggedy blue denim briefcase into the back seat of the cab. "BWI, the airport," I said with no enthusiasm.

The fog enveloped the yellow Royal Cab as soon as we left the curb. My driver, a black man in his fifties, had on a red plaid shirt and wore a tan cowboy hat, the brim rolled up in a tight curl on the sides. I told him I was traveling to Chicago.

"I love Chicago weather," he started. "Cold, mean, and windy. I don't like warm with wind, only cold with wind. The kind of wind where you have to back around corners of buildings. The kind of wind where the trees bow down and greet you."

"They call it the hawk," I interjected, feeling at home moving through the foggy city.

"The doublehawk," he replied, his voice taking on a strange ecstatic quality.

On the highway the fog reduced visibility to fifty feet. Cars swerved and red taillights glimmered and swayed in front of us. My cab driver was unperturbed, his hands gesticulating, his voice gliding up and down in cadence. I needed encouragement for this trip. The full impact of the death of Tom Woods hadn't yet arrived. But I knew I couldn't hold it back much longer.

"Americans love money. That's the problem," my driver intoned. "They spent all that money making rockets that go to the moon, and those special space suits that fit over people. Then they went out there and spent a few days floating around! They thought they had made a breakthrough. But I say we've learned nothing."

"God did a better job," he went on. "He took Jesus without any space suit and went right by the moon in less than five seconds."

The fog was clearing as we ascended the airport ramp for flight departures.

"Countries will wage a Holy War against the United States. We are so divided, disunified, uninformed," my driver spit in denunciation.

"You may not agree with all I've said," he calmly concluded, handing me a receipt.

"Close enough," I replied, waving the receipt away.

"Can't get no closer."

I took my window seat and hoped that no one would be assigned to the middle seat, which would eventually lead to elbow fights and conversation. The 90-minute flight to Chicago was a time for sleep, reading, and daydreams.

My grandparents on my father's side had gotten off the train at Chicago's Harrison Street Station in 1887 and walked fifteen blocks to Pilsen, the teeming neighborhood of Bohemians, Slovaks, Poles, Lithuanians, and Germans that hugged the South Branch of the Chicago River. They eventually built a wooden frame house on the back of a deep lot on South Throop Street, erecting a three-story brick building in front of it when my grandfather's bakery on 18th Street began to thrive. Now there were only a few Spivaks left in Chicago, at least connected to me, and they lived in Berwyn and survived off anger about how America had betrayed them. Ronald Reagan photos had replaced old country pastoral scenes in the front windows of their modest cottages. My only sister escaped Chicago and now lived in New York with her girlfriend.

Commotion in the aisle of the plane interrupted my memories of Chicago. An older woman, with a package or bag hanging from every appendage, was bashing passengers' heads and faces as she made her way down the aisle. A flight attendant followed behind her, soothing irate passengers.

Despite my prayers, the gray-haired woman stopped at my row and gave the middle seat the satisfied look of a homesteader. She aimed her boxes and fired. I recoiled and turned back to the window.

I hadn't grown up in Chicago. My father learned the rudiments of electronics during the war in the Army Air Corp and, as a result, got a job with a defense contractor. We traveled the corporate byways across America in the 1950s, ending up back where we started in a Chicago suburb just as the country was erupting in a cultural civil war in the mid-1960s. All that traveling made me want to stay put, which I did for twenty years, attending Northwestern University and its Kellogg School of Management.

An elbow jabbed my side and I knew the battle had begun.

"Excuse me. Do you have my seat belt strap?" the gray-haired woman asked, barely disguising an accusation of wrongdoing on my part.

"No, I don't believe so." But I began checking to satisfy her. "Ah, there it is, stuck in between the seats," I murmured in surprise, which did nothing to ease her look of reprimand.

"Thank you."

No more daydreams of Chicago, land of the wild onion. My reward for finding the seat belt was a mixture of prickly questioning and soliloquy. The overweight businessman in the aisle seat pulled out all the stops to create social, psychological, and physical distance from my interaction with the woman.

"Visiting family?" she asked sweetly, a forgiving tone in her voice. She would give me one more chance.

I looked appreciative.

"No. The death of a friend," I replied, hoping the sad, unfortunate truth would buy me mental space.

"Are you married?" she asked, skipping easily to another dimension of my life.

"No, I'm afraid I'm divorced," I replied again, my politeness beginning to freeze into a fortress mentality mobilized when under attack. Stiffness gathered in my chest.

"That's the difference today," she continued, unimpeded by the plane lifting off. "Commitments are so thin, not worth fighting for. We trade them in so quickly in the name of happiness or boredom. What's your reason?"

I noticed the slits of businessman's eyes opening slightly, no doubt intrigued by my being grilled.

"I don't know. My wife asked me for a divorce."

She looked at me suddenly with a piercing seriousness. "That's stupid. You don't know? You haven't learned anything yet. What have you been doing?"

"Surviving."

"Pitiful young man!"

She turned to the left, catching the open eyes of the businessman and his vicarious attentiveness

"And you're a voyeur."

Now it was my turn to sleep. Dreams about a life hurtling along in slow motion.

CHAPTER 2

▼

A small, ebony-colored man with receding, wiry black hair sat on his haunches in the square of grass at the corner of Halsted and Van Buren, near the spot where Harold Raymond had found Tom Woods. He stared up at the 110 stories of the Sears Tower ten blocks away, much as he might have observed a stampede of Cape buffalo in his native Kenya. Chicago was indeed a global city.

I had walked from the Halsted train station, known as the El, one block away.

My first order of business, after arriving in Chicago, was visiting the location where Tom had been found. I had called Sergeant Radachek from the airport and set an appointment for the next morning. Radachek told me that Tom Woods was attending a seminar at the Urban Pastors Convocation.

Walking down the grassy embankment I witnessed, and stumbled over, the debris left behind after the destruction of a homeless warren—old sneakers, a stool, a soggy sleeping bag, and assorted pieces of cardboard. Most of the clearance had been done by hand axes, saws, and scythes. I wondered whether this attack on the homeless had caught them by surprise, one more dislocation in lives marked by dislocation.

I picked up a rusty beach chair from the brush and, with some difficulty, spread its legs so that I could sit and ponder the destruction in front of me. Cars pulsated below, speeding up and braking to survive the perils of Monday morning traffic and the deadly curves of the interchange.

"Quarter for some coffee," I heard.

As I turned to see the source of this eerie phrase, my beach chair collapsed and I found myself splayed on the embankment looking up into the face of a wizened old man in blue denim overalls and a straw hat.

"Live around here?" was all I could muster.

"Naw. They drove us out of here three weeks ago. Now I'm at the mission on Dearborn. How about some change for coffee?"

"You around here on Saturday when they found the body over there," I pointed up the hill toward the intersection.

"Might have been. You a cop?"

"No."

"Why you want to know then?"

"He was my friend," I replied, desperately trying to keep my patience in tow. "I'm trying to find out who killed him."

"Well, that's the truth," the old man livened up. "Somebody stabbed the man good. I'd never seen him around here."

"What were you doing here?" I asked, still sitting on the garbage-strewn embankment.

"Believe it or not. Mistah, I come back every Saturday to look at the old place. I spent three summers and falls in those bushes. A lotta bad memories and wet nights," he stammered.

"I believe it. See anything else I should know about?"

"I didn't take any notice. That body reminded me of the old days when those bushes were full up."

We both realized that we had nothing more to say, so we went our separate ways. He wandered toward downtown and better panhandling opportunities. I headed north on Halsted Street in search of the Reverend Lee Sampson and the Urban Pastors Convocation. I gave the old man some loose change before I left. He tipped his straw hat.

The Urban Pastors Convocation had moved three times in the past twenty years, following the destruction of Chicago's skid row and the gentrification of the West Loop. In the early 1980s, it had occupied the first floor of a cast-iron loft building across the street from the Red Star Hotel, the notoriously sleazy, skid-row dive in which police had captured Richard Speck—the murderer of eight nurses in 1968. Most of the old skid row, what had once been called hobo-hemia by a slew of Chicago sociologists, had burned or been torn down as part of the real estate scheming that had wedded real estate greed and machine politics. Upon the rubble of wasted lives and urban renewal public subsidies arose two high-rise complexes called Majestic Towers, which were built with a generous government-backed mortgage and housed downtown executives in comfortable condos. As with many big real estate deals of those days, Majestic Towers was in default.

Now the Convocation was located in an old church school building on West Monroe Street. The UPC as it was known in social activist circles, was a relic of the social justice commotion that engulfed the United States in the 1960s, including the usually staid mainstream Protestant denominations. The Interfaith Commission on Urban Affairs set up UPC as a training and retreat center for wild-eyed seminarians, newly-minted pastors, and middle-aged ministers in search of their own second coming.

As with other reality-shock training of the era, at the core of the UPC's curriculum was a two-day, experiential learning adventure in urban survival, fondly referred to as the "Gauntlet." After one and a half weeks of lectures, discussion groups, and site visits, the class was thrown out on the streets of Chicago, each supplicant armed with only a quarter and an emergency phone number, and told to sink or swim. Most found a safe spot to catch a few hours sleep and wait the night out. The more adventuresome joined the roving packs of homeless seeking warmth, food, and safety.

Many programs like UPC thrived during the heyday of the 1960s and early 1970s, when a sense of optimism reigned even in cities that had burned from riots, arson, and disinvestment—a belief that the good at heart would be protected in the vortex of social chaos. By the 1980s, that sort of innocence had become the rare exception, particularly after a few incidents of missing or mauled seminarians convinced the elders that cities were indeed dangerous places. Yet somehow the UPC, despite its location on the edges of gentrification and downtown, continued its survivalist education in urban reality under the leadership of Reverend Lee Sampson, a tall, gangly minister who charmed mainstream as well as progressive religious folk.

Over the years, UPC lore accumulated, true or not, about the adventures of the well-meaning religious initiates thrown onto the streets of Chicago. Most made it through the Gauntlet with only minor injuries and emotional scars. There were even a few heroic episodes—delivering babies on buses, saving tourists from Iowa who got off the expressway at the wrong exit to get gas, or battling police brutality against the down and out.

Reverend Lee Sampson relished recounting these antics as if they were horror stories told to a bunch of greenhorn Cub Scouts anxiously sitting around a campfire awaiting initiation rites. Each story evoked horror-stricken looks, shaking heads, occasional tears, and fear-drenched silence.

The most famous of these UPC tales concerned a young seminarian from a small town in Western Maryland who was held hostage for twelve hours by the Vice-Lords, a notorious gang that operated out of Henry Horner Homes public housing project, to the west of UPC headquarters. He had the misfortune of crawling into a boxcar on the Northwestern Railroad right-of-way on Lake Street, in search of safety and a place to sleep. Unfortunately, the boxcar contained a contraband shipment of Uzi machine guns destined to feed the escalating drug wars of Chicago's ghettos. To make matters worse, the gun buy was part of a sting operation by the FBI, and fifty federales roamed the rooftops and alleyways of the two surrounding blocks.

UPC's seminarian became a bargaining chip for the Vice-Lords in their protracted negotiations with the FBI. During one eerie interlude at 2 in the morning, he told a camera crew that had been allowed to peer into the boxcar that the Vice-Lords were the true apostles and that the FBI was under the control of the Devil. When finally released, he was in a near-vegetative state. He had cigarette burns on his arms and his clothes were soaked with gang members' urine.

Reverend Sampson told me this story with a mixture of self-righteous horror and glee that typified those who considered themselves chosen. We had known each other since the Chicago 7 trials, following the yippie's rebellion of the 1968 Democratic Convention. I arrived at UPC to find an older Sampson, a little less hair and a lot more weight—a mature man.

"I would always end that story," he smirked knowingly, "by asking everyone to hold hands and join in reciting the Lord's Prayer. The connected arms shook in a kind of spastic rhythm as if one of the group had stuck his finger in an electrical outlet."

The Reverend Lee Sampson, born and bred in Oklahoma, migrated to Chicago as a graduate student in social work, and became, in the 1970s, a community activist on Chicago's north side. He had been one of the most boring people I have ever met, and still was, but his apparent purity of principle had ignited the juices of lakefront liberals. After two unsuccessful campaigns for City Council, neither of which harmed his standing since repeated loss was a mark of liberal virtue, he matriculated at the Chicago Theological Seminary. An almost life-sized photograph of Sampson in his white robes and paisley stole, with his hands outstretched as if beckoning to the flock, hung on the wall behind his 1950s-issue desk piled high with books, magazines, and correspondence.

I had always looked down on the lakefront liberal crowd although I agreed with much of what they advocated. I just couldn't stomach their self-righteousness, preferring the gritty activism of Chicago's neighborhoods.

But Sampson and I knew each other, and maybe even had a bit of respect for each other's divergent paths.

"Tell me about this round of missionaries in the Gauntlet," I started, hoping that Tom Woods' disappearance was connected to someone or some event in the class itself.

"Please, no cynicism about our participants, Nick," Sampson drawled, getting up from his beaten wooden desk chair. "We've known each other too long."

He moved around the room, contemplative, with his hands clasped behind his back.

"Okay," I nodded, knowing he was right but not feeling up to a full admission of guilt. "Tell me who was in this class. What were they like? Did Tom bond with others?"

Sampson settled into an old rocking chair with a wicker back in the corner of his office, and began to rock slowly.

"Every class has its own spirit and its own center of gravity," he began earnestly. "It usually is shaped by one or two people who, by the strength of their personalities and convictions, set the tone. This year's class was no different. In fact, it was worse. Had I known in advance about Alphonious Jackson, I might have rejected his application."

Later that afternoon, after leaving UPC and Sampson, I meandered the formerly gritty edges of the Loop, Chicago's downtown, chewing on the illuminations of Lee Sampson. Most of the grit had become condos, lofts, grills and taverns with full plate-glass windows. The area had been renovated, gentrified, or as one cynic described, all-Roused-up, named after Jim Rouse of Baltimore, the developer of shopping centers, new towns, and waterfront districts. The condo developers transmogrified the original factory names to anchor their spots in history, like Printer's Row or Haberdasher's Square, as if one hundred years of immigrant women sewing and forming unions had relevance for yuppies, buppies, and empty nesters.

That's what made the Par-a-dice a special anachronism on the endangered species list of urban character. I'm not sure how it survived the tax increases that came with gentrification unless the elderly couple, Mr. and Mrs. Beleckas, who owned the place, received some type of special tax break. Maybe they were just waiting for the highest bidder. I couldn't blame them. The Par-a-dice was located on Randolph Street, around the corner from what's left of Haymarket Square, where anarchists reputedly threw a bomb that killed four police officers at a nighttime rally for the eight-hour day in 1886. Five of the anarchists were hung or died under suspicious circumstances while in prison. The statue of a police-man on the site, commemorating the fallen officers, became a target for mindless left-wing sectarian activism until it was moved inside City Hall in the 1970s.

That night the Par-a-dice contained a crew of silent drinkers ending another work day. The husband and wife team barely spoke English, having only emi-grated here after the war from what once was Lithuania. It kept conversation to the point, I learned over time.

I grabbed a stool, ordered an Old Style, and checked out the refreshingly seedy joint before I let my mind wander to Sampson's story of Alphonius Jackson. Sampson's story was tantalizing but inconclusive.

Alphonius Jackson was no innocent hick preacher come to the city in search of street smarts, as Sampson had told it. He had plenty of street smarts, which were cooked up in the inferno of the Robert Taylor public housing high-rises over-looking the Dan Ryan Expressway. A stint at Joliet followed. Scars, tattoos and a missing ring finger on his left hand, the result of a mishap during a robbery get-away, were his urban signs of courage. He was, in a word, bad.

Against all odds, he graduated Joliet with a GED and a bedrock belief in Jesus Christ, the Bible, and salvation. The Reverend Jackson emerged six years later from the Missionary Evangelical Seminary of Birmingham, Alabama, the home of his grandparents, to take charge of his first flock in downtrodden and largely abandoned Chester, Pennsylvania.

On October 7, 1991, he arrived at the shabby iron-grated storefront of the Urban Pastor's Convocation on West Monroe.

The two-week UPC session opened with a grueling, and frequently boring, round of introductions from the band of new recruits. Several were fresh faced and soaked in anxiety as if entering bootcamp; others had the confident look of peace and enlightenment. Reverend Jackson, surveying his comrades with a downcast eye, couldn't help noticing that he was the only black among the twenty religious activists.

The two-week ordeal moved predictably through stages of awkward guilt, emotional breakdown, revelation, and finally communal hope. By the middle of the second week, Jackson had become leader of a Gauntlet team that included Tom Woods.

Alphonius and Tom were joined by Sister Mary O'Conner, who had worked in Latin America for two decades. The fourth member of the group was Omar Jutland, the son of an insurance salesman from southwestern Minnesota, who was a lawyer in Milwaukee.

After describing the group, Lee Sampson spelled out the philosophical under-pinnings and group dynamics of the Gauntlet.

"It's not survival as individuals," he explained with a clarity that annoyed me. "That's difficult, no doubt, but most of us, with our backgrounds, could find our way eventually. Working in a small group presents the larger challenge—cooperation, trust, community!

"Alphonius immediately took the lead in his group. While we suggest that groups stay within ten or fifteen blocks of UPC on their first night, he wanted to take his group south through Maxwell Street and the industrial districts along the south branch of the Chicago River. I reluctantly agreed because of the size of the group and his persistence."

My mind wandered to my favorite railroad bridges across the Chicago River. My reverie came to a halt when the husband barkeep pointed at my mug, making a grumbling sound in his throat and furrowing his forehead in a question mark. My eyes opened to the Par-a-dice interior decor, liquor bottles and a mirror.

"No thanks," I retorted in a burst of conversation.

Sliding three quarters on the bar, I pulled on my coat, my mind returning to Alphonius, Tom Woods and company and their trip to Chicago's south side.

Little did I know that I was about to begin my own Chicago journey.

CHAPTER 3

▼

I left the Par-a-dice with a buzz in my head and no clarity about what to do next. Mine was an outmoded reaction to the old Chicago. No bums, hobos, or miscreants lurked about. They couldn't afford the prices. The reek of old urine was long gone. In the old days the chance that a public phone in hobohemia would work, assuming one could find one, was slim indeed.

But now I was in luck. I took advantage of the amenities of the new city by calling Helen Trent, the only person I knew who has walked every inner city industrial district from Goose Island to Lumber Street. We had been friends and colleagues for years, working together inside and outside of city government. Our most infamous project together was protecting struggling manufacturers from yuppie developers in the Reagan days of the 1980s when pundits believed the United States economy was only fueled by services, information, and real estate. Helen and I became drinking buddies at the Blackstone Hotel, sipping brandy and listening to one of the best jazz jukeboxes late into the night. Not until I was about to move to Baltimore did we entertain the thought that something more could happen between us. Nothing did, although my wife at the time thought so, and eventually left in no uncertain terms.

What my wife didn't know was that I craved conversation and someone who actually liked me. That's a tall order these days in relationships muddled by two jobs, high expectations, and low barriers to exit, as my economist friends advised me. That's not to say that I didn't have an affair or two, but not with Helen.

By some chance Helen answered my call and invited me to her office and apartment in UK'ee Village, short for Ukrainian Village, on the near northwest side of the city. This neighborhood represents a swan song for white ethnic solidarity in the midst of urban chaos. Immigrants settled there after World War II, many of them fleeing Communism or other dim pasts in the shadows of the Carpathians. They built churches with gold copulas pierogie by pierogie, regularly broom-washed their sidewalks, and fought the incursions of everyone who didn't look like them, which was almost everybody. During the Cold War, their children, dressed in brown and gray uniforms, proudly marched down State Street every fall in Captive Nations Day Parade. I'm still not sure why I enjoyed that parade so much.

A good place for a single woman to live. I decided to take the train.

Standing on the Clark and Lake El platform at 9 PM meant loneliness. I felt abandoned, in jeopardy. Forty years old, five foot, ten inches, and 185 pounds—dressed in jeans, a work shirt and wool tie, and a leather jacket. Tapping my right foot.

"Why Chicago? Why Now?" I murmured, staring at the small gray rat scurrying along the garbage-strewn steel rails, at home in the dark, damp tunnels beneath the city.

The station's a rush-hour kind of place, dead after 7 PM. A few lost souls arriving from or on their way to O'Hare Airport hang near the stairways and emergency call boxes with blue lights on top. Their tentative looks and innocent faces draw attention to their overstuffed suitcases or sleek black rectangles on wheels, marking them as tourists or professional travelers. Because the station is a transfer point for other El lines, intermittent stampedes of people up and down the stairways suggest safety in numbers. But that is a momentary illusion. Those who enter the Clark and Lake station after hours experience cavernous emptiness, echoing footsteps, and ominous nighttime silence.

And so I waited on the El platform with low-grade apprehension as two trains rushed past. The system was obviously out of sync, a regular occurrence, particularly when the humidity of summer or snow of winter interfered with the magic electrical qualities of the third rail. I feigned nonchalance as I monitored the comings and goings of other platform folk, prepared to take evasive or protective action.

"Why Chicago? Why Halsted and Van Buren?" the Sergeant had asked. The Reverend Lee Sampson had not provided an answer. I was bothered by his lack of concern: UPC was his goddamn outfit. He should have made it his business.

I traded glances with a young white male who had just entered my territory. He wore sunglasses and a worn blue denim jacket. As our eyes locked he about-faced as if he was in a practice drill at boot camp, goose-stepping beyond the stairway. I was alone.

The flickering glow in the tunnel indicated that my train was leaving Washington and Dearborn and would soon arrive. It was during this brief moment of psychic relief, and the letting down of my guard, that I heard shuffling steps behind me. As I turned, I was blinded by a bright blue light and then overwhelmed by a feeling of flight, as another train rushed by our platform.

A pain jack-hammered my body. I rolled over and the jabs became a black shoe and a pumping leg. I screamed and grabbed the leg, tears of pain running down my lacerated face. A voice above demanding…And then silence.

I was unconscious and dreaming about Baltimore. I was having lunch with Tom Woods in a greasy spoon on Boston Street called the Sip'n Bite. We were sharing our blues about Baltimore: our personal diasporas from the backwoods and the city of big shoulders.

Suddenly the crack of what sounded like a gun exploded behind us and somebody screamed "Down!" Glass shattered on our backs as we scrambled beneath the tables. As the explosions continued, I looked up cautiously and saw a young black man swinging a baseball bat at the front plate glass windows. It was a very effective weapon. This was the same young man who had angrily stormed out of the restaurant as we came in, having just been unfairly fired, at least by his reckoning.

Waking up, I realized this was Chicago. The memory of what had happened came floating back. I had been pumped for information about Tom Woods, information I refused to cough up—which explained the kicking foot.

Two hours later I sat on a wooden chair in a small dreary room with a tall window covered with a thick metal mesh. It was dark outside. A medic had cleaned the cuts on my face and checked for broken ribs; the jabbing shoe had produced a ribbon of black and blue across my chest and down my left side.

Before me sat a middle-aged stump of a man, barrel-chested with fleeting brown hair, obviously losing his patience at my lack of responsiveness to his questioning. He introduced himself as Sergeant Radachek, the cop who had called me in Baltimore.

"So, you screamed that Tom Woods was your friend and that you didn't give a damn what they wanted to know. They could go to hell! You wouldn't tell them a thing. Real tough guy." Radachek mimicked as if he were talking to a recalcitrant teenager.

"That's what happened," I said.

"Sure it was."

"Believe it, Sergeant."

"I'm a cop, Mr. Spivak," Radachek replied, his sweaty forehead drawing near. "And we share something: we're both looking for the killer of Tom Woods."

I nodded.

"A few of my City Hall pals that I play poker with told me about your reputation when you worked for the City. They told me that you have the habit of getting in the middle of business you shouldn't be in, something about a plant closing on the west side? You're on the shit list of Gene Burke and Alderman Devereaux, two pols I don't mess with."

I nodded.

"Help me out, Spivak. I just want to know what hot information you could possibly have about a DOA dumped on Halsted Street while you were eating crabs and listeng to the Colts marching band in Baltimore?" Radachek growled, proud of his arcane knowledge about the ways of the world outside of Chicago. "Why would anybody kick you in the gut on the Clark and Lake El platform? Any thoughts?" he concluded, his voice rising several octaves as he threw back his head and sweetly crossed his hands over his bulging stomach.

Radachek was certainly hostile for a peacemaker, I thought. But I, too, wondered who could possibly think that I knew something. And on my first day back in town.

"I dunno," I grumbled, staring through Radachek's tired eyes at the drab green precinct wall and the spider making its way on a caravan route to the far northwest corner. No doubt another trap to check for entangled prey.

I replayed the past two hours—my small urban nightmare. Someone clipped me from behind and stuck a muzzle in the small of my back while two sidekicks prevented escape. A Spanish-accented voice, probably Mexican-American, asked in no uncertain terms, "Where the fuck's the Reverend gringo? Speak up man!"

All I remembered was the ear-splitting scream of the trains. A few more pops to the head and I was down, the bobbing foot pounding my flesh.

Later, a gaggle of faces stood around me clucking incomprehensibly as the fog and pain began to clear. I tentatively lifted myself into a sitting position, but fell back, with memories of the Sip'n Bite crowding out the present.

"Mistah, don't move. You're hurt," a voice said.

"Make way! Get back!"

Two transit policemen cleared the crowd and waited with me for the paramedics. The Fire Department ambulance took me—with a face full of grit and blood—to County Hospital. Radachek escorted me to the Monroe Street Station after I got the once-over in the emergency room.

Radachek swung around in his green swivel chair, sputtering, "Listen, Spivak, let's talk straight about Tom Woods. No more bullshit. Okay? I've got five murders and a pissed-off Lieutenant chewing my tail."

We sat in the war room of the homicide division: rows of desks and silent phones. It was 2 AM and I was wasted, but sleepily amused by the turn of strategy. The last go around of unresponsive answers must have convinced Radachek that I was stupid or unusually committed because his face relaxed after my expected "I dunno" and he said, in a low voice tinged with resignation, "Let's go."

Radachek extracted a bulging accordion legal file from the seemingly random debris on his desk. He pawed through it, spitting out truncated gems like, "panhandler by his side, gangbangers at the Brewery, a missing nun, and dead on arrival."

We spent the next two hours talking about the last days and hours of Reverend Tom Woods, sorting through meager clues and hunches amidst large gaps of time and motivation. Between us a rough picture emerged from the darkness of Chicago's near-south industrial district.

Tom, Alphonius Jackson, Sister Mary O'Conner, and Omar Jutland left UPC headquarters at 7 PM, the previous Friday and headed south. Sampson demanded that teams carry no more than $2 between them, a pad and a pencil, and a water bottle. Smart teams stuffed their pockets with gum and candy bars, so I had learned years before from Gauntlet survivors, contrary to the tough rhetoric of Sampson. Some even brought flashlights.

They moved south along Halsted Street looking the part of sightseer missionaries in the tow of a black tour guide, according to witnesses Radachek had dug up. Students at the University of Illinois remembered being panhandled by a towering man and an older woman who barely came up to his chest. Tom and Alphonius were seen hanging about fifty feet south at the fence surrounding a remnant of Hull House, the settlement house opened by Jane Addams in 1889 that had been moved to save it from the university's wrecking ball. The purpose of the Gauntlet was to push people into the survival tactics that low-income people adopted out of necessity. The students—on the down-and-out side themselves—were short on compassion and loose change.

The hot dog man at Halsted and Maxwell, six blocks south, had looked up from his four-inch pile of frying onions to tell a patrolman, "They bought two brats and coffee, without cream. I told them to be careful down here after dark."

Maxwell Street was no longer the Jewish ghetto and marketplace formally designated as a public market by City Council in 1912 and home to luminaries ranging from Benny Goodman to Jack Ruby. Maxwell Street had now shriveled to less than a block surrounded by acres of vacant land that on the weekends became a street market for everything under the sun, including what was stolen out of your car last week. Blues singers drew crowds on street corners. Pork chop sandwiches were a specialty. During the week, and especially at night, Maxwell Street became a gloomy tableau of men huddled around fifty gallon drums burning urban driftwood, urban anarchists announcing the ecological apocalypse, and hubcap dealers who built elaborate, wooden-pallet displays for their wares that doubled as makeshift homes.

Across the street, the sock man—who had been peddling the same white gym socks for an eternity—was just closing up shop when he saw the four crossing the empty lot where the five-story, 12th Street Store had stood until the late 1970s. They were heading south on Ruble Street.

Their trail grew cold, disappearing into the east end of the neighborhood called Pilsen, named after its namesake city in Bohemia. There was a gap of several hours before the police report on the gang fight and fire at the Schoenhofen Brewery at Canal and 18th Streets.

Police picked up two underage Latin Aces in the back of the Brewery Administration building bleeding from minor gunshot wounds and punctured egos. Squealing tires and gunfire interrupted the planned showdown with the Canalport Boys, another under-the-radar street gang. Four people seen running in different directions met the general description of the Gauntlet team. At that point, according to the gangbangers, gunfire spewed from a beat-up blue Chevy truck that fishtailed out of gravel parking lot onto 16th street. A dumpster full of waste paper from a printing company on the lot exploded into flames after the truck veered past.

The day after Tom Woods' death, Sister Mary O'Conner called Radachek from the rectory of Assumption of God Church, a few blocks west of the Brewery, saying that she had sought refuge there because of what happened that night.

Radachek grimaced, slamming the accordion file down on to his desk.

"She don't know what happened. Just that suddenly there was yelling, gunfire, and that she was hiding. The last she saw of the others was Alphonious and Tom running towards 18th Street. She has no recollection of what happened to Omar Jutland."

Radachek looked up, his sagging face and bloodshot eyes saying his shift was over. "She's not telling us the whole story," he grimaced.

My head started to slump.

"Can you talk with the good Sister?" he asked.

"Sure, if you let me get some sleep."

"You promise, Spivak?"

I nodded, pleading, "Can I go?"

CHAPTER 4

▼

The Balboa Arms Hotel is one of the last cheap residential hotels in downtown Chicago, and its days are numbered. The South Loop is a mish-mash of a neighborhood south of the Congress Expressway that the big-boy CEOs and the civic planners have played with since the 1970s when they built the upscale Dearborn Park. Their intentions weren't all bad, but their plan, with the help of ample public subsidies, set off a speculative boom in the surrounding blocks that pushed out the remaining printing firms, converted transient hotels, and made the homeless the enemy of the people—or at least the middle-income people who buy lofts, condos, and cappuccino.

I had stayed at the Balboa, as old time residents called it, on and off since the mid-1980s. Walking in on the frayed green carpet to the caged registration window brought back memories of late nights and stolen afternoons.

I rapped on the cage. "Wake up, Sam! I need a room and you need the business."

A mountain of muscle and greased-back hair turned on his stool, revealing heavy-lidded eyes, a broad face and neck, and a mouthful of good-looking teeth.

"Nick, my friend. Long time..," Sam murmured in a drawl, signaling his long-ago home of New Orleans. "Sure I gotta room, Number 517, if you got the cash!"

Sam and I met under less than inspiring circumstances in the fall of 1985. I was doing get-out-the-vote door knocking in the South Loop and had wormed my way into the Balboa Arms. I worked for the City at the time; a few of us who wanted to be remembered as more than bureaucrats were helping out a grassroots effort to elect a new alderman in our spare time—the ward's first African-American alderman.

Not likely in the First Ward, a river ward known for its ties to the mob. But with new downtown development, empty-nester housing, yuppies and buppies, the voting public of the ward was changing.

There's nothing like doing door-to-door once you firmly put on your game face. Rejection occurs frequently. Most people don't answer. But once in a while you make a connection that makes it all worth it, like the eighty-year old hobo who had ridden the rails in the 1930s.

Unfortunately for me, I struck a mother lode of ill-temper when I knocked on the door of Room 621 in the Balboa.

Dressed in boxer shorts and a not-so-clean undershirt, the old and fat tenant spoke with a heavy accent, and as I learned later from Sam, he was fighting deportation by INS for his duties as a member of the Civilian Guard in Croatia during World War II.

When I handed him the election literature he tore it up with barely a look.

"You're sick! You betray your own people. Get out of my sight!" he bellowed in disdain.

Starting to slam his door, he opened it and shouted, "I'm calling the police. You're not permitted in this building to solicit. It's illegal."

He was right on that point so I decided I'd better finish the building by shoving flyers under the doors. Enough of my soft sell at the Balboa.

When I returned to the lobby to complete my escape, a large black man I had seen inside the caged office when I walked in was talking to two police officers.

"Hey you!" one of the officers yelled at me. "You hassling people in the building?"

Sam intervened: "As I was saying officer, we gave him permission to pass out information. Most of the people don't get out and there's no harm in it."

"Whatever you say, Sam," the officer replied. "It's your watch. Tell the Nazi we stopped by." They walked out the front door.

I stuck out my hand, "Nick Spivak. You sure saved me some grief."

"Sam," he replied, omitting his last name.

I slipped him five twenties to keep me under roof for a few days, swiped the key, and turned toward the elevator.

"Hold it," Sam bellowed

Sam slid his stool on wheels slowly across the cage floor to the peeling cubby-hole cabinet with felt numbers on about half of the boxes.

"Yeah, there's one here that came in a week ago, or so. A guy named Tom Woods. I told him you weren't around but he said your Baltimore phone didn't work."

Sam worked his way back to the window and stuck his beefy paw through the window slit with a piece of paper in his hand.

I stumbled to my room clutching Tom's note on which Sam had scribbled, "Call Him" and the UPC phone number. Before losing consciousness for eight hours I called Helen Trent, leaving a message that I wouldn't make it to her place last night. I gave a short list of my wounds and indignities, hoping to garner sympathy and to soothe my own disbelief at the past twenty-four hours. I said I would call her later that afternoon.

After I woke up I made my way to El Torta, a hole-in-the-wall, ten-seater at the corner of Wabash Avenue and Balboa Street. I dived into a plateful of huevos Mexicana, with hot peppers, beans and rice. Chicago's cognoscenti of ethnic food derisively dismissed my designation of El Torta as real cuisine. Apparently a lot of in-the-know people held this prejudice because a colorful mix of hotel workers, street people, mailmen, and bikers inhabited El Torta. Greasy food with an edge.

"Mas café, Senior Nick?" Jacinto Alvarez, owner of El Torta, queried with studied politeness.

"Si Bueno," I said, stumbling on the most elementary restaurant Spanish.

After Jacinto refilled my cup with coffee tinged with cinnamon, my mind drifted from the plate glass window facing the street theater of Wabash Avenue to 1988 and my first meeting with Tom Woods in the basement office of the Baltimore organization he ran at the time—Dockland United Neighborhoods, otherwise known as DUN. DUN was a feisty grassroots organization made up of parochial white ethnics, hyper-participating middle-class professionals, and left-over sixties radicals with bright ideas about struggle and democracy. Water, working waterfront, industry, railroads and Fort McHenry, home of the Star Spangled Banner, surrounded their neighborhoods.

I had met Tom while volunteering with a community coalition that fought neighborhood redlining by banks who refused to make loans available to qualified home buyers, usually black or Hispanic. Tom invited me to talk about a part-time job.

We never talked about a job at that meeting or at any other time. That was typical of Tom; linear discussions were not his forte. In fact, they were impossible. Unfortunately, this quirky trait explained Tom's failure at directing almost any kind of organization, whether community-based, church, or school.

That day our talk ranged from base communities in Nicaragua to the Mondragon worker cooperatives in Basque, Spain, from micro-enterprise, to working-class organizing. His flights of commentary about each was occasionally interrupted by the present, what was currently happening at DUN, and he comfortably, at least for himself, interjected me into the middle of things as if I was an old hand who had signed on for unlimited surprises.

Tom took a call from the lawyer for the Harbor Neighborhoods Coalition, a group of activists fighting speculative, high-rise developments around Baltimore's fabled Harbor. What had once been Cannery Row now was pumped up by public incentives, developer bravado, and the bitterness of working class angst about being displaced.

The Coalition lawyer called from a bar in Fells Point, the headquarters of the Coalition, that resembled a public house of the 19th century. Tom put me on the phone as an expert from Chicago who might be able to help.

"Yeah, we want to avoid what happened in Chicago with the wall of high-rises up and down the lakefront on the north side. That's what we're fighting here," the lawyer concluded, with a maximum of authority and a minimum of facts.

I wondered to myself whether anyone in this rebel crew had visited Chicago or observed the existence of Lincoln Park along the lakefront or that Chicago is flat, without a lot of views. One more example, I thought, of small city afraid of big city.

I pledged non-specific support to the community lawyer and mouthed, "Sounds like you got a real fight on your hands. Let me know if I can help," before shuffling the phone back to Tom. He chattered for a few minutes more about the next meeting and the most recent factional fight between the yuppies and the ethnics.

After a few more rounds of story telling we walked two blocks to the Cross Street Market, one of a handful of public neighborhood markets that still thrive in Baltimore, for a crab cake sandwich. We sat on old-fashioned diner stools around the oyster bar.

"I grew up in North Carolina," Tom began. "My family owned a furniture business until the early 1970s. I decided, against the wishes of my father, quite a religious man, to become ordained as a Presbyterian pastor.

"The transformation of my life occurred when I was pastoring a church in rural Georgia in the early 1960s. I joined a civil rights vigil against the wishes of the elders. I was asked to leave within a week. The same thing happened a few years later outside of Atlanta where I pastored a church that attracted members from nearby military bases. When I spoke out on the war, I was on the road again.

"I truly love writing and delivering sermons each week, beginning from a biblical passage or metaphor and constructing a story of moral meaning that has relevance for today. It's a mixture of poetry, teaching, and common sense," Tom said, not having given a sermon in ten years.

Tom became an itinerant preacher and community organizer after those life-transformative events, making the rounds of southern and mid-Atlantic cities and towns. Eventually the stress of the road and so many changes led to a break up of his family and an affair with another community organizer with similar bad habits.

They settled in Brooklyn for ten years where they started a school. Somehow, as always, the bottom fell out of this scene for Tom, although he was the last person to see through his own larger-than-life adventures on behalf of social justice. He moved to Baltimore while his wife stayed in Brooklyn picking up the pieces.

I never did get that job with DUN and Tom Woods. But we became friends as his journey continued through Baltimore to the dying steel towns of western Pennsylvania.

"No mas!" I almost screamed as Jacinto brought his pot of decaf around for the fifth time. It was a special pot for me. But even decaf could give you a buzz; that damned one percent.

He scowled and busied himself behind the counter.

Radachek knew why I had left Chicago but had only smiled. A redeeming feature, I thought. Yet he knew. And it wasn't the divorce, although that provided me enough reasons to run as far as I could.

I had gotten fucked by just about everybody.

An appliance plant owned by a multinational decided to close its facility on the west side around Christmas and lay off 500 workers. Plant closings happened all the time except for two things: most companies had the good taste or better lawyerly advice not to shut down during the holidays; and this company drank deep at the public trough of subsidies and incentives and made big promises for jobs and neighborhood improvements. In fact, they had lost jobs in recent years.

My job was special projects, and this was special. We organized inside government and out in the community to oppose the closing and urged the City to enforce its rights in court and collect on all the promises made by the company. The City filed suit in court along with workers, community groups, and religious leaders. It was a big deal.

And then there was big flack—eventually aimed at me. The new mayor didn't want to make waves and his advisors told him not to cross the business community. And some advocates thought we were selling out by bargaining with the company, even though our court case was smoke and mirrors at best.

Anyway, I was hung out to dry. They fired me and tried to stick a charge of bribery against me, something about soliciting campaign contributions from businesses that received City largess. Only a few stalwarts like Seth Greenburg and Helen Trent came to my defense as the City cut a bad deal with the company about the re-use of the facility. The advocates cheered because they got money out of the deal to study employee ownership.

To make matters worse, the company sent its lawyers after me for defaming their reputation during the height of their holiday business season.

I left town in Spring 1988. Good riddance, Chicago.

And now I needed to reconnect with my Chicago past, most especially Helen Trent.

CHAPTER 5

▼

My journey on the northwest elevated subway, or El, was pleasantly uneventful, except for the overweight, elderly Polish woman who sat next to me—more precisely, on top of me—and destroyed a bag of DayGlo orange Chitos in minutes, leaving a cloud of hazardous-looking dust on everything, including me. She got off at the next stop, her mission accomplished.

With three stations before my stop, I realized that my compassion for Tom Woods was turning into a job, and a complicated job at that. The cuts on my face and bruises on my ribs were proof. And things were just getting started. But there was no client to speak of, no source of deep pockets and motivation, except me. This was beginning to feel like another bad life choice, like my divorce or move to Baltimore. I had a propensity to quit when the going got tough or to jump headfirst into troubled waters.

Strangely, in those moments as we careened around the curved track on our way to Division Street, I missed the smallness, insularity, and subtlety of Baltimore's rowhomes, alley streets, waterfront views, and public markets. A kind of exile down the urban hierarchy from the big cities. Comfortable but no buzz.

I had run out of steam in Chicago, or passion, in 1988. My own staleness, as well as the boot from City Hall drove me away, despite my umbilical attachment to the city. I became obsessed with Chicago ever since dropping acid with two friends from Bridgeport in 1971 during the dead of winter. I lost control; Chicago took over. We walked for hours, the hawk biting our faces. Wealth and poverty. Night people. Blurred boundaries between the glitter of downtown and hobohemia. The soulful pleasure of kicking a soda can; the lonely buzz of a tractor-trailer truck idling in the dirty snow. Luckily, I made it back from the shadows reborn: a Chicagoan.

Thank god for the jarring station stop at North and Damen before I became submerged in a pool of nostalgia and self doubt, a dangerous mixture that encouraged drinking, naps, and more bad life decisions.

Bad life decisions were on my mind in part because of the white panel truck that tagged behind me as I walked six blocks from the station to Helen Trent's home. I guessed that my presence had made an impact in Chicago. But who was betting? The truck creeped along, not even trying to be subtle; that was intimidation.

How did they know my station stop?

Tom Woods and my compassion. I needed a partner to untangle this Chicago mess, one who was prone to bad life choices like myself. I pondered my pitch to Helen Trent as I rang her bell, a condo in a red-brick six flat on a treelined street in UK'ee village.

She buzzed me in.

It took an hour of concocting fancy arguments, subtly invoking favors due, for Helen to agree to join my investigation of Tom Woods' murder. She was reluctant because of the reasonable insight that this was a fool's errand better left to the Chicago police. All the while, I sipped exotic herbal teas and stroked her thirteen-year-old enfeebled calico cat. I showed my nurturing side, no matter how much it drained me.

After all the preliminaries we got down to business, reviewing the facts of Tom's murder, drawing maps of how the Gauntlet group moved south, and making lists on yellow legal pads of next steps in our investigation.

"You know," Helen said, pointing at our crude map, "they landed right in the middle of a Tax Development District, what they call TDDs. And TDD's are special. They're part of the casino scam."

"Tell me about this TDD stuff," I told her. "It's after my time."

Helen laughed.

"It's the new scam, Nick, the new flexible funding for real estate development. It makes a difference on some deals; in most cases, it just lines the pockets of the favored few. And the administrative costs, the City likes them. No federal oversight. Deal by deal approval once zones have been designated. A developer's and politician's dream come true. You pay for development out of expected property taxes generated after project completion. Of course, that means the tax dollars are not going to schools and parks. But that's the development biz."

"What's the mechanics?" I asked, deciding I'd better sound technical.

"Two steps, Nick. First, City Council designates geographic areas to be eligible for these tax incentives. The usual stuff—demonstrated need for development, slum and blighted. The downtown wins big as usual, but neighborhoods have received their share of TDDs as well.

"The second stage is when the fun begins. Each year the City sells TDD bonds. The amount of the bonds is based upon the projected property tax revenues that can be generated in each TDD district from development coming on line during the next three years. It's a simple capitalization rate they've worked out if you want to know the details. Then the City slips in transaction costs and administrative fees and takes the TDD bonds into the marketplace."

"And then?" I asked raising my eyebrows in mock horror.

"And then the City sits on a pot of money until the deals reach closing and require payouts. Most of the deals are solid. But there are exceptions."

"Sounds like a cash cow," I said, showing off while I stroked Norma.

"Yes. But the guys are getting smarter, Nick. They're using part of the float—the interest from the money sitting in the bank—to pay into a social linkage fund for affordable housing and other goodies."

"Doing good and Chicago don't taste right," I grunted.

"Yep!"

"Is anybody keeping an eye on those TDDs? You know the City will never make information available about its deal making unless somebody asks real hard and makes a fuss."

"Ask Seth," Helen grinned. "Information about the City's business is not part of Chicago democracy according to the machine."

"So tell me, oh knowledgeable one. Is the Brewery in a TDD zone? And if so, where's the development?"

"That's the point, Nick. The Brewery's one of those deals that's dead in the water."

We made assignments. Mine were the morgue and Sister Mary O'Conner. Helen took the Brewery. And then I told her about the white van.

"Good work, Nick! And now they know my address," Helen snapped. "I'm not in this to get beat up or raped just so you can make a point."

She stalked the room with stomping footsteps, stopping to peer out between her off-white designer window blinds at the street below and the parked white van.

"You're right. I'm losing my edge. It's those mild Baltimore winters. Don't worry, love, I'll leave by the front stairs and face my enemies."

"Cut the bullshit," Helen said. "I'll call the bad boys from next door who like to pretend that they take care of me. You go down the back stairs."

"I love you, too," I smiled.

I left by the back stairway. We agreed to meet at the Billy Goat the next night to compare notes.

CHAPTER 6

▼

The next morning, I sat in a damp, white-tiled room in the bowels of the Cook County Morgue reading Tom Woods' autopsy report. I was dressed in blue protective paper pants, shirt, cap, mask, and booties over my running shoes. A faint, distinctive smell pervaded the morgue. Dead people.

I saw Tom for the last time stretched out on the stainless steel pull-out tray in the morgue's cold storage room. His wispy white hair fluttered in the breeze from the fans in the ceiling. His next stop would be the funeral home that I had chosen from the worn yellow pages at the hotel, and cremation.

The Assistant Medical Examiner was a small, dark slender man in his late forties. He handed me the autopsy report after a flurry of double talk about rules, procedures, and authority worthy of the British Empire. I put him out of his bureaucratic misery by calling comrade Radachek, who obligingly told the doctor to give me the goddamn autopsy report and to answer all my fucking questions. He then ordered me back on the phone and told me in no uncertain terms that my ass was required at the Monroe Street Station that afternoon: Lieutenant O'Malley wanted to talk.

The autopsy report told me what I already knew. I was surprised, though, by key facts that Radachek had overlooked or left out of our late-night bullshit session. Woods had died from a knife wound to his heart, entering from his left side, more like an ice pick than a blade, crudely inserted. Puncture wounds in the back of the neck indicated drugs but the toxic screen hadn't come back yet. Tom wasn't murdered at the place they found him, although he died there; abrasions and a broken wrist suggested that his killer had thrown him from a slow-moving vehicle. Death occurred at approximately 6 AM, October 19, 1991.

The rest of the report was incomprehensible medical-speak so I leafed through until the end. Tom's shoes and pants legs had particles of dried mud with bits of hardened red clay. His pockets were empty except for a wallet that contained the usual assortment of licenses and credit cards.

The morgue made me extremely hungry: the allergic reaction of my life forces against the inevitable. I disposed of my blue costume in a designated medical waste receptacle and saluted the presiding doctor. All I could think about, as I walked up the cement ramp to the sidewalk, was the hot dog stand on the corner of Harrison and Wolcott. I'm a ninety-five percent vegetarian, who allocates the five percent to character-building, nostalgic food, that is almost always bad for my health, like an occasional hot dog, souvlaki, or chicken satay. I remembered that I was meeting Helen at the Billy Goat, and would undoubtedly partake of sliders—cheeseburgers for the uninitiated. Maybe I should revise my definition of vegetarian, I mused, bursting into the sunlight.

Transfixed by hunger, I failed to notice the white van parked on the street and the two gorillas who grabbed me by the elbows and launched me through the sliding door of the van and on to the floor. A burlap bag was roughly pulled over my shoulders as one of my kidnappers garbled, "Keep your mouth shut! We're taking you for a ride. To Cicero if you know what I mean. Someone wants to talk."

The reference to Cicero made me giggle in a delirious way, which earned me a sharp poke on top of my new bruises by one of my caretakers. A ride to Cicero was an old Chicago joke, much like getting fitted with a cement shoe. But it wasn't as deadly unless you ended up in the trunk of an abandoned car in a forest preserve along the Desplaines River or in the concrete forms for a new highway bridge. Cicero at one time contained a large population of white ethnics, some tied to the Mafia and many of whom were racist. Cicero became one of the prized targets for open housing marches, along with Gage Park on the south side, when Martin Luther King Jr. came to Chicago in 1965.

Since that time, Cicero had changed. The giant Hawthorne Works of Western Electric, that had eighteen miles of railroad track within its factory gates and employed 23,000 people after World War II, closed in the 1980s, its vast footprint of land parceled out for shopping centers and industrial parks. Cicero had also become Mexican-American, the third stop of families from former port-of-entry neighborhoods like Pilsen who moved westward along the same paths traversed decades before by Bohemians, Slovaks, Poles, and Italians.

So, why was I being taken to Cicero, and to see whom? This was the second time in two days that I had been bushwhacked, so even a smart ass like me realized that I was in somebody's face. But whose face, I wondered, as we turned right and then veered right again onto a bumpy road. Tom Woods wouldn't, and couldn't, hurt anybody.

The van stopped suddenly, throwing me against the headrest of the front seat. The side door opened, and two hands yanked me onto the ground. Gravel stung my hands and knees as I pulled myself up; somebody jerked the burlap sack off my head and shoulders, almost knocking me back to the ground. Noonday sun blinded me, but my eyes managed to make out that I was in the middle of an old freight-switching yard that had once served the Hawthorne Works. Now it was mostly empty, piles of rotting railroad ties and oily gravel the only reminders of its past.

"Hey Bro," I heard, turning my head to see a middle-age Latino hulk in a three-piece suit, his face swelled with the fruits of a life of gangbanging. He stood in front of a black Town Car.

"Where's my stuff, man?" he growled. "I got people waiting on me. That's not good for you, Bro."

I was about to ask a clarifying question when my knees buckled and a sharp pain shot up my back. I fell to the ground screaming, as gangbanger number two, who could have been a pulling guard for the Bears, finished his follow through after whacking the back of my knees with a baseball bat. For a few seconds all I saw was red, as consciousness quivered. I dug my hands into the sharp edges of the gravel, hoping to get a grip on the pain, and the situation.

"I'm not waitin' much longer, Bro," gangbanger number one spat as he walked up to me and slapped his patent leather black boot on my left hand. "You got a day to return the stash that your fuckface friend Woods took from me. Times up, Bro!"

His full weight crushed my hand against the gravel. He turned, my hand still beneath his foot, and walked back to his car. A few moments later the Town Car spit up dust and gravel as he accelerated out of the abandoned railyard. The van followed.

My howls died down in a few moments, leaving dull aching pain that ran up and down my torso, arms, and hand. Lying sprawled on the gravel, I pondered my cuts and bruises and the new meaning of a ride to Cicero.

More hungry than before, I flagged a cab on Roosevelt Road. This wasn't prime taxi territory, but I lucked out with a return ride whose driver was not in much better shape than I was. An unlit cigar butt stuck in his mouth and his head shook slightly; he dropped me off at 18ᵗʰ and Damen, at Phillip's Chili

I grabbed a stool and ordered a large bowl of chili mac, Phillip's all-star chili on top of macaroni, and iced tea.

"Tough day, ah?" the old man commented under his breath as he slid my bowl of chili across the counter. Tattoos of glorious women and proud patriotic sentiments covered his thin arms and stringy muscles.

I nodded. "Yeah."

I was hoping the conversation would stop there but somehow I knew it wouldn't. I must have looked like white-trash wreckage: a magnet for the emotionally dead and dispossessed. I ate quickly; my body craved sustenance.

And then it came as it always does.

"I know just how you feel. This neighborhood ain't the same as when I was growing up. Not by a long shot. Those spics multiply like rabbits and throw their diapers out of their top floor windows. The sidewalks and alleys stink. A few years ago a family died in a fire because they couldn't understand English. They were barbecuing on the back porch in the middle of winter. Do you believe it?"

I finally interrupted. "Where's your family from?"

"Don't got one," he evaded, looking at me as if he might have misread my physical cues.

"How about your parents or grandparents?"

"Slovenia," he mumbled, wiping the counter with a checkered red towel, an unlit Camel hanging from his lips.

"They speak English?"

"Not much. They made sure I learned English."

"So what's the problem," I concluded, taking the last bite of my chili mac. "Pilsen's a port-of-entry, a slum where Poles, Slovenes, and Mexicans settled and then moved upward and out. That's the American way."

Now he was looking at me with narrow eyes, the towel hung over his shoulder.

"Why do you have a bug up your ass? Maybe cause you got nowhere to go," I finished.

"That'll be four dollars," he snarled.

I tossed a crumpled five-dollar bill on the counter and walked out. One more disgruntled American blaming everybody else for their bad times and lost dreams. Chicago was full of them.

CHAPTER 7

▼

Sister Mary O'Conner had short-cropped graying hair and a trim physique that masked her sixty years. Based on her work protecting Indian peasants in the Nicaraguan borderlands, she was not an obvious candidate for debilitating fear. And yet that is what had taken over her the night of the Gauntlet.

"Call me Mary for God's sake," she demanded as we sat down.

We sat at a long kitchen table covered with a light blue plastic tablecloth in the refectory of the Assumption of God Church, the basement kitchen of the rectory. I had been there several times in the past for strategy meetings with community leaders, most of whom belonged to the parish. An ageless, white-haired housekeeper, who occasionally muttered shards of English, served us coffee and a plate of cookies with pink frosting. Sunlight showered the refectory through two half windows at the top of the southern wall.

Leaving Phillip's and one more behind-the-counter racist, I had walked the fifteen blocks to Assumption of God church, passing through the heart of Pilsen's vibrant commercial world. Of course I drew stares, the only juaro on the street. So what that Assumption of God was one of the first Lithuanian churches in Chicago; now it was largely a Mexican-American parish. Lithuanians had moved southwest from Pilsen.

"I'm still not sure why I joined the UPC retreat," Sister Mary began in a slight Boston accent. "I hardly needed an introduction to the effects of poverty after my years in Brazil and Nicaragua.

"Maybe that's the reason after all. U.S. poverty is different: the contrast of wealth and poverty; expectations fed by television and the movies. I hardly knew what being in the U.S. was like after twenty years abroad."

Her earnestness was convincing as her story poured out, faster than she wanted to tell it. Tight lines in her face revealed that there was another level of thought and feeling that troubled her.

The housekeeper interrupted us by clearing her throat and pointing at the old percolator coffee pot on the stove, her way of saying that there were refills at this refectory. We nodded yes.

"Why did you choose UPC and how did you hook up with Tom Woods?" I asked, moving the story into the zone of relevance. Doorbells and muffled voices reverberated from the floor above us in the rectory, a center of community life in the Mexican east end of Pilsen.

She hesitated, the stumbling of a strong person. I said, "Mary, just tell me about your time at UPC."

"UPC was really a fluke, an accident," she finally replied. "I don't know Chicago and I never heard of Lee Sampson. A friend of mine who was in the convent with me outside of Boston, told me about UPC. She left the order years ago during the mass exodus of the late sixties and has worked for the Bishop's Campaign for Human Development in Washington D.C. for fifteen years. She wrote that Sampson was a pompous ass but that the UPC experience was the best introduction to U.S. cities in the 1990s."

She looked up at me and continued. "I wrote her last year as I was planning my move back to the U.S. and asked her to help me sign up for UPC training. You see I…."

This time her words were lost in a disconcerting mixture of silence and tears. She stood up and walked around the kitchen, grabbing a small plastic container of tissues from her handbag. She dabbed her eyes in privacy as she struggled to regain her composure. The refectory grew darker as the afternoon sun moved westward. Minutes passed. She circled back to the table and sat down, her green eyes alive with emotion.

"You see…I get panic attacks, a recurrence of dread that I first felt after hiding for three days from marauding bands of guerillas who ravaged their villages. I saw too much death, too much butchery of women and children. Innocents! After six months in recovery in Boston, I thought I was ready to begin work again, but I'm afraid I miscalculated. And now I'm to blame for Tom Woods' death."

I let that misplaced guilt sit for a moment before I asked if she wanted to postpone talking anymore about the Gauntlet. She shook her head vigorously in a show of strength.

"Was UPC what you thought it would be?" I prompted, my stomach turning at the sight of the pile of pink cookies still facing us.

"Yes and no," she replied. "Sampson was like many priests I've met. Full of himself. Unaware of a certain level of being. Men!" She laughed. "But the speakers he brought in to talk with us were real—welfare moms from the projects, gang members, community organizers.

"I gravitated to Alphonius and Tom because the rest of the group were so wooden—from the suburbs, insulated religious orders, do-gooders. Omar came later. He really didn't belong. He didn't connect with anyone except Sampson.

"By the end of the two weeks we were spending a lot of time together, really good time. Alphonious, or Al as he emphatically asked me to call him on day two, had a genuine mission, and once he had a sense of who you were, he dropped the, 'Why are you white people trying to understand something that you'll never comprehend?'

"On the next to last day, before the Gauntlet, Al challenged Sampson during our reflection after lunch.

"I can remember he said something like, 'With all due respect, Reverend Sampson, recognizing your long history of championing liberal causes, we've spent close to two weeks listening to each other's social justice blues and the aspirations of a lot of folks to make things better. That has been okay but the approach is limited. I've been surprised beyond belief that we have talked so little about power, racism, the mayor, gentrification, what we see happening right outside this building. I'm not looking for the sixties, but this is nowhere close. Not by a long stretch. Somehow you think poverty and hopelessness can be solved with a good dose of sensitivity. I've just seen too much for that to ring true.'

"The room grew silent for a few awkward moments, everyone waiting for Sampson to respond. A red-haired woman from New York finally broke the silence in a quivering voice, 'Al, I think that's unfair. We all know what is happening out there. Why belabor what we already know? We need to build our own resolve!'

"A few people laughed.

"'Respect,' she retorted, looking around.

"Then Sampson finally spoke.

"'Reverend Jackson, I've fought a lot of battles,' he said. 'Battles for rights, justice, for representation, for getting what you paid for. You've known me in this hardest of cities to achieve justice. Let us talk again about justice after the Gauntlet,' he said. 'Now is the time for you to focus your thoughts and feelings for the day ahead. You will need all the sensitivity and guts you can muster to make it.'

"With that, Sampson spread his arms and said with unbelievable sincerity, 'Go forth, my friends!'"

"And so we did, after last-minute preparations and the addition of Omar Jutland to our group, making us the only Gauntlet team with four members. We set off. Al set a humorous edge by singing in a deep resonating voice, 'We're inchin' along, inchin' along…inchin' along like an old earthworm.'

"In fact, we moved a bit faster than that. Tom was exuberant. He shouted, 'Freedom from Sampson, now! Freedom from Sampson, now!'

"Only Omar was quiet. His spindly legs, in ill-fitting khaki trousers, set a breakneck pace.

"I finally said, 'Omar let's slow down. We're not in a hurry. We don't have a destination.'

"He replied, 'It's getting dark. We need to find cover, maybe in some old buildings.'

"Al poked his head over Omar's left shoulder, 'Inchin' along…'

"Omar flinched and flung himself forward.

"We walked down Halsted Street towards the University of Illinois. Students mingled outside the student union. Al playfully challenged Omar and me to panhandle the students since we looked the most respectable, that is, straight.

"Omar was horrified, saying, 'We have no time for this!'

"Al replied, standing erect, 'We must honor the hopes of Reverend Sampson that we challenge our assumptions about life during the Gauntlet. We wouldn't want to disrespect him, would we?'

"And so we panhandled, with very little success. Out of the corner of my eye, I saw Al and Tom breaking into laughter as students looked at us without contributing, with a gaze of dumbness, fear, and distaste. In fact, one neat-as-a-button student said under his breath, 'Get a job,' as he passed us by.

"I think we netted about a dollar and a modest loss of self-esteem. Omar, however, was about to burst into rage or tears or both.

"Let's move it, he ordered, in a voice of authority none of us had experienced or even believed he could muster.

"Our pace picked up as we moved southward on Halsted and into the Maxwell Street district.

"Al told us, 'Get anything you want here on Sunday. But they're fixin' to tear it down. Too much of a good thing. Mr. Mayor don't like the look of it. Too messy, I guess.'

"We pooled our meager change and bought coffee and a sandwich from a Greek at the ramshackle hot dog stand and then walked across a big empty lot, passing a man in blue overalls and a stocking cap who sold socks. Al greeted him, as if an old friend.

"The darkness of Ruble Street and the elevated Dan Ryan Expressway enveloped us. A shiver ran up my back. It was suddenly very quiet, except for the distinct whizzing above. Omar was becoming more erratic, which inspired Al to poke fun at him. Tom and I tried to intervene but we were too late.

"'Leave me alone, Al,' Omar screamed, walking toward him with adolescent anger erupting in his face. He came a little too close because Al's demeanor and tone abruptly changed.

"'Listen white boy!' Al flung back at Omar. 'This is my city, not yours, streets that I've lived on, not you. You were last aboard this train and nobody asked for you. Now you better straighten up, calm down, ease up or we're packin' you back to Daddy Sampson, that is, if he'll take you. He might just make you sleep on the doorstep.'

"Omar unexpectedly knocked Al off balance with a spastic reflex of his right arm and then ran off to the east through empty lots, backyards, and alleyways.

"Tom and I pulled Al to his feet. He was bubbling with mirth cut with a small dose of guilt.

"'Oh well, I'm sorry. That boy's scared of something bigger than me if he run off like that. Let him go, I say, that's the beauty of the Gauntlet. Reverend Lee be proud of us,' Al mimicked. 'I know a friendly little camp of homeless families that live below Cermak Road near the river in a clump of old tractor trailers. Warm fire. Good conversation. We'll be safe.'

"We should have followed Al's advice but we didn't. Tom and I felt obliged to at least look for Omar and make some kind of peace overture. All we knew was that Omar had introduced himself that first day as someone who had never set foot in Chicago. Could we really abandon him to the Gauntlet knowing that?

"The sounds of barking dogs, slamming doors, and sporadic yells in Spanish led us east and through several blocks of old frame houses, two per lot in some cases, sunk five feet below grade level. As we turned right on Lumber Street we caught a glimpse of Omar moving between two multistory brick industrial buildings, part of the Brewery complex we later learned.

"As we followed Omar between the buildings our pace slowed and the frightening question of what we were doing here in the dark gripped our throats. We were right to be worried because Omar stood about fifty feet from a panel truck, talking with two men dressed in coveralls, one shorter than the other. They seemed to know each other. One of the men gestured at Omar as if he were scolding him.

"It took only a few seconds before they saw us, and then fifteen minutes of bedlam ensued. The men pulled Omar along and pushed him into the truck. As they started the engine, another pair of headlights flashed on one hundred feet in front of them. Engines raced, dust flew up, and gunfire popped in the night.

"At that point we split up. I huddled against the brick wall of a building, stumbling through an opening and falling on my knees. I saw Al and Tom moving toward the truck. Gunfire continued, and suddenly an explosion rocked the night. I curled up and lay still.

"I hid for an hour and then crept out of the building, making my way to 18th Street, away from the flashing lights of police cars parked at crazy angles at the Brewery entrance.

"I walked west three blocks and found Assumption of God Church. I rang the bell next to the rectory door, hoping to find sanctuary."

CHAPTER 8

▼

Sister Mary O'Conner was exhausted when she finished her story, her thin, transparent hands shaking visibly. Chicago was not consumed in a third world civil war but it had its moments. I admired her commitment and resolve, and asked about her plans.

"Back to Boston in a day or so," she said, "after I confront Lee Sampson. I feel betrayed; Sampson should not have enrolled Jutland in UPC. I don't exactly know what Jutland's problem was but he didn't belong in UPC. Sampson has to take responsibility. Al's missing and Tom's dead!"

The housekeeper interrupted us by turning on the lights and starting dinner preparations. She rescued the plate of cookies.

Sister Mary O'Conner and I shook hands warmly and I left her in the refectory, a slim figure tired in the waning light. Her story put me in the middle of the Gauntlet, but what happened to Tom and Al? And Omar?

Retracing the steps of the Gauntlet team north on Halsted Street to meet with Radachek and Lieutenant O'Malley, I bought a hot dog smothered in onions, using up a couple of weeks of my vegetarian quota, and nodded to the sock man. It was nearly 6 PM, and rush hour traffic unfolded like a ribbon of Xmas lights. It was the end of the workday. Not for me.

Monroe Street Station is a standard-issue precinct house built in the 1940s and adorned with assorted new bells and whistles—like air conditioners and elevators. The density of police cars increased dramatically as I drew closer, balancing the feeling of emptiness and vulnerability that existed among the hulking warehouses on the near west side as darkness enveloped Chicago. The desk sergeant, entombed in a sagging belly and neck, barely acknowledged my presence, absently pointing to a conference room around the corner before I could even get Radachek's name out of my mouth.

My entry into the bland green conference was not well received. A lively spigot of conversation was immediately shut off, leaving inquisitive cop looks aimed at my chest and forehead.

"Glad you could make it, Spivak," said Radachek, with a short staccato laugh. "Thought we might have to send a squad of uniforms after you.

"This is Lieutenant O'Malley," Radachek pointed to the forty-something man in a pressed dark suit on his right. "And Pelegrino, from the organized crime unit," he turned to the short, excruciatingly thin man seated on his left.

I didn't know much about Chicago cops but everyone had heard of Jack O'Malley. Son of a famous Chicago fireman, young Jack was known for his brutality and womanizing, both of which had earned him several high-profile transfers. Worse than that, he was known to be a mean son of a bitch.

"So we hear you took a pleasure trip with Javiar Centeno, the Latin-King gangbanger," Pelegrino said. "How's the weather out in Cicero?"

I stared at him, saying nothing.

Radachek chimed in, "Same guys who kicked your ass at the El? Or maybe you didn't see them again," he added for the sake of his partners.

O'Malley remained quiet, a hard guy waiting for the right moment. All of this was warm up for him.

"Okay, chitchat's fine," I retorted in anger. "I've had a rough day. What do you want? You called me, so if you have something to say, say it. If you know who's been trashing me, tell me!"

The three looked at me with weary cop eyes, Pelegrino chewing a toothpick out of the side of his mouth. I wondered whether they had rehearsed this act, or maybe this was what the business gurus called teamwork or organizational culture. They were certainly on the same page, of a comic book at least.

O'Malley, signaling the next act, pushed himself off the gray steel table and walked around the room. He limped, dragging his right leg after him. I remembered something about a prostitute on the south side stabbing him with an ice pick in the back of a squad car. He turned, anger flashing in his blue eyes.

"Why the hell are you here, Spivak, obstructing our investigation? You were supposed to come to Chicago, identify the body, make arrangements, and answer questions. Cut and dried. Back to Baltimore! Instead, you're running all over town, getting the shit kicked out of you, hassling our witnesses, and generally interfering with police business."

As he delivered this opening salvo, his face turned from light pink to red, and he limped over to me, so close his spit splashed on my glasses, a frothy mixture that I had little taste for.

"This is bigger than Tom Woods, drugs, and gangbangers," he snarled. "That's your sideshow! This is Chicago. We got the FBI, organized crime units, and who knows who else screwin' up my business."

Radachek and Pelegrino nodded with choreographic precision.

"Why?" I interjected, knowing that his speech wouldn't stop without a dose of cold water.

My interruption jarred Pelegrino and Radachek out of their chairs. O'Malley stared at me with his dull blue eyes, his neck muscles tightening.

"Get out of here Spivak," was all he said.

My abrupt dismissal felt like being fired from a job and having my mother yell at me for not cleaning up my room at the same time. Maybe I wasn't cut out to be a detective. An assortment of retreads kept beating me up. I wanted a drink.

As I reached the sidewalk, I returned to the vision of the monotonous row-house streets of Baltimore. I walked into the street, almost getting flattened by a bus on Halsted Street. I jumped back onto the curb, inhaling bus exhaust and doubling over.

A wino, disoriented by the upscale environment, bumped into me as I was bent over, knocking us both to the curb. After fumbling to disentangle his limp limbs and grimy clothes from mine, he asked, "Can a fella get a drink around here?"

"Not anymore," I replied, regaining my feet and crossing Halsted.

My calves and feet ached from the abuse of the day. Even after eating the hot dog, I was ravenous. The thought of the Billy Goat comforted me. I knew I would eat greasy food, drink too much, and ingest enough second-hand smoke to file my own class action suit against the tobacco companies. I couldn't wait. It was ten blocks east along the Chicago River.

I stood for a moment on Wacker Drive looking down at the derelict piece of land where the south and north branches of the Chicago River part. This was Wolf Point, home of McCormick Reaper, multiple grain elevators, and river barge traffic. The original Chicago. Now a bulky hotel sat on the point in the shadow of the huge Merchandise Mart, owned by the Kennedy clan, measuring Chicago's progress in landfill and concrete.

Walking on Hubbard Street east of State, I entered a different dimension of downtown Chicago, a dark and musty labyrinth of below-grade streets, alleys, and parking lots along the Chicago River, with Wacker Drive serving as its curvilinear spine. This is where the Billy Goat Tavern reposed, made famous as a hang out for reporters, writers, rugby teams, and home of the infamous sliders. Opening the red front door, I took another ten steps down into the smoky, noisy combination bar and greasy spoon.

Helen Trent promised to meet me at the Billy Goat by 8:30 PM at the latest. I had at least a half hour to burn given her propensity for being fifteen minutes late for everything, a habit that I learned to tolerate because of its consistency.

I patted the side of my coat for reading material when someone shouted at me. "Spivak, you old shit! Get over here!"

The voice and cadence told me, before I had even looked up, that I would be spending thirty minutes with Seth Greenburg, troublemaker and history buff who had gotten himself at the center of every big fight about real estate in Chicago during the past three decades. He'd battled Worlds Fairs, airports, football stadiums, and many lesser deals that inspired greed and corruption, all the while looking like he had wandered in from skid row.

Unfortunately for me, Seth was not alone. Across from him, looking dog-faced into his half-empty beer, was Jack Delaney, a splotchy-faced drunk who wrote about neighborhood affairs for the Chicago Bugle. He had a long track record of ingratiating himself into civic and neighborhood coalitions, particularly when they opposed City Hall projects, and then stabbing them in the back, revealing a deep ambivalence that undoubtedly had to do with his father. He was on my list of least favorite Chicagoans.

"Sit down, Spivak, have a cold one," Seth ordered. "One more time you don't call me when you're coming to town. I catch you every time. You can't hide. We're tied together. It's a matter of grace and your fuckin' bad luck."

Delaney couldn't help chiming in, his rosy dimples moving up and down as he talked. "Last time I saw you, Spivak, you were leaving City Hall with your tail between your legs, running fast from a bribery charge."

Out of the corner of my eye I saw Helen walking down the stairs, fifteen minutes early. That is, on time. A miracle.

"I'll catch you tomorrow," I blurted. "You at the Center?" I asked, walking away without acknowledging Delany's silly wisecrack.

Seth nodded, "Tomorrow's cool, Spivak."

What makes sliders addictive must be atmospheric because they only take minutes to fry and contain simple if not identifiable or healthy ingredients. I amply doused my sliders with pepper, onions, and ketchup for taste and hygiene. I brought two back to our red and white formica table on the quiet side of the Billy Goat. Helen had secured draft beers.

"I have no idea why Seth agrees to sit at the same table with Delaney after what that guy has written," I complained, taking a long pull on my frothy beer. "It makes it seem like there might be something redeeming or transformed about him. I don't like that possibility. Do you?"

"You abandoned Chicago," Helen replied, pulling her long dark brown hair into a ponytail in preparation for feasting on her slider with cheese. "Those who stick around have to play with the cards dealt," she chided, taking her first bite.

We chewed our sliders, occasionally gulping beer to clear our palates for the next bites. This didn't take long.

After I relived my side of the day we tallied our knowledge, or lack thereof. Jackson was missing. Centeno wanted to kill us for drugs he thought Tom stole. Omar Jutland disappeared with two men in a panel truck. Tom had mud on his shoes. And O'Malley had a bug up his ass.

"Hmm," we both hummed, finding no pattern but lots of loose ends, some even frightening.

"Let me fill you in on my day," Helen started, extracting her day planner from an overstuffed brown leather briefcase while holding her pen between her perfect teeth, obviously the product of braces.

"My day was not as exciting nor as geographically expansive as yours," she started. "But I made some headway. I snuck by Assistant Commissioner Gene Burke's office, pal of Alderman Devereaux, and comrade Sweeney showed me where the urban renewal files for the Brewery were hidden, the real stuff, not the public file," she said, flipping to several pages of notes. "It's two file cabinets of stuff at this point."

Her words barely registered. The incessant bar chatter and television sports buzz combined with the aftermath of the slider and the pleasure of watching the movements of her high cheek bones and full-lipped mouth put me in a trance, one that I didn't want to give up. It had been a tough day.

"Come on, Spivak," Helen chided, a mixture of laughter and exasperation. "Wake Up!"

I nodded submission just as Jake the bar runner slid two more cold ones on our table. I saw Seth climbing the stairs to the red door and underground Chicago. He waved without looking back.

The Brewery was an old story for Helen and me, at least through the early 1980s. We both had been spectators, and at one time active—to some people obnox-

ious—combatants in a psychodrama involving artist hallucinations, city government arrogance, and community anger. In short, it was the familiar saga of
higher-income people displacing lower-income people that played out in many
urban neighborhoods in the 1970s. In this case, the community held off big-time
developers for a few years. Jack Delaney told it as a parable of community organizers stopping progress.

But I knew little of the Brewery saga in recent years, and Helen had also lost
track as she became embroiled in citywide fights to protect manufacturing.

Beer was actually brewed in the complex of 15 buildings named the Schoenhofen Brewery from 1859 to 1918 when it brewed 700,000 barrels. It was the
home of Edelweiss beer, "…a taste of good judgment," in a neighborhood called
Pilsen, named after the brewing center in Bohemia. The Brewery was located in
the east end of Pilsen, what had been the Lumberyard District. Before that, it was
part of the shantytown of Hardscrabble that housed German immigrants who
dug the Chicago Sanitary and Ship Canal in the 1840s, across the river from rival
ethnic settlements of Kilgubbin and Swedetown. Canalport Street, which dead
ends at the Brewery, ran through the center of Hardscrabble.

Pilsen's development exploded after the great conflagration of 1871 that
burned a large part of Chicago to the ground. The City banned frame houses east
of the River, so they sprouted up, or were moved over on logs, to the unregulated
district of Pilsen, sometimes called Gads Hill after the notorious town in Mis-
souri. Pilsen became a factory district overnight, and the home to eastern and
central European immigrants, bitter labor struggle, and hard times.

The Brewery buildings represented typical industrial architecture of the 1880s
and 1890s, but Richard Schmidt of the Chicago School designed the Powerhouse
building in 1902, a premier example of the "prairie school," a style of functional-
ity and simple beauty, whatever that meant for factories. Unfortunately, the German owners of the Brewery intermingled with Kaiser Wilhelm and his ilk
through marriage. That didn't sit well with anti-German sentiments during
World War I, and the federales closed down the Brewery in 1917 because they
claimed its water tower was being used as a signal tower to broadcast vital war
information back to the Reich. Prohibition dug the hole deeper and led to the
federal seizure of the Brewery in 1919 and its sale to William Kellogg of the cereal
family.

The Brewery became many things during the next fifty years, almost all
food-related. Mushroom farms. Pickles. Glue. Grain storage. Food packaging. It
became the home of Green River soda, one of the most popular carbonated

drinks during Prohibition. It was also used to make chemicals and became an assembly and a chop shop in the 1970s.

Finally, in the mid 1970s, after the last big manufacturer moved out of the Brewery, the City of Chicago declared the 20-acre district an urban renewal zone and sought to have the most dilapidated buildings torn down. It would have cost millions of dollars to restore these beat-up industrial hulks. Even in its state of collapse filmmakers used the Brewery as the orphanage set for the movie Blues Brothers; the FBI used it as an escape route for Pope Paul II on his visit to Chicago in 1979.

This was when the fun and games began. Pilsen's east end had become an artist colony, with lofts, courtyards, and high heating bills. The main culprit was a former buildingl inspector who had grown up in the neighborhood, a Lithuanian, who knew how to make the right payoffs while creating an arty tone from minimalist renovations that artists and their hangers-on craved.

Like any frontier, Pilsen attracted pioneers who, after not too many years, sought to plant roots of a bigger sort, and not just deck porches off the backs of their brick tenement structures. A group of artists in cahoots with developers conspired to have the Brewery designated a historic landmark and put together a proposal to turn the buildings into condominiums, a holographic arts center, and a micro-brewery. Meanwhile, a small number of jobs and businesses flourished in the remaining Brewery buildings, jobs held by Pilsen residents.

The whole thing blew up in community conflict. Pilsen ceased to be the exotic old neighborhood in which everyone got along, meeting on Maxwell Street or Bill's Hardware on Halsted Street. Some people had plans, friends with power, and resources. But the urban pioneers resented their game being called what it was. One more Chicago scam.

What this meant was that nothing happened, except lots of meetings and bad feelings. Meetings with the alderman. Meetings with the City's Department of Urban Development, Gene Burke in particular. Meetings with lawyers. Community meetings in the basement of Assumption of God Church to debate strategy, elect leaders, and embarrass foes.

It took years before the historic landmark status was lifted to allow the worst of the Brewery buildings to be torn down. In true Chicago style, the demolition crew accidentally knocked down part of the highly prized Powerhouse building, producing a new round of accusations, court filings, and little action.

As far as I was concerned, doing nothing with the Brewery was just fine. My interest had been to stop bad things from the point of view of the community, not to see the Brewery as the grand strategy for bringing in new businesses. Tearing down dense, multistory buildings produced some fresh air and sunlight, but not much developable land. Other players, on all sides of the fight, had different ideas about the role of the Brewery in Pilsen's future. They started to take things too seriously, for me, at least.

Helen's information made me realize that time really had passed and that although the city landscape changed at a snail's pace, it nevertheless changed. And the Brewery was in the midst of the change.

"Two files cover transactions for the site during the past year," she said. "The City sold the Powerhouse and Administration buildings to N&M Ltd in 1989, one of those semi-mysterious real estate and financial brokers with offices on La Salle Street, in the epicenter of finance and deal-making.

"Several transactions show that the property leveraged other public and private resources, but the wheeler-dealers operated through secret trusts so its hard to pin down exactly how this happened," Helen continued, her amber eyes moving back and forth between her notebook and me. I was getting dizzy.

"The Mayor gerrymandered the Brewery into a Tax Development District that he created for his Riverboat Gambling plan that never got legs in Springfield. Most of the development action was east of the river, but somebody saw the potential for secondary development in the east end of Pilsen. The TDD's still in place; so this same somebody's sitting on a goldmine depending upon their connections."

"In short, the Brewery's become a real hot spot again, if you ask me," Helen concluded. "There's a new owner and cash for development. Somebody's going to take an interest eventually. What I don't understand is why, given the market values, guards weren't posted. I can't believe they don't want to protect these assets."

Helen closed her notebook and drank the last of her beer. "I set up a meeting with N&M at 2 tomorrow afternoon. It's all yours, my friend. I've got another appointment that I can't break. Sorry, Nick."

I mumbled defeat.

"Nick," Helen said, taking my hand. "Making things right for Tom Woods is becoming dangerous. I don't think you fully appreciate the pile of dog shit we're stepping into. Maybe we should let things cool down. This town is a lot worse than when you were here. Everybody's hungry to score on real estate and they don't like obstacles."

I mumbled agreement.

"Why don't you spend the weekend with me up at Union Pier? You need a rest. And we need to talk strategy. Plus, I have a surprise to tell you about"

"Whatever," I responded. "I'm beat. Drop me back at the Balboa. I'll owe you big time."

"You're no fun," Helen laughed.

We left through the red door at the top of the stairs.

CHAPTER 9

▼

Sam interrupted my trajectory to the Balboa Arms Hotel's only working elevator with a "Nick, gotta talk to you boy. Hold on. Don't go up there!"

I froze in my tracks and turned to Sam. Face pressed against the cage, he said, "Lee Sampson's been calling for you all day. And Sergeant Radachek left a message saying the white van's out of commission."

I felt immediate relief. Now at least I could sleep in peace knowing that Centeno wouldn't kick my dreams. Radachek was becoming downright customer-friendly.

Sam hesitated, "And you got somebody waiting for you upstairs. I let her in for you."

Sneaking in that third item was not a simple accident of random order, and Sam's feigned innocence was about as convincing as junk mail. He looked up, sensing my glare and disbelief.

"You loved that poor girl and then left her for Baltimore with no one to look out for her," Sam pleaded, an awe-inspiring emotion in a 300-pound man. "I promised I'd let her know when you came to town again. I've been keeping an eye on her as best I could. Don't give me no shit, Spivak! Get up there!"

Good advice, I thought, considering I was nearly comatose, and could not mount a counteroffensive to Sam's sentimentality. The elevator, as usual, stopped at every floor regardless of which floor buttons were pushed. It baffled the elevator company as well, so they said.

More Chicago history. My little secret. That's what made it so alluring and ultimately so wrong. Relationships don't grow on secrets, but on honesty and straight talk. I learned the hard way.

Opening the door as quietly as I could given the resistance of the antiquated deadbolt lock, I slipped into the darkness of the room. It only took a few minutes, without lights, to grope my way into the bathroom, rinse off the outer layer of grime from my body, and slip into bed, a double bed that would normally land you in the sagging middle within seconds. Luckily, Sam had honored me with a special room that had the extra comfort of a full sheet of ¾-inch plywood as reinforcement between the mattresses.

My eyes gradually acclimated to the darkness, the outlines of my companion becoming clearer, her shoulder-length blond hair splayed out on a pillow tucked under itself, as if in a contortion. I rested my head against the wooden headboard from another era and listened, my heartbeat quickening and a feeling of warm expectation moving like a tide incrementally up my body. Sarah Larsen, all five and half feet, rolled over, clothed only in my worn t-shirt, breathing the cadence of sleep.

This all changed, as I knew it would, as the heat and subtle movements of our bodies intertwined. No words were spoken in the next hour.

Sitting up in bed, I saw the first blurry evidence of morning creeping through the worn curtain that masked our view of Wabash Avenue. I relished a cigarette, but that was ten years out of date as a stylistic option. Sarah slept.

Sarah Larsen was a small-town refugee from the southern Iowa burg of Keokak who had found her way to Chicago in search of a life and a mission. She volunteered with the Center for Neighborhood Options, having studied architecture in college for a year before dropping out to cook in a health food restaurant. By her thirtieth birthday, when I met her five years ago, she had more than enough experience with dysfunctional relationships. She needed her own life.

We eyed each other for about a year before we engineered the beginnings of our affair after listening to jazz at Andy's one rainy Thursday night. We were both seeking escape, she from a troglodyte boyfriend, me from a failing marriage. We had a secret and we still do, I thought, watching her sleep.

Our secret. Sam rented us a cheap room in the rear of the third floor, a seldom-used room, more like a big closet, in a hallway of permanent residents, mostly pensioners, who seldom left their rooms. They also kept our secret.

One of the pensioners, as if misplaced from a Russian novel, greeted us regularly as if warned in advance by Sam or because of their sixth sense for pent-up sexual energy, perhaps their own. Soon, the whole floor was part of the act. Whoever was on duty winked or gave us a thumbs up. We felt like Olympians. One little old woman in a babushka awarded us a granola bar.

All we did was make love in the sagging bed, drink red wine that we picked up at the take-out liquor store on Wabash, and hold each other for a few hours in the embrace of post-coital sleep. Baby sleep. The world and its demons—ignorant bosses, unloving spouses, brutal boyfriends, and other bad guys—melted away. And then we would depart for other parts of our lives, winking our way to the elevator as doors cracked behind us.

I talked freely about all parts of my life because there was no good reason not to. After all, we were a secret. That was the deception. Great sex and communication eventually became caring and obligation without the normal trappings of love, furniture, and mortgages.

The morning light revealed worn hotel furniture, a faded painting of a Chicago railroad bridge, and clothes scattered on the floor. Sarah had eventually broken up with the boyfriend and had begun to construct a life based upon her needs and decisions. It was tough going. She didn't know how to live by herself on her own terms, or had forgotten.

Sarah stirred as if jarred by my thoughts. She looked up at me, blinking her eyes and tossing her hair to the side.

"Nick, I know you don't really love me, like in a relationship," she said lifting her head. "But why do you make me track you down when you come to town? If it wasn't for Sam, I wouldn't be here now. It's a pain, Nick!"

"Sorry, I mumbled," with more honesty than I thought I could muster. "I'm trying to make sense of the death of an old friend, but I keep getting the shit kicked out of me. Chicago can go to hell!"

"I know you can do two things at once," Sarah said with a chuckle.

My departure for Baltimore after walking the plank at the City and losing my marriage had ended our regular visits to the Balboa Arms, undoubtedly wreaking havoc on the third-floor pensioners. Another loss. Sarah and I suffered as well. There was hardly a goodbye.

That was four years ago. We managed secret meetings in Chicago and elsewhere every three or four months, brief encounters, as full of fantasy as reality. We grew apart.

I must have sounded like a stray dog coming in out of the rain because Sarah began to lightly caress my right leg. I turned towards her. Here we go, I thought, smiling. I didn't know stray dogs were appealing.

The desperate sounds of a couple squaring off in the next room—the product of a morning after and paper thin walls—shattered our mood. The words of accusation and betrayal, high-pitched and angry, were too familiar for both Sarah and me. We had lived them, and still had scars.

Sarah shuddered.

I threw my shoes, one at a time.

While I lay on the tousled bed, warm and pleasantly unconscious, Sarah took advantage of the Balboa's startling hot water pressure. We had some time before I had to meet Seth Greenburg and pay a visit to N&M Ltd.

My empty mind couldn't last. It was a ripe target for guilt. I remembered the old lady's pronouncement on the plane that I was pitiful when I said my wife had asked me for divorce and I didn't know why.

To tell the truth, I didn't know whether to think of my ex-wife as my liberator or oppressor, or both. I had given up on our relationship and was willing to hunker down and let life run its course, a peculiar fatalism that strikes many apparently experienced people in their thirties. It must be desperation driven by the uncomfortable feeling that you haven't formed enduring relationships amidst flings, live-ins, and fantasies. All my remaining personal power was directed at making our time together miserable, from withholding sex to fighting about the piles of papers I had left in the living room. Not that she didn't make a fatal contribution. She avoided risks, going for control rather than a life of give and take. I didn't know how we made the decision to marry, one more illusion of love that made two relatively reasonable people act stupid.

We met in 1983 at a protest rally against the planned 1993 World's Fair in Chicago, the centenary real estate celebration of the 1893 Columbian Exposition. Chicago corporate elites planned this billion-dollar boondoggle to revitalize downtown, finance new mega-infrastructure, and make Chicago a global city. Its flaws matched its ambition if one was only willing to take off one's booster blinders and look. Who, for example, would really come to a fair of this magnitude in the age of television, cable, and computers? And who would pay the bills?

My ex-wife worked with Seth Greenburg and others to expose the World's Fair for the expensive pipedream that it was. She taught city planning at the University of Pennsylvania, and was on leave for a year to do action research on grassroots oppositional politics, as she named her work in the plethora of professional papers she wrote up for academic conferences.

I couldn't believe it. Same interests. Activism. A love for Chicago. Physical attraction. It was a good year, although I really didn't get to know who she was or what I wanted.

By the end of the year we were married, to the chagrin of our friends and families. We began commuting almost from the start of our relationship; I traveled two weekends per month, she traveled one. We rested on the fourth. We had exotic vacations and longer stays in Chicago or Philadelphia during holidays. It worked but we never made a home life together.

She took another year of leave in 1986 to be in Chicago. We fought all year about where to live, sex, whether I respected academics, and all matters domestic. The fights grew mean and we discovered parts of ourselves that we didn't know about. Like outright anger. I finally buried my head in the ground, and focused on work, colleagues, and anything that bolstered my sense of self.

Why I didn't leave I didn't know. I started up with Sarah, which seemed to stabilize things but really only enabled me to withdraw. By the end of the year Grace and I were barely talking. She asked me for a divorce on the same day that things crumbled for me at City Hall. She left the next day. We had talked twice since.

CHAPTER 10

▼

Meigs Field is a tiny airport on a strip of landfill on the Chicago lakefront that serves the vanity of corporate CEOs and as a reminder of the unbridgeable political chasm between the mayor and governor. Flying out of Meigs in small prop planes is a near-death experience for the neophyte flyer, the wind unexpectedly whipping the plane up and down so that your guts are on the ceiling and floor at the same time. Its days are numbered; fewer and fewer homegrown CEOs exist to make a fuss.

I walked to the observatory—my old running route when I worked for the city and lived downtown—after Sarah left the Balboa for her job. She had recently left Seth's outfit to work for a community literacy program on the north side. She now knew where I was, and I was sure that Sam would let her into my palatial room any time she asked. Despite the pleasure of our time together, I sensed that we were at a dead-end. To bring the relationship out of its secret status would expose it to the deadening effects of normalcy. But to remain secret imposed its own harm.

I still had an hour to kill before meeting Seth Greenburg at El Torta, so exercising my body seemed like a sensible course of action since I didn't know what physical damages today would bring. The pain from yesterday's bruises on my chest and knees and my swollen finger were ever-present. But I needed to stretch.

It was a cool, clear day and Chicago's downtown glistened as if carved from a huge block of ice. Only a few sailboats rocked in the harbor.

Tom Woods had become a case, a mission, a torment. His presence was almost palpable, saying, "I'm more than that. Not just a mystery to be solved, but also a person with a history of success, failure, and love. Don't lose me in your muddled Chicago quest!" And then the image fluttered away.

My exuberant one hundred yard dash beat Lake Shore Drive traffic coming gangbusters in both directions. I was on a mission. Deliberately stomping through a multicolor pile of leaves in Grant Park, I kicked Chicago in the ass with great satisfaction.

Jacinto hustled me a mug of decaf before I had grabbed a primo window table for two facing Wabash Avenue next to a black-leathered couple of indeterminate gender. Art students from Columbia College, with psychedelic orange and blue hair slicked back or sticking out in all directions, lounged in a human cluster on the sidewalk, possibly their only performance art that would ever command an audience.

"Como sta?" asked Jacinto.

"Muy bein, gracias," I replied as if transported back to my one-day-a-week, third-grade Spanish class, an effort at cross-cultural sensitivity on the part of my enlightened suburban grammar school of the 1950s. We had made a pinata, I recalled. Jacinto laughed, a juaro he liked whose Spanish stunk.

"I'm waiting on Seth, Jacinto," I said. "You haven't seen him, have you?"

"No Nick. Seth rarely graces my restaurant since you left Chicago. I'm not sure my cuisine agrees with Seth's stomach."

"That's hard to believe," I countered. "Seth loves greasy street food like gizzards and knishes…"

"You cannot possibly be comparing the food of El Torta with that kind of food," Jacinto opined with great drama. The biker couple looked our way for a moment in disbelief, their mouths ringed in salsa and bits of tortilla chips.

As if on cue, Seth pushed open the door, a big man with a rabbinical, brown curly beard and a gold ring in his left ear. Seth was a secular Jew, whose grandfather sold suits on Maxwell Street in the old days before moving the family west to Lawndale to escape the grime and chicken coops in the tenements. Two years earlier, Seth got himself baptized at Antioch Baptist Church in Lawndale by Reverend Theobold Jones, a long time civil rights activist and friend of Seth's for thirty years. It all fit together, although Seth had a look of disarray that suggested otherwise.

"Hey babe," he said, squeezing my neck with the thumb and forefinger of his right hand and then grabbing the other seat.

"What's the real scoop on the tamale murders, Jacinto?" Seth parried. "And I still can't understand how you make rent on this place and avoid the wrecking ball. You belong on 18th Street, not in the heart of hotel row."

"You see, Nick, this man insults me when I am ready to extend my hand and bless him with our special breakfast taco. But now..," he trailed off.

"Just coffee, Jacinto," Seth responded. "And a bowl of them chips if you have any left the way they've been eating," he added, gesturing behind him.

Seth pushed back his chair a few inches as a way of emphasizing his message, accidentally jarring one of the biker couple so that he or she stabbed her or himself in the cheek with a triangular chip.

What ensued was silly. Jacinto stopped it before the bigger of the bikers revealed himself to be a man and growled at our table, showing a checkerboard of yellowed teeth and a red slobbering tongue.

"Be cool," Seth said to the hovering biker. "Wasn't talking about you. And sorry about the chip. This damn place ain't meant for guys and gals our size. You know what I mean?"

Jacinto ushered the bikers to the door without collecting his meager bill. When he returned to our table he said to Seth, "Two extra Diet Cokes on Seth's bill."

"Not hardly!" Seth shot back. "Fucking Spivak's picking up this bill. He invited me out for brunch at El Torta, not the other way around."

"Okay, fine, it's on me, Jacinto," I answered, figuring now was as good a time as any to start our real conversation.

I gave Seth the ten-minute version of the last few days, of Tom Woods and UPC, of white vans and panel trucks, of the Brewery, Radachek and Lieutenant O'Malley. That last name drew a guffaw from Seth. I left out Sarah and a few other things just so I had reserve ammunition once Seth dismissed my story, mission, and reason for existence.

He passed on that opportunity for reasons unknown to me. He was a mystery. So I jumped in.

"I need you to help me find Alphonius Jackson and Omar Jutland. Jackson is probably hiding out in the neighborhoods and Jutland's looks like he's in cahoots with somebody connected to the Brewery. He's from Milwaukee," as if that explained everything.

Seth looked at me with wide-eyed seriousness. "I've heard rumblings on the south side about how Reverend Jackson was treated. Some angry people. Tell you what. I'll follow up on Jackson and you check out Milwaukee. Ain't my kind of place."

I threw Jacinto a ten-dollar bill and a wink. Seth stuck out his hand in a gesture of mock friendship. Jacinto turned the other way.

We opened the door and joined the mayhem of noontime Chicago.

Zigzagging ten blocks northwest to the financial district, I bought a Daily Times at the ramshackle newsstand on Jackson and State. There was no doubt that the Bugle was a better paper, but I preferred a rag that was more plebeian, the kind of paper people read on the El. I also didn't like supporting Jack Delaney.

The big bold headline read, ***FUTURES BREAK RECORD***. The story didn't reveal much except the belief that grain derivatives—the latest abstraction in Chicago's history as premier agricultural market place—caused the blip in the futures market. Several dealer names sounded familiar, but my pleasure-soaked brain cells were not performing at capacity. A story buried in the metro section announced: *Casino Bill Unveiled to Questions*. I walked the remaining two blocks and entered the LaSalle Bank building, now owned by a Canadian group, unless it had been sold again.

The security guard directed me to the narrow corridor of pay phones to the left of the elevator bank designated for floors 12–25. I wanted the 17th floor. The corridor was empty except for a harried woman who spoke anxiously on the phone. She turned her back as I drew near. I needed to call Lee Sampson and ask him why Tom Woods had been looking for me.

I reached the answering machine at UPC, so I began to leave a message at the beep that I would call back later in the afternoon. Sampson picked up—a cautious or introverted man who monitored his incoming calls. At least he had one trait I admired.

"Spivak," Sampson started. "I left two messages for you this morning. Where have you been? I thought you were taking care of the Woods problem."

Sampson's voice cracked and I heard a scared man. Pomposity and self-regard dissolved when confronted by the unthinkable.

"Someone named Centeno burst in here yesterday afternoon and demanded that I hand over Tom Woods' personal effects. He said he had already dealt with you," Sampson said.

"And did you?" I prodded.

"Of course I did, Spivak. They broke into the storage cabinets and knocked over my bookcases. Our administrator, an older woman from Elmhurst, fainted on the floor. I''e been on the phone all day with her son—a lawyer with Penn, Oak, and Daley—and with my board of directors. First Woods' death and now Centeno! Our support is not like the old days. Enrollment is down and we depend upon on the generosity of a few donors who themselves are having questions about our mission. I promised them that you would explain what this all is about at our board meeting next Tuesday. Can I count on you, Spivak?"

Unfortunately for Sampson we were still hooked up to his answering machine and time ran out, cutting off our connection before I could answer, "Sure."

As I walked out of the phone corridor the woman's voice had become hysterical.

N&M Ltd was located at the end of a hallway, two rights and a left out of the elevator. My footsteps echoed amidst tinted glass, pale yellow halls, and designer doors. N&M was strictly low-key but expensive. Simple gold letters announced their home.

I negotiated the entry buzzer with all the finesse of a middle-aged man who had barely figured out how to work a VCR. My excuse was that my ex-wife took all the electronics and expertise with her. No wonder I felt ill at ease in the world.

A slim, black-haired woman greeted me as I burst through the door, saying that Mr. Affazzi would be with me in five minutes. The robotic quality of her words and gestures puzzled me as she took my coat and beckoned me to sit in one of the modern-looking blue chairs arranged around a glass table piled with magazines.

Catching my breath, I idly leafed through the magazines; they were all about grain, shipping on the St. Lawrence Seaway, and the futures market.

A softly accented voice interrupted my reading. "Mr Spivak, I believe?"

Turning, I saw a dark man in his early fifties dressed in an expensive but conservatively cut suit, with a great deal of gold on his fingers and wrists. He must have been watching me devour his magazines. We shook hands.

Affazzi's face was tranquil on the surface but I detected an undertow of nervous tension that characterized someone going into battle. The rest was camouflage.

Helen had given me a manilla folder that contained two sheets of paper. The first was a brief description of Affazzi's background, drawn from the Who's Who in Finance for the Midwest, 1990. Born in Lebanon, Khalid Affazzi attended the London School of Economics and worked for multinational natural resource companies in the 1970s. The next entry referred to the formation of N&M Ltd in 1985, a gap of six years. His civic and business affiliations included the University Club, the Society of Industrial Realtors, and the National Association of Mortgage Bankers. Not much to go on.

A throat cleared and I looked up.

"I am so sorry that Ms. Trent is unable to attend," he began. "I've heard remarkable things about her work, however much I disagree with protecting the economy of the past. But please, come into my office and we can be more comfortable. I understand you want to know about our real estate holdings in Chicago."

I sat on a tan couch and crossed my legs while Affazzi relaxed in a desk chair on the other side of the wooden coffee table. Our view was of the boxlike federal center and one of Chicago's real beauties, the Monadonock, the tallest building in the world with masonry bearing walls.

Affazzi started, "Mr. Spivak, I've learned quite a lot about you in the past day since Ms. Trent called. I must say, though, I almost cancelled our meeting after examining your dossier. You can imagine that a business like ours might feel awkward being associated with a troublemaker like yourself."

Affazzi remained composed as he complimented me, a sphinx in control of the flow of gesture and emotion. I wasn't sure I'd ever been called a troublemaker, and if I had, it hadn't been for twenty years. I wondered from whom he had obtained the dossier, as he called it, so quickly.

At that moment the young woman returned with a silver tray with small white cups of espresso. Her stoic look and perfect posture made me nervous and prompted thoughts of brainwashing.

"Please!" Affazzi gestured towards me with his small right hand, pudgy fingers, and gold ring. I was afraid that asking for decaf would signal something about my manhood.

"Thank you," I said, downing the high octane espresso in one gulp.

"I'm interested in why a partnership like N&M would bother with a lemon like the Brewery, and the complications of City incentives, regulations, and politics," I spit out, the espresso boring a hole in my stomach. "N&M's about grain from what I can tell, not industrial real estate."

Affazzi sipped rather than gulped his espresso, showing how gentlemen drink, I supposed, and carefully formulated his answer, his facial muscles tightening slightly. A razor-sharp edge perfectly parted his jet-black hair.

As he sipped, I remembered the second sheet of paper in Helen's folder. A photocopied article from the New York Daily News in September 1979 recounted the deaths of Helen and Hussein Affazzi, killed in a head-on collision on the West Side Highway. A car of drunken teenagers from Stamford, Connecticut—making their way home from an all-nighter in the city—crossed the highway and hit a cab. The reckless teens survived with minor injuries. The deaths of

Affazzi's wife, born and bred in Wisconsin, and his son were instantaneous. The article referred to Mr. Affazzi as a financial broker on Wall Street.

"I think we should discuss your motivation rather than N&M's business strategy," Affazzi said. "I know your background and why you have come back to Chicago. What I'm not sure about is why you are inventing a conspiracy when it's obvious that street gangs shot your friend, the late Reverend Woods, in the middle of the night. The unfortunate result of profound naiveté."

Affazzi was meeting with me to deliver a message, not to share information. This interview was about to terminate, so I jumped in with both feet, throwing questions at Affazzi in hopes he would trip over himself.

"Look Mr. Affazzi, we're not discussing grain futures, we're talking about murder and mayhem at one of your properties. Who was in the other truck parked at the Brewery on October 18th, the one so-called gangbangers forced Omar Jutland into? Or was somebody exchanging something? And what happened to Alphonius Jackson?"

"Ah," Affazzi said, rising from his chair, a look of patient exasperation on his face. "I see you have been talking with the good Sister. She's quite fragile, I understand, subject to periodic breakdowns. I do hope she recovers."

Affazzi walked to the door.

"I'm afraid our time together is concluded, Mr. Spivak. I have a pressing business appointment. I hope you realize that your investigation, if I may call it that, is unnecessary.

"But," he hesitated, "perhaps it soothes your loss."

With a superbly refined sweep of his hand he gestured toward the door where the receptionist stood waiting to guide me out. He didn't even offer to shake my hand.

"I'm sure we'll meet again, Mr. Affazzi," I blurted out, trying to beat the clock. "N&M is mixed up in the Brewery and in Tom Woods' death. Arrogance and good manners won't save you. If my time in Chicago has taught me anything it's, 'Follow the money!' You can be sure I will."

I walked slowly to the entrance door, struggling not to show a scintilla of anger, fear, or stomach pain. I was rewarded. Assistant Commissioner Gene Burke of the Department of Urban Development had just entered the office. We stumbled into each other. Burke and I were long-time adversaries, and finding him in N&M was a pleasing coup.

He noticed my victory face and sputtered, "Looking for a job, Spivak?"

My return look, I hoped, was equal parts disinterest and conspiratorial humor, a sure combination to set Burke's sensitive insides aflutter.

Affazzi waved at Burke with annoyance. "Goodbye, Mr. Spivak."

"Why all the bother about a troublemaker like me?" I shot back, opening the door to leave.

"It's the Brewery."

CHAPTER 11

▼

It was already growing dark when Helen picked me up in the Loop and we headed south in her cluttered 1984 Nissan sedan. A Midwest red horizon flashed as we drove past the expanse of rail land south of the Loop, slowly being filled in with a post-modern potpourri of pastel-colored townhouses. Who lived in these new suburban enclaves, the newly gated neighborhoods of Chicago? I had no idea.

Finally, up ahead rose the dark hulk of the Brewery Powerhouse, dominating the vista like a death star as we topped the bridge over the rail yards and the Chicago River.

It was not the ideal time to reconnoiter the Brewery since we could hardly see. Flashlights helped some. That the darkness made us less conspicuous was important because the Brewery was becoming quite a busy after-hours marketplace according to Sister Mary O'Conner.

"What are we looking for?" Helen asked, as the industrial hulk grew closer.

"I don't know," I replied. "I just think we should look around, and probably more than once."

"Well, I guess we'll see if N&M smartened up and hired a security guard," Helen laughed.

"That would make Affazzi's day if he caught us. Let's not give him that pleasure," I said.

Picking up on my ambiguity, Helen said, "Listen, Nick, maybe we should just go to Healthy Foods in Bridgeport. We can skip this visit."

The thought of my favorite Lithuanian restaurant and a bowl of borscht appealed to me but I held firm. "No, Let's stick with the program. Then we can eat."

"You're the detective," Helen snickered, turning right on Lumber Street and parking on an empty block. Everything was dark except for a few house lights down the street. No vans, panel trucks, security guards, or cops in sight.

We grabbed the flashlights and closed the car doors with as little noise as possible, mainly to impress each other with our collective stealth.

"Now what?" Helen whispered, taking my hand.

"Let's walk the perimeter and get down to business," I answered, squeezing her hand.

Those strategic deployments yielded little in the way of clues. Helen and I exchanged friendly banter about the past and present. When we ended up at the car for the second time, I said, "Let's check out the building Sister Mary fell into."

"Go for it," Helen said.

Edging along the southern wall of a brick two-story building that was once the Brewery stables, I leaned my shoulder against the wall to keep my bearings. About two thirds of the way along the wall a space opened up without warning, and I tumbled through it and onto the ground.

"Holy shit!" I exclaimed.

It was a permanently open door. Luckily, Helen and I had dropped our hand-holding and her light flashed on me within seconds. She stuck out her hand.

"Here ya go, partner."

I got to my feet. Our flashlights revealed a large open, two-story room, the ceiling held up by thick wooden beams and posts. I considered searching for a light switch or the electrical box but thought better of it. Flashlights would have to do.

Further inspection showed tire tracks, mud, and sliding doors that opened to reveal a narrow pockmarked dirt road running down the middle of the Brewery buildings. Broken wooden crates and cardboard boxes littered the cement floor. A clump of boxes drew our interest and flashlights. Behind the boxes we saw what looked like a freight elevator. Helen pressed the call button.

"Might as well give a try," she said. The elevator motor kicked over and the elevator jumbled up to our floor, stopping with a jerk. We opened the gates, entered, and slammed them shut. Pressing the green button, we descended.

Leaving the elevator, I found a bank of light switches that illuminated the entire basement. I'd rather be caught than break a leg down here, I thought. The basement walls were built of large, quarried stone block. An earthen floor had been hammered into a hardened cement-like surface, except in the corners where protracted water leaks had produced canyons of erosion. Rows of wooden pallets sat empty.

"One more 19th Century industrial building," Helen said. "The only difference is that it's eight at night, we're trespassing, and the owners left the door open. But then again, there's not much to steal or destroy from what we've seen so far."

"No argument from me," I replied, tramping around the basement. "Let's wrap it up and hit Bridgeport."

We started to make our way back to the elevator. I swung the flashlight in arcs against the four walls, playing games, watching the shadow play and strobe effects.

"That"'s making me sick," Helen complained.

"What's that?" I said, ignoring Helen's comment and pointing at a steel door barely visible in the southeastern nook of the basement. We walked over to it, stumbling over pieces of broken pallet. I yanked the door open and entered a small storage room. Not much there except another door, secured by a rusty hasp and a new lock.

"Why not?" Helen said.

I pried off the hasp with a two-foot-long steel rod that I found on a sagging workbench in the corner of the room and opened the door. Behind it, a fifteen-foot wooden staircase descended into darkness. We both pointed our flashlights toward the bottom. There was a rusty manhole cover and nothing else.

"I feel like a juvenile delinquent rather than a professional investigator," I complained to Helen.

"Go with your feelings," she laughed.

"Am I really a constitutional troublemaker?" I laughed back. That's what Affazzi called me.

"You're just fine," Helen soothed.

We pried up the manhole cover with the same pipe and flipped it to the side. It was lighter than I expected, but I still jumped out of the way when it careened against the wall and clattered to the floor. We pointed our lights into the darkness.

"Believe it or not. I think we've found an entrance to the Brewery's old drainage system that emptied into the River. Breweries produced a lot of waste, to say the least. It must extend a couple of hundred yards to the east and the river."

"Such knowledge you have!"

"Yes, I do!"

"Let's take a look," Helen urged, pushing me lightly on the elbow. "It's obvious someone else has been scouting this tunnel from the looks of the lock and the cover. Bring the pipe!"

"Sure, me first," I replied, sitting on the edge of the hole, my legs dangling into space. It was about a six-foot drop. I jumped, landing easily on a flattened surface. I helped Helen down and we inspected the tunnel. We found a switch to turn on the makeshift lighting system of wire strung on the walls and light bulbs in metal cages. The bulbs threw off just enough light for us to see. An aluminum stepladder leaned against the wall of the tunnel.

The tunnel was oval-shaped and made of bricks. Slippery green moss held the decaying mortar together, most of it anyway. The tunnel was about eight feet in diameter; someone had recently leveled the bottom with a red clay material to create a smoother surface.

"Why would anyone go to so much trouble? This tunnel isn't worth an archeological dig," I said, speaking to myself as much as Helen.

"Let's take a walk," she replied.

It was an easy walk along the well-traveled path, as long as I kept my head bowed. Toward the end, the moldy brick tunnel widened into a fan shape. At the widest part of the fan, steel doors of modern vintage opened no doubt into the Chicago River. A ladder rose above the doors to the surface. Then we saw him— or it. Slumped up against the doors was a lanky man with light brown hair and a bloody shirt.

"Omar Jutland, I presume."

Chicago's three musketeers—Radachek, Pelegrino and O'Malley—immediately decided Jutland's death was connected to drug smuggling, stolen electronics, and undocumented workers. Sand and gravel barges brought the contraband to Chicago each year from down south on the Illinois and Mississippi Rivers. The Brewery was the drop-off and distribution point. Nothing like a half-abandoned, city-financed facility for illicit trade. Somehow, Jutland got caught in the middle.

Helen and I stood back in awe as the loose ends were tied together with the lightning speed of a basket-weaving contest. The cops simultaneously thanked us and slapped our wrists for sneaking around other people's property.

I pulled Radachek aside when we returned to the basement. We walked over to a corner, pretending to be searching for new clues.

"What gives? This is freeze-dried before it's even cooked," I snapped.

Radachek looked at me, a quiver of humanity momentarily showing on his broad Slavic face.

"Give it up, Spivak. You're only making more trouble for yourself. Let it rest!"

"Doesn't anybody care about Tom Woods?"

"Not really," Radachek barked back. "Random killing on the streets of Chicago is how that's going down. Go back to Baltimore, Spivak!"

"I don't think so," I replied. "It's just getting interesting. Who knows where it will lead, Sergeant." My voice had risen.

At that moment O'Malley emerged from below, and upon seeing the two of us talking, called, "Radachek, wrap it!"

He glared at me in silence as the Brewery shut down.

Helen and I exited Chitown.

The next morning, I woke up at 9 o'clock, startled into consciousness and all that had happened during the past five days. I was lying on an old-fashioned cot, under a ragged quilt, on a glass porch that stuck off the rear of a two-story cottage, sun streaming in through the greenhouse windows. I smelled a wood fire and coffee. This was Union Pier, Michigan, Helen Trent's cottage that she owned with a couple of Chicago friends.

Union Pier was named after a 600-foot-long pier built in the 1860s to facilitate the transport of lumber and agricultural products to the growing behemoth across the lake. The blazing demise of much of Chicago in 1871 fueled its growth. By 1900, Union Pier had evolved into a vacation spot for Chicago's working stiffs.

Although I had pledged to fight during my tangle with Radachek, I was tired and felt a terrible sense of loss and confusion. There were too many angles to this story—Centeno, Jutland, and Affazzi. The cops closed down the investigation of Woods' murder even as the loose ends and troubling questions multiplied. There was no hunger to go the extra distance. Maybe someone warned them off. And I was operating near empty, not bringing in revenue; quite the opposite, I was expending resources that I didn't have.

Helen and I had picked up a few things at her condo and at the Balboa after departing the Brewery. For once Sam shrugged "no" when I asked if there were any messages. Maybe he was being protective. We headed for Union Pier, having missed borscht at Healthy Foods, but we stopped to have Jacinto fixed us burritos. A good alternative. We drove south through Chicago's industrial wasteland and the devastated city of Gary, Indiana, home of what was left of Chicago's steel producers. Union Pier is the first resort town on the Michigan side of the lake, still reachable by the South Shore Railroad Line, and a lot more attractive since the air and water have been cleaned up. Unfortunately, that meant a dramatic loss of jobs.

We hadn't talked much on the way to Union Pier, listening instead to late-night jazz and falling into ourselves, wherever that took us. Walking around old industrial buildings late at night had exhausted our mental and emotional reserves, particularly given the unexpected presence of another dead body. Figuring out what, if anything, to do next could wait another day.

At mid-morning I walked along the Lake Michigan beach. It was in a state of shifting erosion, indifferent to the public gestures aimed at its protection. Fall colors splashed the crowded trees on the dune embankment, and the lake was blue cold. The beach was empty.

My mind went back to Tom. He and I had grown apart in the past few years. He became the pastor of a dying congregation in a dying steel and coal town in western Pennsylvania, the elders holding on to the reins of the little church as if it were Noah's Ark. The wife of the previous pastor held court on the committee of elders, a bad sign for anyone trying anything different. Tom survived a few years but his passions were not about winning battles for power. He had no aptitude for sustained intrigue.

For myself, my need for concreteness—completing tasks, uncovering mysteries, and achieving stability—made me impatient with Tom's flights of spiritual and political fancy. Maybe I was growing old and becoming intolerant of a life lived on the messy edges of things. I lost the ability to take him seriously, or to make him a priority in my life.

And now I felt guilty. Maybe Affazzi was right. Reverend Lee Sampson's UPC was a profound act of naiveté, one wrapped in a lot of deception and performance art. Tom hardly needed an introduction to big city poverty and social justice; he had more experience with these issues than I did. So, why had he come? Because he had lost his way? Because all he had left was the performance art of social justice? I didn't know.

And why had Tom called me at the Balboa instead of in Baltimore? I must have told him that Sam was my ex-officio manager. But why call me? Tom felt my skepticism, although we had never talked openly about it. I guess it wasn't a barrier because he called; maybe he was more oblivious than I thought—more forgiving. Distracted by Sampson's anxiety, I had forgotten to ask him about Tom's call.

In any case, I was committed to discovering who murdered Tom Woods. It wasn't guilt about neglecting Tom, the need for a goal to give definition to my life, or my troublemaker nature seeking to battle the power structure of Chicago. Tom and I had connected in the mysterious ways of friends, creating a bond that each of us could call upon, a lifelong credit. Neither my skepticism about him, nor his distance from me, diminished the strong feelings of obligation that tied our lives together.

Back at the cottage, I climbed a steep embankment where the stairs had rotted away, leaving only occasional wooden posts sticking their heads above the sand. I stared down a mixed-breed black dog guarding the top of the embankment. I breathed hard as I vaulted the three wooden steps onto the cottage porch.

The long and short of it was that Helen had a boyfriend who had been around for a couple of years. All this was new to me. A couple of years was a record for Helen's checkered love life, but maybe this was her winning roll of the dice. I felt good for her, maybe. His name was Alex Bexton, and he was a commercial loan officer for a big downtown bank.

Alex and I avoided contact, skirting each other as much as possible, our antennae always up. I was the potential other guy, or so I dreamed. Those are the worst; they represent all the fantasies of what could be better—fulfillment, intimacy, and love. It was hard to believe that I could be sized up in that way, but such is the power of fantasy.

When I returned from my walk, Helen and Alex sat at the big table in the living room drinking coffee. Jim Majors, a United Church of Christ minister, lounged on the couch with his wife Ellen. They owned a cottage down the street. Another friend of Helens, Kim Snowden, a writer and long-distance runner, semi-permanently camped out in the front bedroom. She stood in the doorway to the kitchen.

"Welcome back, Mr. Spivak," Jim's baritone voice boomed. "And how was the lake today? Full of existential pleasures I hope."

"Indeed," I replied, grabbing a coffee cup. "Gorgeous! Glistening! All those things! Simply post-industrial!"

"I didn't know you had such a way with words," Kim said.

"I don't," I smiled, realizing how attractive she was in an athletic sort of way.

As I grabbed a chair from the kitchen I caught sight of Helen giving Alex a "don't do it" look. He obviously didn't register the message because he attacked before I had settled in my chair.

"Helen tells me," Alex fired, everyone else observing us with amused attention, "that you two were tramping around the basements of abandoned buildings last night. And of course the body," he exclaimed, sitting up straight in his chair.

"What about holding hands?" I added, watching a tide of red engulf Alex's face.

"Let's stop this before it starts," Helen said. "I don't need that kind of protection, Alex. And Nick, you should keep your mouth shut." She stood up, her fists on the table.

Ellen took Jim's hand and said, "It's time for us to go. We'll see you for dinner."

A new social pattern took form before my eyes. Kim Snowden grabbed my hand and suggested that I accompany her food shopping. We left Helen and Alex trying to decide if they should make up or have a real fight.

Everybody behaved at dinner. Including me. We cooked up a large pot of spaghetti and three or four different sauces to meet the group's lifestyle, health, and cuisine sensibilities. It was easy and fun, and the buoyancy of the group had recovered from the lunchtime dose of relationship angst.

Not surprisingly, dinner conversation turned to politics and the question of what should be done in a time of political machines, patronage, and untrammeled growth. Alex listened as if he were visiting a zoo, intrigued by the colors of the birds, but happy there was a fence. Jim Majors and Kim Snowden squared off, Jim calling for local action and Kim arguing for careful public disclosure. Ellen swayed between the two sides, while Helen and I remained agnostic.

About 9 PM Jim suggested that we all go to the Double B for beer and country dancing.

"We got ourselves three couples here, at least the way I count. Let's have some fun."

"That place is dangerous," I laughed.

"This ain't Uptown in the 1970s," Jim replied. "There are reputable people there who like to jiggle."

We all gave in after being prodded and cajoled by Jim, and walked the three blocks to the Double B, howling upbeat country songs like, "My Dog Done Left Me At the Altar."

No fights broke out while we were at the Double B, although there were close calls. I knocked someone's coat off a chair, only to find out that it was a vintage ENCO gas jockey jacket from the 1960s. I put it back with reverence. As a tall sort with an untamed dance style, Jim threw a couple of wild elbows that were not well received. Other than that we had fun, failing miserably at the line dances that had come into vogue, doing better on the free form.

There was a moment, when Kim and I were dancing, that I thought of giving up on Chicago, Tom Woods, and Helen Trent, and settling down with Kim in Union Pier. Our eyes met, and the moment passed. I didn't know why.

We got home after midnight. I was on my cot and asleep within minutes.

CHAPTER 12

▼

The jerking of the train flipped my mental channel from its fixation on the mottled commercial strip of South Chicago. Undermined during the past two decades by the collapse of the steel industry, South Chicago is a landscape of abandonment: no more South Works, Wisconsin Steel, or Republic Steel. And so went the working class and stable community of white ethnics, blacks, and Latinos. Disinvestment undermined the community but the political machine still lorded over South Chicago, siphoning off public dollars and preventing independent political action from upsetting its fiefdom.

Sam's call at 6 AM had interrupted a perfectly good sleep. Helen stuck the phone in my ear. "Spivak, catch the 7 AM train back here," Sam said. "Sarah's been beat up pretty bad. She's at University Hospital on the West Side."

I dressed and packed my few things as I absorbed Sam's words.

I explained my sudden departure to Helen, who was making coffee, without revealing secrets like who was Sarah and why I cared. Helen had a look of utter dismay, concluding, I supposed, that I was inextricably drawn to lost causes.

"Sure, I'll drive you to the station. Let me tell Alex. Grab breakfast before you go. There's nothing to eat on the train anymore."

I guzzled a cup of decaf to stoke my furnace and munched on a health muffin that Kim Snowden had baked the day before. I needed more sleep after all that dancing. Maybe on the train. It was two miles to the train platform, not really much of a station, for the South Shore Line that rolled through the center of Michigan City, one of the last inter-urban trains.

"Nick, we've got a few minutes before the train comes. I'd like to talk about something with you," Helen said, after we shut the car doors and snapped on our seatbelts.

"I'm sorry about Alex," I said, anticipating a critique of the day before. "I'm such an ass!"

"I know."

"Honey?"

"Look Nick, you may not like Alex, but he's the best thing going for me. He's stable and he loves me. He's asked me to marry him and I've said yes," Helen said.

"Lucky you," I replied, instantly regretting my bitterness about marriages and skepticism about Alex. "You deserve some happiness," I added, trying to water down the bitterness. "I mean it. I'm serious."

"I believe you," Helen said, letting a tentative smile creep over her face. We were only a couple of blocks from the platform. Union Pier never looked so good, the result of baby boomers buying and renovating the cottages previously owned by working stiffs.

"There's something else," Helen said. "This is the hard part, Nick. Alex doesn't want me working with you on the Woods' case anymore. He thinks it's too dangerous; finding Jutland's body was the last straw. He's also heard rumors about Affazzi. N&M is one of the bank's customers and nobody quite understands where their money comes from. N&M's known for being tough on anybody who asks too many questions. The bank shipped off one of Alex's colleagues who handled the account to Des Moines after Affazzi complained about his unconstrained curiosity."

"A double kiss-off," I laughed. Helen didn't join in. "Are you making this call or is Alex?" I asked.

"Does it matter to you?" Helen said.

"Yes it does. We've worked a lot of industrial hulks together."

"Well, it's my decision," Helen said. "I've listened to Alex. Finding Jutland really scared me. We could be next on the hit list. And the cops don't give a shit."

"You're right on that!"

"I care for you, Nick, and believe in what you're trying to do for your friend and yourself, but not enough to risk my life, business, and boyfriend. How many times have you been beaten up this week? You look like shit! And the noble ride to Cicero! You're lucky you got a ride back. Were you than close to Tom Woods to risk your life?"

Helen pulled the Nissan into a diagonal parking place next to the train platform, in between two pick-up trucks. Commuters and shoppers waited in clumps on the platform, clutching coffee cups, folded newspapers underneath their arms. Another workday. Another shopping day.

I opened the door, but sat back and paused.

"It's okay," I said. "It's my business, not yours. I'm happy for you Helen. I'll keep you in the loop."

"Do that, Nick"

I touched her right hand that rested on the seat and got out of the car, grabbing my brown leather overnight bag out of the back seat.

The site of an oversized black man standing alone in the hallway told me I was approaching Sarah's room. The security guards downstairs instructed me to take the elevator to the fifth floor and then follow the thick blue line on the cracking tile floor to Hospital Room 321. I hated following directions but had little choice.

Sam hugged my shoulders when I reached him, a gesture that was both dangerous to the receiver and one reserved for situations of extreme gravity. That worried me.

"Hold on, Nick," he murmured. "Sarah's groggy and nobody's saying much. All they talk about is taking tests, rest, wait and see. All those words tell me they don't know when Sarah's going to wake up."

"Can I see her?" I asked

"Yeah, you do that. Hold her hand for a while. It will do both of you some good," Sam said. "I need some sleep before my shift. New owners are waiting for a reason to fire me. Can't give them that. All they want to do is run the place down, kick out folks, and build lofts. No way!" he shouted, drawing the attention of two women in white lab coats walking down the hall.

"I'm cool. Don't worry," Sam said. They smiled awkwardly and kept moving.

"What happened? Tell me before you go," I asked.

"You remember our old friend, Randy Blevins?" Sam asked.

"How could I forget," I replied.

"Well, hold on Nick, Blevins is involved in this."

"What do you mean?" I snarled. "Sarah didn't know Blevins? How did she get connected with that piece of shit?"

"Well, there's only so much I know, and even less that I'm going to tell you," Sam said. "You'll just make things worse. It's your way!"

"Give me a little credit," I pleaded.

"I'll think about it," Sam replied

"Thanks for the support."

"Sarah's been okay for a while," Sam began, "but her younger sister visited a couple of weeks ago and set her back. She hadn't seen her for a few years. I guess she didn't tell you about that the other night?"

"Yeah, and I didn't ask," I replied.

"Something went down because two days later she stopped by to say that an old boyfriend from her hometown wanted to see her and that she was thinking of moving back to Iowa. I told her people change a lot slower than what they tell their girlfriends and boyfriends. She laughed and said, 'Sam, I love you'."

"I'm not following this," I said. "What do old boyfriends and Iowa have to do with Blevins? That deadhead is all Chicago."

"That's for you to find out," said Sam. "I'm just saying that Sarah was getting ready to leave when this happened.

"Hospital called at 3 this morning saying that a guy named Blevins had dumped her unconscious in the emergency room. He said he had found her on the street near Greektown. Then he left in a hurry before the cops could talk to him. My business card was in her wallet. You'll have to find out the rest for yourself."

He grabbed my shoulders again and we hugged. It went unsaid that we had screwed up and failed to protect Sarah.

"You take care now. And don't do anything stupid, if that is possible," he said, walking down the hall towards the elevators.

I waited a few minutes to let my feelings settle before entering Sarah's room. She lay in bed, her face bruised and swollen, and her left arm in a cast. Bandages swathed her head. I held her right hand and told her things would be okay. What I really meant, but didn't say out loud, was that I was going to find out who had done this and why as soon as I left the hospital.

After about an hour the attending physician entered and checked Sarah's chart and vital signs. His haggard face showed no emotion. I asked him questions about her condition and prognosis but I received the same answers as Sam in a weary, monotone voice. Wait and see.

I stayed with Sarah for another two hours before the nurse kicked me out.

"More tests," she said. "Come back in the evening."

First things first. I transferred to the Howard El downtown at Jackson and headed north to Uptown, exiting at Argyle Street after an uneventful ride in a half-empty train. My anger must have given off bad karma because the roaming pickpockets, blind entrepreneurs, drunks, gangbangers, and evangelists steered clear of me.

In the 1970s Argyle was the upper limit of No Man's land, known as Appalachian Chicago and the north side skid row. It had the pockmarked look of equal parts urban renewal and arson. It had become Asia town north, and Appalachians had fled west or back home. Gentrification was bubbling full blast.

I walked east towards Andersonville, the Swedish enclave that had turned Middle Eastern during the past decade, except for a few holdout Swedish restaurants, bakeries, and gift shops. Blevins lived in a four-story walk-up apartment building on Carmen Street, in a brown U-shaped courtyard building. Sam had told me that much. He had his own contacts but I was smart enough not to ask how he had come upon this information.

Blevins and I had crossed paths too many times over the years. It was too much of a coincidence that he had delivered Sarah to the hospital and hadn't tried to hide his identity. He knew I would find out, meaning he would know that I was looking for him. So much the better.

You couldn't tell by looking at him that he was purely mean: five foot eight, brown curly hair, and dumpy thin. He looked vulnerable, not violent. Nor did he visibly show the effects of the drugs and alcohol that he had abused since adolescence. A lot of folks were taken in by his soap opera good looks until he opened his mouth.

Blevins did have street smarts. His real ace in the hole was that his father was the top precinct captain for Alderman Ed Devereaux, head of the Finance Committee and a City Council powerhouse from the 23rd Ward on the southwest side. Blevins' father, when not collecting graveyard votes, worked for the Sanitation Department. Everybody called him the "Sheik," because of his magic touch. A touch to be feared.

Randy Blevins was a small-time hustler who used his political contacts to feed his habit. He was a common critter in Chicago, part of the big and happy patronage family. He was known among housing rehabbers as a regular, if not reliable, source of cheap drywall, lifted from the Park District warehouse with the help from a few friends from the Police Department.

Last time I talked with Blevins I told him he had better pray we didn't meet again. He grinned stupidly, saying, "Go tell the Sheik! He'll fix things for you."

I picked up a chunk of wood from the garbage can on Broadway. That should help me make my point, Sheik or no Sheik.

Blevins wasn't home, or at least no one answered his bell. I went around back and ran up the stairs two at a time. I peered into what I thought was his rear window, seeing nothing but a sink piled high with dirty dishes and a cheap bottle of gin on the kitchen table. The opening of the back door on the floor above and the growl of a dog encouraged me to make a quick retreat from the staircase. Blevins would have to wait.

After the failed Blevins encounter, I retreated to the Siam Café on Bryn Mawr Avenue under the El tracks—another beacon of urban character amidst mediocrity, known for serving white-bread toast with its chicken satay, the perfect food sponge for excess peanut sauce. The rumble of trains above interrupted every other bite, the appropriate soundtrack to city life on a rainy day.

No guard was posted outside Sarah's room when I returned at eight that evening. Opening Sarah's door I wondered whether I would find a miraculous recovery, a comatose young woman, or an empty bed. It was maudlin, but that's what went through my mind. What I found was somewhere in between recovery and comatose. Next to her was a younger woman who bore a striking resemblance to Sarah, except she was not as thin and wore her dirty-blond hair short. She had a stern look on her face.

"You must be Nick Spivak," she said, looking directly in my eyes and rising from the corner of the bed where she had been sitting. She didn't shake my hand. I didn't offer. "I'm Sarah's sister, Margaret," she said. "I caught a plane from the Twin Cities as soon as I could after Sam called."

"Okay, okay," a slight voice said. "Enough introductions. What about me?" Sarah propped her neck up slightly on a pillow to deliver these words, and then slumped back. We moved to opposite sides of Sarah's bed, each of us holding one of her hands. We took turns caressing her brow as she moved in and out of sleep.

At 10 o'clock the attendants brought in a blanket and pillow for Margaret to use in the chair near the window. She had promised Sarah she would stay with her through the night.

"Let's have coffee before they put her down for the night," Margaret said. "They've got to give Sarah her pills and take some blood anyway."

"Sure," I said. "Good idea."

We took the elevator down to the second floor and followed the yellow line. Margaret wasn't good with directions or authority either. We got lost twice.

There was no line in the cafeteria so we served ourselves, paid at the lone register, and sat down in the far corner of the room, away from the few clumps of interns and worn-out nursing aides. We knew that what we had to say required privacy.

Margaret fired with both barrels.

"I'm not sure whether to thank you for supporting Sarah or condemn you for taking advantage of someone as vulnerable as Sarah. You only allowed her to keep functioning without dealing with the fundamental problem of why she attaches herself to losers. And you are one more version of the same, no matter what you think."

Somehow I knew this was coming, had known for a long time that I deserved a verbal thrashing.

"I know what you're saying, I've been saying it to myself for years," I responded. "It's one reason I left Chicago three years ago. It's why I don't call Sarah when I'm in town," I continued, not quite knowing who I was trying to convince. "I thought she was doing better."

"That's bullshit," Margaret snarled. "Don't tell me you didn't have any sense of the consequences. That it was all a momentary lapse. I don't believe it. You don't either!"

"No excuses," I said. "I was lonely, mixed up in my own problems. You're right."

"So now we have the consequences," Margaret said, the self-righteousness climbing in her voice.

"We really don't know what happened yet," I replied. "It may have more to do with the case I'm working on."

"We do know what happened," she said. "Sarah's almost dead! Are you blind!"

I didn't mind taking my licks, but I did object to piling on.

"You know, I've got a feeling this isn't the whole story," I countered. "Sam says you were here a few weeks ago and that your visit precipitated a change in Sarah. She started talking about leaving town. That's a big change to make overnight. I know I'm responsible but something else is going on."

I'm always astounded when an attractive face turns mean and ugly. But that's what happened before my eyes. Margaret grew rigid and grabbed her purse, ready to leave.

"You stay away from Sarah," she ordered. "You're responsible for this and none of your stupid questions will change that. I'm advising the police about your role. We'll take legal action if necessary. Stay away from Sarah!"

"Is that what Sarah wants?" I asked.

Margaret Larsen stormed out of the cafeteria. I sat back and stared at my coffee. I clearly wasn't getting an answer.

C H A P T E R   13

▼

I pulled into the asphalt parking lot of St. Augustine's Lutheran Church, a plain brick building of 1970s design and construction, located in an ex-urb of Milwaukee named Warascota, about thirty miles from downtown. This was Omar Jutland's home, church, and funeral. I arrived to witness the pallbearers pace out carrying the extra-long casket to the black hearse.

Seth Greenburg had loaned me his 1981 Chevy truck, guaranteeing nothing and strongly advising against the whole idea. But I was feeling lucky: why not after the last few days? The trip to Warascota was an uneventful buzz through a cloudy Midwest morning and the rolling flatland of northern Illinois and southern Wisconsin. No mean little valleys to obstruct one's imagination, just a couple of steps above desolate, even with the fast-food embellishments of civilization.

My impeccable timing allowed me to play caboose as the funeral procession drove a few miles to Fairlawn Cemetery, a large expanse of land reserved for the eternal rest of Protestants—any kind of Protestants, I was told later. Omar Jutland had more friends than I would have expected, or a large extended family with time on their hands. And then there were the hangers-on like me and, in the car that almost ran me off the road, Radachek and Pelegrino. They waved as I jammed on the brakes.

It began to drizzle, a cold penetrating wet. I felt sorry for Omar.

The funeral procession wound around the cemetery a few times, much as one would drive through a housing subdivision, perhaps to remind the newly dead inhabitants-to-be of their past lives as suburbanites. The wagon train finally stopped near a tent set up thirty yards from the road. Piles of rich Midwestern prairie loam sat on either side of the plot. People moved from their cars under umbrellas to the tent. Some ran with coats arched over their heads. A few—unwilling to grant the rain priority status—walked at a reflective pace, daring the drops to fall on them. About fifty people gathered by the time the hydraulic lift lowered the casket into the ground and family and friends threw handfuls of dirt on top of the smooth black casket.

A middle-aged woman and two teenage boys dressed in black sat stiffly in the middle of a row of folding chairs perched on the far side of the hole. An older couple, whom I took to be Jutland's parents because of the man's height and angularity, sat next to them. This was Jutland's family. They looked grim—a natural disposition, I suspected. I wondered if they knew that their father, son, and husband had been in Chicago on a doomed Gauntlet expedition.

I tossed the last handful of dirt atop Omar Jutland. The backhoe operator respectfully waited to turn over his engine until I had retreated ten feet from the hole.

Back at the church hall, about thirty survivors milled about, nibbling on carrots and celery sticks and drinking sodas and coffee in a room more suited for square dances. The family sat together in one corner, in a protective huddle against the world and the unknown, the pastor ministering to them in hushed tones. Every few minutes someone would break off from the clumps of milling people to pay their respects to the family. I didn't know there was a plan behind this movement until Radachek elbowed me in the side, saying, "Get up there, Spivak. You're next."

"Don't cause any trouble," Pelegrino said.

Reaching the family I said, "My name is Nick Spivak. I'm very sorry for your loss."

They nodded. The two boys tried to stare me down.

"I didn't know Omar personally but I'm the one who found him in Chicago. I'm investigating the death of a friend who was with Omar the night of his death, the Reverend Tom Woods."

My words elicited more cold stares as if the family couldn't fathom the reason for my presence or had some deeper personal pain that they had not yet dealt with. Omar's wife broke into tears, and pulled her black veil down over her face. The boys turned their heads. Omar's father strode to me, took my arm, and said we should talk outside. I obliged.

"Mr. Spivak, is that right?" he said, his voice cracking voice.

"Yes," I said.

"Your presence upsets us so much because none of us have seen Omar in six months. He simply did not come home from work one day. No message, no phone calls. He just disappeared."

"I take it you talked with the police," I asked.

"Of course. But they were of little help," he answered. "In fact, they made things worse. After a few weeks they offered an explanation, if you can call it that, to Evelyn, Omar's wife. They said this kind of disappearance happens more frequently than you might expect. Middle-aged men seeking new lives, new families perhaps.

"Evelyn refused to talk with them again. She wanted to hire a private detective, but I advised against it after talking with the police.

"It just didn't make sense. Omar's my son. I must say the notion of Omar seeking a new life is out of character. It would require courage and imagination. That's not our strength, I'm afraid."

"Was he in trouble at work or at home?" I asked, hoping that Jacob Jutland could shed some much-needed light on Omar's state of mind. Out of the corner of my eye I saw Radachek and Pelegrino eyeing us through the bay window of the church hall. They didn't look happy. Then again, they seldom did in my limited experience.

"Things were stable at home as far as I know," Jacob Jutland stated. "I'm sure that Omar wasn't the best father or husband. I say that because I wasn't, and Omar and I were alike in most respects. Distracted. Self-absorbed. Not emotional men." He revealed himself and Omar with the matter-of-factness that comes from self-resignation.

"As for work, I don't know. He seemed more remote and perhaps upset in the months before he disappeared. Evelyn told me that he was working extra weekends on a special project for the past few months. She didn't know what it was about. Omar didn't talk about work at home. The police interviewed his partners but didn't discover anything as far as I know.

"I'm surprised," he said, looking around. "I didn't see any of his partners at the service or reception. Only a paralegal, a Ms. Edwards. She's the tall, pretty one with brown hair. I guess they forget quickly when there's not more billable hours," he added with bitterness.

"I have to get back to the family, Mr. Spivak," Jutland concluded, his eyes cast downward. "I hope you find what you are looking for and that it will help us understand what happened to Omar. I must ask you not to bother the family anymore about Omar. Call me if you have additional questions," he said handing me a slip of paper with his name and Minnesota address.

"We want the truth," he said with sadness. "Just not now. Not yet!"

We shook hands. Mr. Jutland took long strides back to the church hall. I remained outside, thinking about the strange lives of families.

If I was looking for a few minutes to make sense of what I had learned from Omar's father I didn't get them. Radachek and Pelegrino filled the gap within seconds, tipping their fedoras to Mr. Jutland as they strolled out from the reception on the concrete sidewalk that led to the parking lot.

"Spivak, always on the job, eh?" chuckled Radachek, looking out of place in this semi-rural setting in his city garb. Perhaps we all did, huddled together as if we were on a neighborhood street corner waiting for a gang fight or a game of stickball.

"What is this guy, tough or stupid?" chimed in Pelegrino. He pulled his black trench coat tight, a big smile cutting across his face like a canyon.

"Find any clues, boys?" I retorted, growing weary of the silly interactions that were following me around the Midwest. "Or you just come up for a free meal? A bit far from Chicago for handouts, but after all, you're Chicago's finest. That's got to mean something, right?"

"Shut up, Spivak!" Radachek instructed. "We're asking ourselves whether you're still messing with police business. We didn't like your conversation with Mr. Jutland. That was out of line. If you're screwing with us, Spivak, we can throw you in the Cook County jig for some R&R, or better yet, run you out of town back to Bawlmore."

"All that sounds like a lot of work, something Javier Centeno might do," I said. "Maybe you should ask him for some tips. And if I'm not mistaken, I think you may have a small jurisdictional problem. Don't you agree?"

In the ways that boys sometimes speak when frustrated, Pelegrino shoved me with surprising strength given his small size. I stumbled back, laughing.

"How many times do we have to replay this movie, boys," I said, backpedaling. "I just want to find the killer of Tom Woods, and maybe even Omar Jutland, whether the Chicago Police Department cares or not. First you interrogate me. Then you help me. Then O'Malley busts my chops. You even cut me off in a funeral procession. What gives? Can't you guys make up your minds?

"You know," I continued, improbably feeling more confident—mainly because they didn't snarl or elbow me. "Two dead. Mysterious circumstances. The Brewery. N&M Ltd. Maybe even a City Council connection. This is the kind of stuff that Jack Delaney and his ilk love to bite into for weeks at a time. It's like handing them a big chunk of their future pension."

It's difficult to watch faces go from blank to crestfallen but I was an expert on emotional gestures, like Margaret Larsen's. Maybe I hurt their feelings—impugning the dignity of law officers sworn to uphold civilization and all that, even when they're from Chicago.

"I'll tell you, Spivak," said a Radachek. "Maybe it will help you, maybe it won't. Jutland didn't belong at UPC. That's a lot of bull to make you and the family go away. The guy was a flake. If I were you, I'd talk to your pal Sampson about Omar Jutland."

Radachek and Pelegrino kept walking to their black, police-issue sedan. "You guys getting overtime for this," I asked, waving goodbye. They didn't reciprocate.

The reception was breaking up by the time I went back in the church hall. The pastor immediately descended on me, a stern look engulfing his boyish face. He was acting as if his flock was under attack by the big bad wolves; maybe that was how people felt about a few boys from Chicago. It must be difficult, I mused, for a person of his age to minister to people so much older and a little bit wiser.

"I don't know what you are trying to achieve by asking such hurtful questions," he lectured, "but I would greatly appreciate it you would look inside yourself and honor the Jutlands' request for privacy."

"Tell me pastor," I asked, ignoring his request. "Why did Omar Jutland run away from home, his job, his family, to attend the Urban Pastors Convocation in Chicago? I take it you are familiar with UPC?"

He nodded. There was a long pause.

"I really don't know," he finally replied, looking around perplexed for an ally to help him out. He did not expect to be grilled back. That was disrespectful.

"Was Jutland a religious man? One who cared deeply about the poor, the downtrodden?" I sensed I had him on the run. There wasn't time for me to feel bad about pestering an innocent pastor from up north.

"I don't know what to say," the pastor replied, again looking around, now to make sure that our conversation wasn't being overheard. "He rarely attended church services, mostly on religious holidays, and he never became involved in our committees, volunteer work, or missions. I'm quite surprised."

"Why would he pick Chicago and Reverend Lee Sampson?" I asked. "Did you make this recommendation?"

"I'm sorry. I really don't know what motivated Omar or why he went to Chicago. Evelyn, Omar's wife, did mention that he had a college friend in Chicago, someone he hadn't seen for many years, but that's all I can think of. UPC is not the type of missionary work that we support. I'm afraid we're less activist and considerably more conservative in outlook."

"You prefer handouts rather than fishing lessons?" I asked, holding my breath.

"I'm not sure what you mean. We are..."

"Thank you, Pastor. I'll keep in mind what you said about privacy."

There was no more to be learned from the young pastor. I also noticed that the attractive Ms. Edwards was leaving, so I shook the pastor's hand and walked quickly after her. I caught up half way to the parking lot.

"Excuse me," I said, as I came up beside her. "Jacob Jutland said you worked with Omar..."

"And you are?" she cut off in mid-stride, a look of surprise and interest on her broad but finely featured face. She wore a tailored black wool coat. She observed me observing her.

"My name is Spivak and I'm looking into the death of a friend who was with Omar in Chicago—Reverend Tom Woods. He was murdered two days before Omar. I'm trying to understand his murder and who was responsible. Omar is definitely a part of the puzzle. But I really don't understand how he fits. Do you have a few minutes?"

She stared at me for a moment, running her own mental calculation. After all, this was the 1990s, and nobody's stated credentials were to be believed nor trusted. Least of all mine.

"Listen," she said, "Follow me and you can buy me a drink. Funerals are depressing, aren't they, and I'm freezing from this rain. We have to drive a few miles to the next town. This one's dry. Think you can follow directions?"

I nodded, apprehensively.

I caught up again with Dorothy Edwards at a box-like hotel near the interstate, a darkened bar with tables in the back. It was part of a chain of restaurants with an obnoxious name and even more obnoxious advertising about its after-work rewards. But it served its purpose. We ordered brandies and I coaxed her into telling me about herself.

Dorothy Edwards was a brash and confident brunette who grew up in a working-class neighborhood on the south side of Milwaukee. She had made her way to law school at Marquette and then dropped out to become a paralegal, turned off by the Socratic method, competition, and her ex-husband. Given her aptitude for numbers and computers, she made more money than most of the legal associates.

"So, what was it like to work with Omar Jutland?"

"No one really worked with Omar," Edwards said, sniffing her brandy and looking off into the dark. "He was cut from the original mold for loners. No one got close. The firm tolerated him, in fact promoted him, because no one could do a better jobs at business valuations during due diligence. Omar had law and accounting degrees and a nose for soft financing. Every so often he would call upon my computer skills. But I wouldn't say we worked together."

"What about during the months before he disappeared?" I asked. "Was there anything he was working on that might explain why he left so suddenly? And did he ever mention an old college friend in Chicago?"

I was moving too fast for Ms. Edwards and she let me know it.

"Don't be in such a hurry," Ms Edwards said, chuckling. "Let's take it slow if that's possible. I've just spent the afternoon mourning someone I hardly knew and barely liked. And call me Dorothy."

"So what do you do for fun when not computing or mourning?" I asked, trying my best to slow down, or least head in another direction.

She gave me a look that was hard to read. I waited for her to throw her brandy glass at me or to escape this dark hole and me.

She did neither. We didn't talk much about fun for the next two hours and three rounds. That's expensive with no client to bill. We shared, in gruesome detail, all our love relationships that had crash-dived, burned out, or disintegrated. All the books say not to talk about old relationships on your first date, but we were having a business meeting, not a date. There's nothing like sharing with someone you don't know. There's understanding, empathy, and warmth, all based on a lack of knowledge. Hurrah for ignorance.

By then, Dorothy was ready to tell me about the rise and fall of her marriage, a partnership that had been ended three years before. George, an up-and-coming lawyer at another Milwaukee firm, was not a drinker, abuser, or womanizer. He just preferred men.

It's inevitable that warmth and understanding may turn into lust and desire, especially if the parties are reasonably matched and fed on liquor. We ended up in her loft apartment just south of Milwaukee's downtown in the midst of factories, rivers, and rail right-of-ways. Our clothes began to come off after the first kiss, leaving a garment trail from the living room to the small bedroom, and soon our arms and legs intertwined in a mad rush. We eventually fell asleep on her big bed covered with a handmade down quilt.

Awakening around 8 that night, we touched each other's bodies with more finesse and a little less raw animal hunger. Our bodies and tempos fit naturally. This put us both on guard. Do good accidents really happen?

We returned to the topic of Omar Jutland after Dorothy and I joined forces in the kitchen, concocting a vegetable stir fry with sun-dried tomatoes and pine nuts on top of fusilli. I skipped the red wine, sensing that I would sleep in the Balboa that night. We were both becoming nervous about prolonged intimacy with a near-stranger.

"Omar asked me for a special computer run maybe a month or six weeks before he disappeared," Dorothy said after we began drinking mugs of freshly brewed decaf. "He was working on a due diligence review for the purchase of a grain co-op in Nebraska by a Chicago partnership named N&M, I think."

I gulped out loud when I heard the name N&M, spraying Dorothy with some of my coffee.

"Sorry," I said in embarrassment, handing her a napkin.

"N&M means something?" Dorothy asked.

"Yeah, sorry," I said. "That's my way of saying that N&M is in the middle of things but I'm not sure how and why. What was the computer run he asked for? Maybe that holds the answer."

"Well, it was a rather strange request, but I enjoyed it for that reason. I had to try some new stuff. He asked me to run a time-series analysis on grain output for fifteen co-op acquisitions throughout the Midwest during the past four years, ten by N&M and five by other firms. Corporate farms have taken over what's left of family farming, but they're not equally successful. I think that's what Omar was looking for, but that's just an impression."

"What's the purpose of grain co-ops when corporate farmers are running things?"

"That's the point, although Omar never said as much," Dorothy said, sitting up on the tan couch with her knees crossed under a purple afghan.

"So what's the bottom line?" I asked in a low voice, anticipating a breakthrough of some sort.

"Well," she hesitated. "Omar never picked it up. He disappeared the day I submitted the preliminary findings."

"Did anybody else examine the results?" I asked.

"Nobody."

"How about telling me?" I smiled. "We've shared so much already."

"That's what I'm worried about," Dorothy laughed, lifting my hand off her knee.

"I'll tell you this much. N&M, whoever they are, overvalued those co-ops for purchase based on the ten-year time series. If they would have looked at only the last three years, most of those co-ops were starting to take losses."

N&M was a player in grain futures, industrial real estate, and municipal bonds. This little manipulation seemed like a distraction, a sideline. But maybe it fit with Affazzi's personality.

"Didn't the banks realize what they were doing?" I finally asked.

"Not really. N&M used public pension funds that were accessed through a broker."

"Why would they do that?" I asked. "Kickbacks, scamming loans, politicians?" We both nodded.

"Well, Nick," Dorothy said with a shrug. "You've got it all. I hate to kick a guy out at 11 o'clock at night, half drunk so that you can drive a hundred miles back to a lumpy bed in a seedy Chicago hotel. But I've got to work in the morning. And I think we've shared enough for one day."

Those words would have stung if not for her green sparkling eyes, which suggested something else was on her mind.

I walked over to her and wrapped my arms low around her back, resting my hands on her hips. I kissed her on the lips, looking deep into her eyes. It was scary.

"I hope it's more than one day," I whispered through the kiss.

"I do, too," she kissed back.

CHAPTER 14

▼

Sam handed me an envelope as I stumbled into the Balboa at 2 o'clock in the morning. Sam, it appeared, lived in that cage.

"Last words of Tom Woods," he said. And indeed the letter was from Tom Woods, sent to my Baltimore address and forwarded to Chicago, Balboa Arms being scratched above the crossed-out Chesapeake Apartments.

Sam had more to say. I could tell from his uptight posture. I wasn't sure what I was in for but I knew damn well it had to do with Sarah. We both felt guilt, but both Sam and I knew that I also carried the weight of responsibility, even if I did move to Baltimore.

I beat him to the punch, not knowing until the words came out whether I would sink into self-flagellation about my abysmal record with Sarah or take off on her demonic sister. I took the latter course, not completely out of malice or denial, but because Margaret was hiding something. The moment called for disclosure. I didn't like eating shit by myself.

Sam listened, a solemn look stretched over his expansive face. He was upset and his huge right hand beat a slow rhythm on the counter top, picking up speed as I made my case against Margaret. Paper clips, rubber bands, and pencils kept the beat on the counter.

Finally, Sam said, "Stop, Spivak. Too late for all of that now. Sarah's recovering and she says she's returning to Iowa. She's got some real work to do with her family. And she needs time to mend, without interference. That's all I'm saying. That's what Margaret talked with Sarah about a month ago. Nothing more than that, no matter what you think. You're just being foolish."

I felt like I had run into a brick wall. "As simple as that," I murmured. "Nothing's simple."

"That's what's wrong with you, Spivak. You're scared of simple. It's a dishonor in your twisted view of things. I remember you saying that if a question can be answered, it's not worth asking. That's just bullshit."

"That bad, huh?"

"Yes, my friend."

"Why didn't I pay more attention," I said. I knew deep down about Sarah and her family, but I refused to ask questions or get into it. It was her business, her life.

"That's your story," Sam replied.

"Okay. Okay. Maybe I didn't want to know because it would have screwed up our secret life together."

"Now you're talking," Sam said.

"But she can't be leaving," I protested. "She's hurt. I saw her. There's no way she should be leaving Chicago."

"That's right," Sam replied, "It'll be a few days. And she needs time to deal with the last few weeks."

"Where do I fit in?" I asked.

"You don't fit, Spivak. You blew your chance, baby," Sam grinned.

I hung my head, from total physical and moral exhaustion. "Naw, its not that bad, Spivak. You were just stupid. No surprise. Sarah wants to see you. She made Margaret mad as hell when she insisted. You go see her in a few days."

"Goodnight, Sam."

I skipped El Torta after a fitful six hours filled with images of caskets, fusilli, and railroad tracks. I needed an eating place a notch more depressing and I knew where to find it—the Balboa Arms coffee shop. Located on the first floor on the opposite side of the lobby from Sam's caged outpost, it rarely attracted anyone who lived outside of the cloistered Balboa community. No one dared enter. The flow of customers represented a cross-section of the down and out of humanity—the homeless, those ascending in recovery, those descending in alcohol and drugs, the generic transitions, political organizers, the just-released, illicit entrepreneurs, bad writers, and me.

A seventy-year-old solo waitress brought me a health breakfast of decaf, boxed orange juice, and rye toast with no butter. She snarled while putting down the food as if I was wasting her time and skills by eating such fare. She and Sam were the only solid anchors for many of the hotel residents. They were revered in this culture of loss.

Tom Woods' letter was stuffed in a legal-sized white envelope that had a Pennsylvania return address, perhaps to prevent it from arriving back at UPC, I thought. It was mailed on October 17th, the day before the Gauntlet began and three days after he had left a phone message for me at the Balboa. I wondered why he hadn't called me in Baltimore, then remembered that my answering machine was broken and beyond my electronic capabilities to fix.

I read the letter three times, absorbing every nuance of Tom's state of mind. His handwriting in blue ink was graceful but hurried. Reading the letter the third time made me realize the fragility of relationships and my lack of investment in them.

Dear Nick:

Greetings. I hope my letter finds you in good health and engaged in interesting work. How could it be otherwise with you? Make time for yourself and room for others to share in your life, Nick. It does wonders.

I'm finally enrolled in the UPC training after all these years. It's nothing new, but it's a welcome breather from the death rattle of my congregation. The living dead are immovable. I've met a few good people in Chicago who I'm spending most of my time with. I missed you last time I was in Baltimore. I hope we can spend some time together soon. There is a lot to catch up on.

Lee Sampson lives up to your colorful, and deeply cynical, portrayal. I'm afraid, though, that I've learned something that casts doubt upon his integrity. I need your help to make sense of what I have learned. I don't want to make a mistake.

I think it's another case of a fellow crusader who has lost his way after investing an enormous amount of physical and emotional energy in a cause that is closely associated with him. That's always when temptation strikes. We feel so deserving after what we've contributed, after what we have given up. It's blinding.

In the simplest terms, UPC is in deep financial straits. I'll tell you later how I found out about this. Fewer clergy and lay people are interested in cities and social justice. And there's competition from national community organizing networks. Sampson took donation of the office building of a Catholic Boys School on Monroe Street ten years ago. It needed renovation and Sampson was able to solicit donations and volunteer labor. The main building was empty until a few years ago when developers converted it into loft apartments, using all the public development incentives and historic preservation tax credits that they could get their hands on.

Not long after that, UPC's finances started to crumble. No one was interested in urban survival anymore. But Sampson did receive a number of unsolicited offers to buy the building because of all the upscale development starting to occur around it. UPC turned down the offers. Sampson finally took out a large loan on the building to cover operating expenses and to launch a national fundraising drive to build a permanent endowment. It failed miserably, I'm sorry to say, and UPC's financial condition grew worse.

Now to how I found out about this. One of the participants in our class is an odd fellow named Omar Jutland, an introvert if I ever saw one from Milwaukee. He went to college with Sampson, but has no religious convictions or interest in community affairs whatsoever. For some reason he's in hiding, or that's my guess from the way he behaves: he avoids the more public aspects of our program and I've seen him twice in heated conversations with Sampson in one of the back rooms. He prefers to stay on the margins and never joins in.

Anyway, he's an accountant, and Sampson asked him to take a look at the books and to advise ways to restructure UPC's debt. UPC has a Board of Directors meeting coming up during the last week of October at which time they have asked Sampson to present a new financial plan. From what I've heard, if Sampson's plan doesn't impress them they may be willing to disband UPC or look for merger partners. It's that serious.

Why Jutland came to me I'm not sure, but he saw something in the books that scared him, and something in me that inspired trust. He was desperate when he finally lured me out of UPC for a walk and blurted out the whole story. He gave me a copy of the papers for safekeeping and made me promise secrecy.

Nick, you know details are not my forte, and this situation needs more careful attention for both Jutland's and UPC's sake. That's why I'm writing you. I need your help. You understand development loans and transactions, and you have access to real estate and finance experts, people you trust. You also know Chicago, and I don't. If my gut instincts are right, UPC's problem may be deeper than a poorly structured loan.

Please take a look at the enclosed papers and call me as soon as you can. I'll be staying at UPC through next week. Say you're from the Presbyterian Synod and leave a number I can reach you at. Maybe I can convince you to come out to your old stomping grounds for a week.

We can talk and spend some time together as well. I would enjoy that. Thanks, friend!

Peace and Justice,

Tom Woods

The enclosed documents included a standard commercial mortgage financing agreement and assorted riders and covenants. The usual stuff. I didn't recognize any of the principals until I saw the name Devereaux as one of the trustees for the financing agreement. His name on the papers could refer to a lot of things, including Alderman Devereaux's position as City Council Finance Chair, or his lawyerly role in other private real estate deals. It didn't have to mean anything sinister or corrupt, but then again, this was Chicago.

My waitress wasn't a believer in the metaphysics of the endless cup of coffee, particularly for decaf. Her skeptical eye drove me out of the coffee shop and into the lobby in hopes of laying claim to one of the two ancient and well-used pay phones.

I was out of luck.

A shriveled old man Balboa residents called The Canary had a firm grip on one of the phone booths He had the unsettling habit of repeating verbatim out loud and in a singsong voice anything you said to him or, for that matter, anything he overheard. And he was good up to twenty feet. His renditions included tone, inflection, and gestures. Needless to say, he didn't have many friends. I had never heard him speaking in his own voice before; but here he was in the phone booth I coveted arguing with his bookie about the day's races at Sportsman's Park. I felt like giving him a dose of his own medicine, maybe even messing up his numbers. The temptation passed.

The other pay phone was under the control of a red-haired Balboa Arms prostitute. She exuded optimism that could only be drug-induced, and was taking appointments for the afternoon bounce. She threw me an officious look—over the rim of her librarian, half-glasses—that said, Look elsewhere, fellah. I'm booked.

I only had fifteen minutes before I had to leave for my meeting with Seth. I made a quick decision to invade Sam's privacy and ask if I could use the house phone for two calls.

"Keep it short, Spivak," Sam said, as he looked up from the Daily Times.

I wanted to call Helen but our parting at Union Pier had left a sore spot and a big hole in Team Spivak. It would take a few more days for me to heal and shore up my bench reserves. Helen would be hard to replace; nobody knew what she knew about neighborhoods and City Hall finances. Deep down I couldn't argue with her preference for safety and somebody to love her. I just didn't seem able to find that combination myself. That made me jealous.

Maybe Dorothy would change all that.

So I called Sweeney at the Department of Urban Development—a planning analyst as they had been called for decades in a department that reorganized and cast off commissioners like a snake shedding skin. Sweeney was special because he preserved a soft spot for rebels and ne'er-do-wells who got up the gumption to say, Fuck you! And he wasn't all that particular about who you said it to as long as they could reasonably be described as a boss.

The Department had recently computerized all of Cook County's real estate parcel records since 1980—sales, purchases, mortgages, liens, and court actions. Sweeney could dig up the original dirt on the UPC building within seconds— that is, if he was holding office hours and was cooperative. A long shot, indeed.

"Sweeney," his cigar-cured voice growled into the phone.

"Spivak here, Sweeney. "Calling direct from the Balboa. Greetings! I'm inviting you to enlist in an attack on the monolith, the iron heel in Jack London's words. Strictly amateur and off the books. Are you game?"

"Tell me, Spivak, does this request have anything to do with Burke acting like he has a bug up his ass?" Sweeney asked. "I haven't seen him so hyper since planning for the 1993 World's Fair collapsed in the mid eighties. A true civic catastrophe. People hear him murmuring your name, the Brewery, and somebody named Tom Woods. He doesn't look so good."

"I can't tell a lie," I grinned into the phone. I saw Sam out of the corner of my eye signaling to hurry up with a twist of his big right paw.

"In that case, count me in," Sweeney said.

"Delicious! What I need is information on the most recent loan transaction for 1024 W. Monroe Street. UPC headquarters. Lee Sampson's place."

"Easy enough. Let me fire up Betsy," Sweeney replied with the intensity of a converted computer nerd.

While Betsy was doing her thing I hand-signaled back to Sam to stall for more time. I must have embarrassed him into submission with my deft finger movements because he turned his back on me.

"Got it!" Sweeney crowed. "What ya need?"

"How about sources of funds and anything on appraisals? Devereaux is listed as trustee on the mortgage documents so keep an eye out for him."

More silence. I knew my luck with Sam was about up. Citizens were not allowed in the business cage, the center of action and protection from Balboa residents. If the crazy set saw me back here they might conclude that Sam was vulnerable and try something stupid that would only waste our time and earn Sam a reprimand. That wouldn't be a good thing given the new owners and their real estate dreams.

"Bingo, baby!" Sweeney cried.

"Tell me," I said in a therapeutic voice, calming Sweeney so that his words weren't garbled and I could write down the information.

"N&M Ltd is the source of funds for the loan. They're on LaSalle Street. Devereaux's a trustee because this has something to do with the TDD program. That's not so unusual. He shows up on all these deals. What's strange is that the appraised value is $100,000 less than the loan amount on the building. Very odd. We usually make the arithmetic add up."

"Remember we're in Chicago, Sweeney."

"How could I forget? Oh, by the way, the loan's interest-free for the first five years and then it's graduated, so to speak."

"Sweet deal! You did good for the people, Sweeney! Gotta go and report back to Greenburg. This will tickle his fancy."

CHAPTER 15

▼

Wabash Avenue between Harrison and Lake Streets is a narrow canyon defined by the Loop El and its centipede-like structure that runs down the middle of the street, casting big shadows and producing a constant rumble. Its steel legs mysteriously attract drunk drivers and the uninitiated, who have unknowingly ventured into the Loop with their oversized cars. The El dampens Wabash Avenue land values and hence the economic incentives for hungry developers to tear down small and mid-sized brick buildings in favor of glass high-rises. For the most part, small stores define the street life of Wabash Avenue, the upper floors of the buildings either being closed off or containing a jumble of jewelry stores, dentist offices, photography studios, and delicatessens. The Center for Neighborhood Options, that is, Seth Greenburg, occupied a hole-in-the wall office on the third floor of the Mansfield building on Wabash.

Greenburg grabbed the office cheap after the feds cracked down on a diamond dealer for smuggling contraband gems out of South Africa. No one else in the business wanted to take a chance on the hot location. A residual number of mysterious calls and unsavory visitors confirmed their fears, but they weren't prepared for Seth Greenburg.

The Center, called CNO by the in-the-know or the lazy, was a one person operation, plus volunteers like Sarah Larsen, that attached itself to community organizations or neighborhoods that have taken on contentious, and frequently hopeless, battles involving the demolition of public housing, master plans, urban renewal, and plant closings. A financial endowment from an anonymous group of progressive grandchildren of successful 19th Century meatpackers and railroad barons enabled CNO to be independent, take on unpopular fights, and stay in the battle for the long haul.

Conservative columnists or business papers occasionally wrote exposes of CNO, lamenting how the dollars generated by good, old-fashioned capitalism were being used to obstruct progress. Fortunately, these laments were just that, and nothing came of them. But there was lingering resentment.

I had worked for a neighborhood organization that received help from CNO in the 1970s. After a few rounds of verbal combat with Seth, we formed a lifelong bond that primarily consisted of arguing and drinking beer in places like the Par-a-dice, Billy Goat, or the now-demolished Tiny Tap on Canal Street. Seth had called early that morning and said I should come over to the office about 10 o'clock.

I hesitated in front of CNO's door, the top half of which contained a smoky pane of glass, before knocking. Who knew what jibes and verbal acrobatics I would encounter when crossing the threshold. I needed to be at my most glib. I knocked.

"Get in here, Spivak," I heard before my hand left the glass. "What'aya taking a piss on my door?" he growled.

I obliged and walked into a two-room suite that consisted of Seth's office and the entry corridor to Seth's office. It kept things simple. Seth Greenburg leaned back in his captain's chair on wheels behind a cluttered wooden desk, a black phone jammed against his ear, his back towards the dirty plate-glass window facing Wabash. A train thundered by causing the windowpane to hum ever so slightly. Seth wore cowboy boots, blue jeans, and his hat of the day, a Russian sailor's cap.

He barked into the phone mouthpiece with hyperbolic finality, "Tell Alderman Devereaux that we're filing a Freedom of Information Act request with the City's information officer to obtain copies for all of the City's Tax Development District agreements. No, we don't need a meeting with him first. We'll meet after we receive the documents that we requested five times during the past six months. Yeah, okay, thanks."

He hung up, his chair crashing to the floor with a thud. Seth sat behind his desk with his hands folded in front of him like a choirboy.

"So, Spivak, you prepared to wrassle with alligators as our favorite mayor use to say? "Out here on the prairie."

"I don't know," I replied. "All the wrestling I've been doing is with women for the last few days. And I'm losing bad."

"Yeah, Sam told me about Sarah, and Helen called to say how guilty she felt about dumping you for a downtown banker. You're quite an operator, Spivak," Seth said. He broke into a long riff of laughter, punctuated by coughs generated by decades of smoking Pall Malls. He had quit on doctor's orders several years ago, but the coughing persisted.

I told Seth about Milwaukee and my falling in love with Dorothy Edwards. I surprised even myself by describing this one-nighter as falling in love.

Seth chuckled, "One at a time, Spivak. Dorothy sounds like the real thing. Don't mess it up like you usually do."

Getting chastised, or advised for that matter, by Seth about relationships with women was a cause for humor. He had two divorces and his current wife threatened to lock him in the doghouse in back of their brick two-flat in Humboldt Park if he didn't start bringing in more money. She wanted more out of life than a non-profit salary and no benefits. "Couldn't do without them," Seth said.

We stepped onto the Englewood El at Wabash and Monroe and grabbed straphanger poles rather than becoming trapped in seats that crushed our knees. This was not the most lucrative El line by a long stretch. It cut through the poor and disinvested neighborhoods of southside black Chicago. By the time we reached Roosevelt Road, Seth and I were the only whites in our subway car.

Seth grinned and said, "It's a free country, ain't it?"

"Sure. Look around at the neighborhoods," I replied.

Seth had briefed me for an hour on the protocols required for our visit with Alphonius Jackson, who was well hidden and guarded somewhere on the south side. Apparently he thought someone was out to shoot or stab him. Seth thought so, too.

I didn't ask Seth about how he made contact with Alphonius, figuring that such a question would violate one of the protocols and land me in deep shit. After listening to the rules of engagement, I concluded that Seth had very solid relationships or that we really were two stupid white guys. We were to meet a young man named Dish at the entrance to the 43rd Street station. He would be wearing a Chicago Bulls hat with the brim pointing forward, an unusual and perhaps dangerous fashion statement. No questions asked, we were to follow Dish and his directions, no matter how they sounded to our tin ears.

"Why don't we wear blindfolds?" I asked.

"Don't go there, Spivak," Seth said. "It's their turf and they know the risks. We don't, so follow the rules if you want to meet with Jackson."

So we followed Dish as he led us down an alley and into what looked like an abandoned building from the rear. We waited for an hour in a room made perpetually dark by boarded-up windows.

At one point I began to say something to Seth and Dish immediately intervened.

"No talking!"

I kept my big mouth shut.

An hour is a long time for me. I've been self-diagnosed as having attention deficit disorder, my personal path to victimhood. Some of my life's oddities made some kind of emotional sense with this diagnosis. Why I have a hard time being a Zen Buddhist. Why I can't read Hegel. Why I can't stand in line at McDonalds. Why I can't set my VCR. Why I can't stand in one spot.

In this case I did, but I had to try. My mind surfed topics and images like a possessed television set in a sleazy motel on South Michigan Avenue. Tom Woods. Alderman Devereaux. Lieutenant O'Malley. Dorothy Edwards. All kinds of things flashed and twisted in my mind as I sat there in darkness. And what really did happen to Centeno? I knew he was waiting to take me for another ride to Cicero. I began to sweat.

Dish must have gotten fed up with my messy brain waves or decided things were safe. He led us out the back and down the alley half a block and through a gate into what looked like the rear courtyard of a church. At that point he actually did put blindfolds on us and walked us around for what seemed like an eternity, or at least ten minutes. Eventually he coaxed us up some steps and then took off the blindfolds. We entered a door and climbed ten steps or so, went through a kitchen and into a study with its curtains drawn. A black man, of medium height and weight stood with his back to us reading a magazine.

He turned, grimly smiling, "Alphonius Jackson."

"So now you've met number four," said Jackson, looking from Seth to me as we sat on worn soft chairs around a wooden coffee table. It looked like some kind of church building because crosses adorned the walls.

"Two dead, one in relapse, and one in hiding. That should give Reverend Sampson an inspiring Gauntlet story for his new recruits."

"*If* Sampson gets any more recruits," Seth said. We all laughed, but our faces showed the pain and loss.

"How's Sister Mary?" Jackson asked.

"Safe but shaky at the moment, I'm afraid," I replied. "The Brewery mess triggered a lot of bad memories for her. She said she's going back to Boston after she's had some straight talk with Sampson."

"Yeah, I owe him one, too," Jackson said. "Sister was the most solid and real. Her life speaks commitment. Tom was fine, your friend, I'm told," he nodded to me. "A bit romantic but focused on the important things. Jutland was a joke, from what I could tell—along for the ride and lost and drowning from who knows what. A sad case."

"Tell me something," I said. "I don't understand what you were even doing at the UPC training. You've got more city smarts, contacts, and exposure than the whole lot at UPC, including Sampson."

Seth stared at me as if my impertinent question reflected on him.

Jackson waved him off with a fluid movement of his left hand. "Fair enough," he said, "but the question also applies to Tom and Sister Mary. They taught me some things."

"Okay," I said. "What about for you?"

"You're right," Jackson continued. "UPC training was a cartoon picture of my life and the neighborhoods I grew up in, if you really want to know. Good intentions at the beginning. Now it's a Sampson thing."

"Why bother?" Seth asked.

"Let's say I was looking at the competition," Jackson smiled.

"Competition for what?" I asked.

Jackson sat back in his chair, staring at me. He was dressed in casual black pants, shirt, and button-up sweater. He had been cooped up here for a week with no one to talk to about what had really happened at the Brewery. But it wasn't that simple, as I was about to find out. Things never were.

"I suppose they asked me to do it because I'd just moved back to Chicago and nobody really knew me except the street punks on 63rd. I went straight from Joliet to the seminary in Birmingham and then to inner-city congregations out East. Haven't been on the streets of Chicago for fifteen years. But that don't mean I've forgotten the streets.

"I was asked back to develop a youth ministry at Shiloh Baptist on 35th and King. Just in case you're wondering, that is not where we are now. I'm smarter than that. Shiloh's a member of the South Side Interfaith Alliance, a group of congregations that have joined to improve our neighborhoods and schools."

Seth gently interrupted, "Spivak, the SIA is after your time, but you can probably guess who's in the mix.

Jackson watched Seth and me trade jabs and looks. I nodded.

"Private bullshit," Seth apologized to Jackson.

Jackson nodded. "SIA's part of a national network of community organizations centered in ten or so Midwest cities. We have more than 1,000 member congregations and 100,000 members. So we face a training challenge to make sure everybody's on the same page, and that cultivating leadership is more than words."

"That's the trick of organizing," I said, "to make the powers-that-be think you're on the same page. Tough to make real."

"Don't be cynical," Seth said.

"The SIA wants to set up a leadership training center in Chicago," Jackson began again. "It's as simple as that. And UPC is a big part of our competition for local funding and leaders."

"So did Sampson know you were spying on him?" I asked.

Again, Seth stared at me with cold eyes.

"Hope you're as tough on Sampson as on the little folk!" Jackson said.

"Tougher," I laughed.

"Well, I don't think Sampson knew. But I can't completely vouch for that. He always seemed uptight around me, suspicious like."

"You're everything he's not," Seth said. "Black, street, real, a leader with integrity, and not afraid to speak your mind. That would scare him as much as the SIA training center.

"Maybe," Jackson said.

"So what was your final verdict on the competition?" I asked, trying to keep us on track.

"UPC was no competition." Jackson said. "Could have written my report after an hour in that place. Old paradigm. Moral witness and guilt. But not empowerment. UPC still has a national reputation but the training was half-hearted and Sampson had given the same speeches too many times. I would have left early but I wanted to experience the Gauntlet."

"Yeah, the spiritual roller coaster," I replied.

"Don't be too quick too judge," Jackson admonished. "There's something to having a lifeboat experience."

"Not when you fall out and drown," I said.

We took a break for lunch. Dish and one of his comrades had brought food from Greens N Things, a healthy soul food restaurant that had recently opened as part of the long-awaited Bronzeville restoration project, an attempt to revitalize Chicago's version of Harlem and home of the Chicago Blues. The area had suffered private disinvestment, urban renewal, massive public housing that appalled Soviet planners when built in the 1960s, and the upward and outward movement of blacks since the 1960s. There had been a number of attempts to spur this redevelopment over the past decade, and it looked like this one would stick. Bronzeville occupied a strategic ribbon of land between Hyde Park, home of the University of Chicago, and the South Loop, and was a stone's throw from the massive McCormick Place Convention Center. Many feared that any redevelopment would set off a land grab and neighborhood residents would lose, again.

During lunch Seth told a few anecdotes about the Land Grab Coalition that had emerged to fight the Bronzeville restoration. Their not-so-obvious slogan and sound bite was "Manhattanization is Discrimination," an oblique reference to the all-to-obvious attempts of Chicago developers to conquer the South Side lakefront. Any one who compromised with the City or development interests in this regard became memorialized on their Black Removal Top Ten List.

We all helped clean up after lunch and returned to business.

"So you want to hear the whole sorry mess again?" Jackson asked.

"The whole thing," I replied. "We know about the University of Illinois college kids, the hot dog stand on Maxwell Street, Mr. Socks, your tussle with Jutland, and the Brewery, at least Sister Mary's version. At this point we need your version of what happened and whether there are missing pieces we need to know about."

"Like why I'm hiding?" Jackson said.

"That's certainly a missing piece," Seth replied.

"Let's start instead with what I want," Jackson said, looking directly into our faces. "I'm the one who's holed up, and maybe I'll tell you about that, but I've got to know what you know. You've been out there chasing the story. If I'm not in on it upfront then you don't get anything."

There was a long pause. And then another. This negotiation was suddenly about something important that hadn't been acknowledged by us. About equal partnerships? About who bears the risk? About the nature of black and white relationships in the city of broad shoulders, patronage, and segregated neighborhoods?

Seth's look told me that it was my deal to make or break. We could walk out of this church, or whatever it was, and be on our way, if Dish would take us, with nothing but bad feelings. Or, we could leave with a full partner. The latter sounded good to me as I thought about it. I had felt alone on this case since being dropped by Helen Trent for a beau. And despite his shushing and scolding, the formal addition of Seth to the team was a godsend.

But it was more than that. There was an unacknowledged racial dimension to almost everything that came down in Chicago—casinos, Tax Development Districts, grain, the UPC, and politics. Any good future for Chicago, and any solution to the case of Tom Woods, I suspected, had to offer a different vision about how local politics should help all Chicagoans move ahead. Alphonius Jackson and the SIA represented one such alternative. This was a no-brainer. I said as much.

"So, now that we're settled on that, what's the game? Jackson asked. "Tell me what you really think is going on. Don't hold back. Tell me a story, Spivak," Jackson urged, with an intensity that was infectious.

As a confirmed introvert, I find thinking out loud to be anathema, messy, and embarrassingly revealing. So I took a long minute to gather my thoughts. I had been following multiple leads and what seemed like scattered inquiries. How did it all fit together? Or did the pieces fit? Maybe there were multiple puzzles and multiple games?

"It's about grain," I blurted out, watching the incredulous looks on the faces of Seth and Jackson. All my mulling about N&M, Affazzi, and Chicago came back time and again to the same plot.

"A real Chicago story about prairie alligators," I continued. "The Brewery is owned by N&M Ltd which is a broker in grain, shipping, and real estate. Jutland was working for a law firm that was evaluating the worth of grain co-op acquisitions, by none other than N&M.

"There's lots of other noise to be sure," I added. "Smuggling and drugs, ripping off public subsidies, City Council, and Alderman Devereaux."

"But it's really about grain."

I didn't know if Jackson still wanted me as a partner after hearing my grain hypothesis. Maybe he thought I was a romantic. Or maybe he knew that Chicago produced schemes like that one all the time. Seth looked at me quizzically, twisting strands of his graying-brown beard. In any case, Jackson felt obliged to fulfill his end of the bargain.

He skipped the preliminaries and jumped right to the heart of events at the Brewery. He confirmed that he had an argument with Sampson, calling him a Double A bullshitter.

"And yes, I messed with Omar Jutland. That was out of line, but I couldn't help myself," he said.

"Didn't look to me that Omar knew the fellas he ran into at the Brewery. Both white. One was of medium height with a mouth; the other was taller and didn't say much. The police invented that Latino gangbanger fight.

"When we first saw them the shorter one was ordering Jutland to get into the truck or else. I could tell by the body movements that things were already not following the plan, whatever it was. Jutland resisted, saying this wasn't what he had agreed to. That's when all hell broke loose and they pushed him into the truck.

"At that point Tom and I lost Sister Mary and were caught between the headlights of the two trucks and the gunfire. Tom found a nylon sports bag on the ground as we stumbled along, and picked it up out of reflex or desperation. It must have been dropped by somebody in the truck.

"We made it to Canal Street after the explosion at the other end of the Brewery, and hid behind a low brick retaining wall running diagonally from the loading dock of the Powerhouse building to the street corner. We didn't know what we were in the middle of or who started what, but we wanted to get the hell out of the line of fire. Tom was out of breath when we stopped by. I knew we had to move south and east to reach the safety of my turf, but that was twenty blocks of no-man's-land, Chinatown, and expressways.

"We had barely caught our breath when a pair of headlights hit the wall.

"'Give it up, Woods, Jackson!' Jutland must have told them our names. 'We know you're back there. Give it up. No time for shittin' around. If you don't come out we'll hurt your pal Omar real bad.'

"Tom and I looked at each other. Jutland gave up our names without much fuss, as far as we could tell. So much for Gauntlet solidarity.

"Tom said, 'I can't make it.'

"He could barely breath and was grasping his thighs. 'My leg is all cramped up. You run for it while I try to calm them down. The police should be here any second. Somebody must have called with all this noise and gunfire, even down here.'

"I didn't argue, although it was obvious Tom was putting himself at great risk. These were not your everyday punks. But we had no other choice. No weapons. But I hesitated, Tom definitely didn't know what he was messing with.

"Before I could come up with another plan, Tom jammed the bag into my arms and stood up.

"'Don't shoot,' he said. 'It's Reverend Woods. I'm alone.'

"'Where's Jackson?' the voice behind the lights shouted.

"'I lost him back in the gunfire. I don't know where he is.'

"'Get in the truck,' the voice ordered. 'Check out the wall,' the voice ordered to his sidekick.

"As soon as Tom stood up I began crawling along the base of the brick wall, moving as fast as I could over all the debris on the ground. Pieces of brick, glass, gravel. Police sirens and fire trucks converged from all directions as I was making my escape. There was a lot of shouting between our pursuers and then the truck was gone. They had taken Tom along with Omar Jutland. I made it across 18th Street and down to Joe's Fisheries on the river two blocks south. A friend of mine from Joliet is a fry cook there; after a dirty look from his boss, he took his break and drove me over to King Drive and I was back on home turf. I was safe, or so I thought."

CHAPTER 16

▼

We sat in silence for a moment, absorbing the story of Tom's capture and Jackson's escape. Jackson walked about the room, sipping from a paper cup of hot tea.

"And so what was in the sports bag?" I asked Jackson after he had sat down again.

Seth laughed. "Cool it, Spivak. We don't even know why Reverend Al is hiding on his own turf. That's unexpected."

"No, that's downright embarrassing," Jackson admitted. "But somebody's very connected and has a lot of pull with the gangs. That's why we put you through the paces. I was shot at twice and almost run over by a truck. And that was just day one after the Gauntlet. And we know that this place is probably staked out right now. Dish and his boys are keeping a close eye on the watchers, though. Don't be surprised if we all have to move real quick. I should have warned you earlier, but I didn't want to spoil our fun by making you worry."

Seth and I looked up with a start.

"Us worry?" I said, unsurprised by our unwanted status as prey.

"Yeah, us worry!" said Seth.

"No way a couple of white guys wouldn't be noticed," Jackson laughed. "That's okay. We're ready."

"What about the bag?" I asked, trying to get us back on track.

"Full of crack," Jackson said. "Given the territory, Dish says it could only have belonged to Centeno of the Latin Kings. So there was a deal going down at the Brewery. We found that out and then heard on the grapevine about your ride to Cicero. Old school. You survived, I see."

"Barely," I replied, showing Jackson the bruised hand that Centeno had stomped on.

"I feel sorry for the boys that dropped the bag at the Brewery," Jackson said with genuine sympathy. "That kind of mistake is a death sentence. And these were young kids. Centeno has the reputation of being real tough with his help. He gets them young and keeps them scared. He's a piece of work."

"Tell me about it," I said.

"Dish dropped the bag off at Centeno's place at the tortilla factory on Blue Island Avenue, more like dumped it out of a fast-moving car. Centeno's got more sentries than a high school soccer team, and about the same age. Dish did not want to linger."

"I put a note in the bag that said, 'You've got your dope back. Now's a time to lay off and let folks alone. No use going to war over this.'"

"Can Centeno read?" I asked.

"Dunno, but I'm sure he has some educated hired help."

"Then no more Centeno, right? So who's keeping watch on us, if not Centeno?" I asked.

"Good question," Seth said.

"Centeno must have confided in Radachek that things were okay with me," I said out loud, remembering the message Sam had given me days before.

"Thanks," I said to Jackson. "One less unhappy customer pounding on my body."

"Unfortunately, the gangs, or whoever, haven't given up on me," Jackson responded. "They don't let go easy, or someone is providing them with incentives to keep on top of me. Either way, I'm beginning to lose my patience."

Dish appeared out of nowhere, vigorously nodded to Jackson and waved his right arm and muttered, "Time to move" all at the same time. Seth and I were the decoys. These punks and their investors were after Jackson, not us. Jackson needed a new and better hiding place.

"Good luck," I said to Jackson. "We'll keep you current, partner."

"You do that," Jackson replied.

"Move!" said Dish.

Dish led Seth and me out the back of the building, thankfully without blindfolds, and down the steps. We moved quickly, fueled on adrenalin. Luck was not with us. Seth stumbled on the bottom step and twisted his ankle. Dish and I pulled him along the cracked concrete walkway to the alley gate. A gypsy cab awaited us.

The driver asked in a high pitched voice, "And where can I take your sad asses?" as Dish slipped back into the yard and out of our immediate lives. We both shouted, Seth drawing upon the very real pain in his ankle, "IC Station at 51st." It was a long two miles.

Our car and driver were not likely to win either bumper cars or a hundred-yard dash. The car was a beat up Chevy Impala from the late 1970s—black with a white top and rust spots eating out the bottoms of the side doors. Our driver couldn't have been more than sixteen, and had the Yellow Pages stuck under a ratty purple cushion so he could see over the steering wheel.

Sounding like a motor launch in idle, our car nosed out of the garbage-strewn alley onto 40th Street. Seth yelled as a late model blue sedan screeched towards us, motivating our teen driver to floor the accelerator and fishtail a left turn as the attack vehicle ricocheted off our rear bumper and into a parked utility truck, crunching its fiberglass body.

That wasn't the end of it. As the sedan backed away from the utility truck, looking like a crushed beer can, a cousin of the proverbial white van lurched toward us, sliding perpendicular to the curb to block our exit. The only escape was down the empty sidewalk and that's where we went. We left our attackers entangled and bent out of shape.

The rest of the ride to the train station was uneventful, just two white guys cruising black Chicago in a gypsy cab. We didn't see the third car tailing us at a safe distance, turning south with us on Cottage Grove Avenue. Maybe the fact that our coats were pulled over our heads explained our few moments of inner peace.

As we arrived at the station entrance under the train viaduct the third car made its move. It cut us off diagonally at the curb. Seth and I lowered our coats in time to see two men in suits jump out of the rear doors and run to our car, guns pulled.

Astonishment passed across their faces as they registered who we were and who we were not. They didn't even bother to scare us or ask where Jackson was, but trotted back to their car, one of them extricating a cell phone from his coat pocket. Their driver accelerated backwards and U-turned with minimal regard for traffic etiquette or basic common sense.

Seth and I limped up the stairs to the train platform and bought tickets from the vending machine. A northbound train arrived within minutes.

Because of Seth's twisted ankle, I rode with him to the end of the Illinois Central commuter line at Randolph Street and walked him the few blocks back to his office on Wabash Avenue. Providing moral and physical support to Seth was a rare opportunity that I didn't want to pass up, even though it took me ten blocks out of my way. It made a small dent in my enormous debt to Seth. Before I left him to resume life in his captain's chair I asked if he knew someone at the Bugle who could give me the run down on grain, the Board of Trade, and maybe even N&M. Defending the plausibility of my grain hypothesis was crucial since I had revealed it to the world. Seth and Jackson were witnesses and I'm sure they wouldn't forget.

Seth smirked.

"No way you can work around Delaney without talking to him," Seth advised after a moment. We were standing at the corner of Wabash and Washington at 4 PM. Rush hour crowds were starting to follow their convoluted pathways to trains, buses, and other after-work destinations. Seth and I moved out of the pedestrian traffic.

"No way I'll talk to that son of a bitch," I said.

"Got to do it," Seth said, shaking his big hand in the air. "Take your lumps and score your contacts. Delaney edits the business pages now, too. Be real, Spivak."

"He'll want something," I fretted. "And I'm not about to hand him this story. Who knows what he'll do with it. He might even pass it on to Devereaux and his ilk."

"Got to give him something," Seth said, shaking my hand and limping towards his building entrance.

"Set it up," I shouted after him, the sour taste of practicality overwhelming me. "Soon!"

"Big man, Spivak!"

I walked the ten blocks to the Balboa in a daze. Pride is a refuge, not an answer, I knew. Although trading with Delaney verged on breaking my personal code of honor, the simple notion that if you fuck with me, I'll fuck with you. Maybe I was growing up. Maybe not.

The walk and the late fall air were good for my clogged emotions. I realized that winter and the hawk, maybe even the double hawk, were descending on Chicago. I had already been in the city much longer than planned, much longer than I could afford, and Tom Woods' death refused to resolve itself.

The Balboa Arms' dirty brick exterior hardly conjured up the safe and warm image of home, yet that's what I felt as I entered its revolving door and saw Sam lunging across the lobby. He was uncharacteristically out of his commercial and confessional cage. I hoped nothing was amiss, but how could it be otherwise in the Balboa.

"Be with ya," he muttered, communicating that he needed to talk with me but was on another mission at the moment.

Settling in the 1940s-vintage sofa with new 1970s upholstery, I picked up a copy of the Daily Times. **CASINO BILL SPUTTERS** read the headline about the emerging battle lines for Chicago's future, at least as seen through the eyes of Alderman Ed Devereaux.

Devereaux sounded like the bugle boy for Chicago, warning that we couldn't let this opportunity for making Chicago a world-class tourist destination die on the vine.

"We've let our lifeblood hemorrhage to the suburbs and beyond," he despaired. "I'm as responsible as anyone, but it must stop. I'm prepared to make a stand for Chicago!"

I almost puked. First Delaney. And now Devereaux sounded sincere and made some sense. My edge of Chicago cynicism was growing blunt.

That was as much as I was able to read because Sergeant Radachek and Lieutenant O'Malley were suddenly standing in front of me. O'Malley ripped the paper out of my hands, folded it neatly and placed it on a wobbly side table.

"Where's Jackson?" Radachek growled, putting on his tough voice for O'Malley, given that the voice had not yet worked its magic on me. "We know about the car chase, the hideout, everything. We want him for questioning."

"For what?" I spit back, jumping up from the couch to take away their height advantage. "I thought you guys had wrapped up the Woods case. 'A random act of urban violence,' I think you said. What happened? Have a spasm of conscience? That's a good sign, Radachek. Be sure to tell your wife if you still have one."

O'Malley shoved me with such unexpected force that I fell back on the couch. I bounced a few times. They sat down as well, real close on either side.

"Listen, Spivak! You're way out of your depth," O'Malley lectured. "I'm telling you for the last time. This is not the kiddie pool of bad landlords and pols on the take. This is bigger and you're interfering in a big way."

"Luckily, Sam lumbered into our midst at this moment and ruffled the greasy feathers of Radachek and O'Malley.

"You want him, read'm his rights or charge him," Sam demanded. "And, by the way, I represent Mr. Spivak."

We all looked up in surprise.

"Yeah, that's right, he's my lawyer," I said, knowing how to follow my dance partner.

Sam hadn't told me that he'd been taking law classes at Roosevelt University, one at a time, for the past five years. Nor had he told me that he had taken the Illinois bar exam two months before and was waiting for results. Such are the surprising limits of friendship and the great mysteries of time.

Sam said he'd have to keep quiet about my business now that he was representing me. I knew enough law to tell him not to advertise me as a client until he passed the bar. But I felt a lot better with Sam watching my back in more ways than one.

"You see Blevins yet?" Sam asked, as he looked for my messages on his desk.

"Still looking," I replied. "I'll find him soon enough."

"Watch yourself," he cautioned, handing me a fistful of folded slips of paper.

I had three phone messages. One had arrived during my cross-examination by Radachek and O'Malley. It was from Seth saying that I was to meet with Delaney at 10 the next morning at El Torta, my office away from home. The second message was from Helen Trent; she said she had some interesting information about N&M. No surprise. The third call was from Dorothy Edwards.

I decided to clean up and return the phone calls before visiting Sarah and attending the UPC Board meeting at 7:30 that evening. I also needed to gather my thoughts about Woods, Jutland, and the Gauntlet for my presentation to the UPC Board if I wanted to make sense. Should I share my grain hypothesis? Not tonight, I figured. I promised Sampson that I would be helpful.

I showered and changed into the rudiments of a professional outfit—red wool tie, blue button down shirt, and a lightweight tweed sports jacket, slightly rumpled. I might as well be ready to play the part at UPC per Reverend Sampson's anxiety-ridden request, even though the evidence seemed to indicate that Sampson was mixed up in this mess. I hoped that his transgressions were restricted to financial machinations related to UPC. That would at least be understandable if not defensible. But I feared that his involvements sunk much deeper.

Helen Trent's phone rang three times before she answered, in a confident, professional voice, "Trent and Associates, Helen Trent speaking."

"Helen, Spivak," I said, trying to get to the heart of things before the onset of awkwardness. I was short on time—psychic or otherwise.

"Nick, I'm glad you called," she said, also maintaining a professional distance. "I have some information for you. Alex told me something about N&M that might help you out."

"What's that?" I asked.

"He said you should see who owns N&M Ltd. He said even you would be surprised."

"And how does he know this?" I asked.

"Apparently it's the gossip in his office," Helen replied. "And banker's gossip is known for being high grade gossip."

"Thanks, Helen. I appreciate your call. That could really help and I know this is hard for us."

I hung up the phone after she weakly acknowledged my acknowledgement. I guess I should have appreciated whatever information came my way, but it would have been easier if Alex had just told me what he knew down at Union Pier.

Waiting for the switchboard to find Dorothy was a kinky turn-on. I caught myself almost licking the phone. I stood up and looked out the window. Lights shimmered in the upper floors of nearby high-rises.

"Nick, honey," Dorothy came on the line, the sound of her voice melting the tensions of the past day.

Her endearment did not go unnoticed.

"I miss you, too, Dorothy," I said in less passionate language than I felt.

"Business first, love," she said, laughing at my inability to say what I felt. "A partner in the firm asked me today if I had completed any special computer runs for Jutland before he disappeared. He said he was closing the file for the client.

"I told him I missed him at the funeral. He mumbled something and turned pink. I handed the data over to him, even though I had heard nothing about anyone taking over Omar's work or closing out the contract. He gave me a strange look as if his asking was just *pro forma*. He seemed surprised that I had any relevant documents. It was strange. Something in his eyes told me that I had become a problem."

"Sounds like N&M stuck him on you, hon. That worries me," I said. "These guys play hardball. Maybe you should skip Milwaukee for a while. Get out of their sights."

"No kidding," Dorothy replied. "He scared me, too. But I need the job for a few weeks more."

"Come on," I said. "I've dealt with these guys and they're not fucking around."

"Okay, okay. I have a compromise," she said. "Why don't I train down to Chicago on Wednesday night for the weekend? They owe me a few days at least."

"Are you sure you're ready for the Balboa Arms Hotel?" I asked, wondering whether Sam might fix us up in the bridal suite, that is, if they had one. Greedy

owners had probably subdivided it decades ago to take advantage of the pensioners.

"You mean, am I ready for the raw and undiluted Nick Spivak," asked Dorothy.

"Something like that."

"Well, I'm ready for a four-episode pilot," she said. "Besides, I've got a few old
friends and family in Chicago if things get too comfortable. I wouldn't want to
mess with the ways of a mystery man."

"Just as long as you're home every night by 9 PM," I said.

"Of course," Dorothy replied, feigning obedience. "Got to go. See you at nine
in the PM on Wednesday, Nick. At Union Station. Ciao!"

CHAPTER 17

▼

Blevins and I collided in the cold, cramped vestibule of his apartment building on Carmen Street. I think I made him nervous. He was dressed for a night on the town, at least his part of town, in a shimmering blue running suit and Air Jordans. I had decided to take another chance at delivering him a message before visiting Sarah, and, inevitably, her sister, at her apartment by Foster Avenue Beach. I forgot my hunk of wood.

"Just the man I was looking for, shithead," I said, pushing him up against a rack of wall-mounted mailboxes.

"Watch it, Spivak!" was all he could muster before I punched him hard in the stomach. He crumpled and I slammed him into the mailboxes again, the steel doorknobs jabbing into his back. My forearm across his mouth muffled his screams. Spittle oozed out of the corner of his mouth. He started convulsing as if he was about to launch his guts for a lunar landing.

"Listen, Blevins," I said, my heart pounding like a piston in my chest. "Don't go near Sarah Larsen again or you're finished as an errand boy for Devereaux. And I'll throw your Air Jordans in the River."

His wild frightened eyes told me that I wouldn't catch him off-guard next time. He would be ready with firepower of one kind or another—guns, pals, or maybe cops.

"You don't know what shit you're stepping into, Spivak! I feel sorry for you," he cried out, tears running down his face.

"That's what everybody tells me," I replied, jamming my forearm under his chin. He gurgled in pain.

"I was doing my job," Blevins cried. He couldn't take pain. That was why he was an addict, and a bottom-feeding, low-life.

"And who had the pull to make you do it?" I asked, not expecting this revelation. It made me furious and nauseous that the attack on Sarah might be part of a plan to pressure me. This was a new low, even for Chicago, and hard to believe.

He looked at me. A mean kid who was fundamentally weak and scared, not of me, although my ferocity surprised us both, but of someone else. He clammed up, saying, "Do what ya want."

"What drama," I replied. "You've already told me that Devereaux or Affazzi, or maybe even the Sheik, told you to beat up Sarah."

Blevins flinched at this listing of somebodies, giving off a palpable shiver when I pronounced Affazzi's name.

"But this is too dumb for those guys. I think you're protecting your own ass, Blevins."

I jammed him against the mailboxes one more time and walked out, holding the door open for an elderly white-haired woman and her little poodle, a white ball of fur wearing a purple, hand-knitted sweater.

Sarah was alone when I arrived at her studio apartment on the 16th floor. She was propped up in bed with bandages covering the top of her head. The bruises on her face were dark with an orange hue sprouting at the edges. A portable phone sat on her blanket along with a few books, a TV remote, a tray with a half-eaten bowl of soup, and an empty glass.

"The least I can do is clean up this mess," I offered. "Or will that make Margaret uptight?"

"Nick," was all she could manage before she broke into tears.

I sat next to her on the bed, pushing aside some of the debris, putting my arm around her shoulders and carefully drawing her fragile body closer to mine.

"It'll be okay," I said.

We stayed attached for at least fifteen minutes, a real achievement given my inability to sit still. But it was important; even I could see that. I wondered if I should tell her about Blevins and the crying pulp I had just left on Carmen Street. Instead, I decided to let her tell me what happened.

"Who did this to you, Sarah," I asked in as soothing a voice as I could muster.

She looked at me with wide, scared eyes.

"There's a lot you don't know about me, Nick," she said. "Maybe you should have guessed if you weren't so concerned with your own stuff. But that's not my problem with you. Margaret won't let go. She's looking for some way to escape her own guilt, and you've made yourself an easy target."

"That's me," I laughed. "Every man and woman's target."

"How could I tell you about my family when I wasn't dealing with it," Sarah continued, sitting up in bed. "You provided a safe space and good sex, and no obligation. The only problem was that I began to want more."

"That's one reason I left town," I replied. "I knew it wasn't good for either of us. Our secret prevented us from doing things we had to do."

Sarah kept staring, her eyes fixed straight ahead. The quivering in her body stopped.

"What about this old boyfriend?" I asked.

"Makes going back more than a mercy visit," she smiled. "We had something going after high school that was pretty good. Maybe there's some of that left. I hope so."

I nodded and popped the question. Now or never.

"So who did this to you, Sarah? How did you hook up with Blevins? You know what he's about and who he runs with."

"A blue van pulled up beside me as I was walking from the El. Nobody else was around. Blevins forced me into the truck with a gun."

"Did you know he lives a few blocks from here over by Clark?"

"News to me, Nick. I wouldn't go near that guy after the stories you and Seth have told about him. He's a loser. I've been down that alley. No more.

"But Nick, Blevins didn't beat me up," Sarah continued. "He was mean but he wasn't drunk or on drugs—not with his father there."

Her words sandbagged me. I lurched up and spun around the room in a daze.

"What are you talking about, Sarah? Blevins wasn't alone?"

"I never said he was alone, Nick. Blevins took me to his father."

"The Sheik," I muttered. "What did he say, Sarah?"

She looked at me intently. "Nick, I'm good at keeping secrets, even when that's not what people want, even when it's not good for me. He told me to tell you to stay away from someone named Affazzi if you really cared about my health."

"And then he hit me anyway, after I said I would tell you," Sarah sobbed. "All he said was, 'Clean up this mess, Randy, maybe take her to the emergency room.'"

I stalked the apartment and kicked the kitchen doorframe.

The Sheik seemed to be chiseled out of granite: a square jaw and sharp-edged cheekbones. I had met him the first time in 1980 when he muscled through the front door of my office in Pilsen like a charging Neanderthal. He wore a black leather jacket, black turtleneck, black pants, and Gucci shoes with tassels. I knew immediately it was the Sheik. And political gossip said he pulled double duty as ward sanitation supervisor and as a political operative for a Ward Committee-man.

"Mr. Spivak, how ya doing?" he said as he barged into the office. "I wanna have a little talk with you…about things."

"Things?" I asked, staring into the dark pools that functioned as his eyes.

In retrospect that was the wrong thing to say to the Sheik. He hid under the guise of a slow-witted but well dressed garbage man, but came out punching when he sensed danger or decided somebody was toying with him. He toyed back and it hurt.

"Mr. Spivak, I've got a very important message that you should listen to," he growled in a throaty voice. He sat on the edge of the old wooden desk I had retrieved from St. Theresa's Catholic Girls School on Roosevelt Road when the Archdiocese demolished it for the benefit of the West Side Medical Center. He grabbed a pile of papers and slowly went through them page by page, emitting animal-like noises that I couldn't decipher.

"You read too much," was all he said, putting the pile back on my desk in a much more orderly stack than the one he had found.

"Let me tell you a story. I think it will help you understand, Mr. Spivak."

"Sure," I said.

"Two boys grew up together on Taylor Street in the 1950s. That was long before the University of Illinois. There were Italians, Greeks, Mexicans, and the projects. It was a rough neighborhood, but we survived.

"One of the boys, call him Willie, started to buy up two and three flats after he mustered out of the army and as families moved to Cicero and Maywood. It was a good business. Willie married a girl from the neighborhood and settled down on Peoria Street and had a son. Call him Jimmy.

"One day Willie was collecting rents and three boys from the projects jumped him on Racine Avenue. It got outta hand when Willie wouldn't give them his rent money. They shot him five times in the face—only four blocks from his home and family.

"I was the other boy. And Willie was my best friend. I swore that I would revenge Willie's death and help raise his son. I did both. The cops found the three boys from the projects in rusty fifty-gallon drums on Maxwell Street. Some-one had hacked off their hands.

"And I helped raise Jimmy while having a family of my own. When Jimmy was old enough he took over his father's real estate business. He had the same lucky touch as Willie. He bought more buildings. He made more money. His business became so successful that he started buying up buildings outside of the neighborhood. The first place he looked was Pilsen. Cheap buildings. New peo-ple moving in who had money. The Mexicans didn't appreciate what they had.

"This is when you come into the picture, Mr. Spivak. After Jimmy buys up a few buildings, starts renovating, and advertising for tenants, he finds out that some smart white guy and his Mexican friends are asking questions about his business, researching all his properties in Pilsen and on Taylor Street. Somebody even catcalled at him, 'Go fuck yourself, gentrifier!'

"Do you believe that?

"Now, we all know that America is a free country, Mr. Spivak. That's why we fight wars for it, and win. But somebody's personal business is just as important. It's what makes America strong. Jimmy don't like people looking into his busi-ness. I don't like people looking into Jimmy's business.

"Can I be any clearer?" the Sheik exhaled, jamming his small, thick hands into the side pockets of his leather coat.

"Yeah," I replied, gripping my pencil like a saber. "Who are these investors anyway? Why should they care if somebody takes a close look at Jimmy's real estate?"

"That's what I mean, Mr. Spivak." The Sheik stepped up really close and stared in my eyes. "You ask too many questions. My advice is that you leave Jimmy alone!"

With that the Sheik turned and walked out of my office, leaving me a puddle of fear and curiosity. Needless to say, there were bigger fish to fry as the City and an array of greedy developers unveiled redevelopment plans for the Brewery in the following weeks and months. We left Jimmy alone, and I never had another visit from the Sheik until now.

Over the years I heard new Sheik stories on occasion, and every so often I had a Sheik sighting myself. He left running garbage trucks to become a political aide to Alderman Ed Devereaux, an unusual cross-ethnic alliance that was becoming more frequent as whites became a minority in Chicago. Stories flourished about the antics of the Sheik's stepson, Randy Blevins, the street punk I had just punched out.

Maybe it was time for another visit from the Sheik. I hoped so. The Sheik would crush me, I had no doubt, even though he was pushing sixty, but I owed Sarah that much and undoubtedly much more.

CHAPTER 18

▼

A reckless taxi ride delivered me to the UPC Board meeting on time for my presentation as requested by Reverend Sampson. The cab flew down the four lanes of Ashland Avenue, a hodgepodge of new and not so new shopping centers, century-old commercial strips, and used car lots. The sprint afforded me the emotional space to digest Sarah's revelation that she would be returning to Iowa in the next few days. There was a good chance that we would never see each other again, but neither of us acknowledged that likelihood. It was probably best. Margaret returned before Sarah and I could say goodbye in the way we wanted to, her scowl penetrating my armor of obliviousness. I decided we would ever hit it off.

The UPC held its quarterly board meetings in a private dining room at the Como Inn, a labyrinthine institution off the Kennedy Expressway near Grand Avenue. I arrived at the magic moment as a group of balding waiters in tuxedos served the dinner of chicken scaloppini with a side of pasta and salad. Everybody present had already downed at least two drinks and several chunks of fresh Italian bread. I would have to catch up.

Reverend Lee Sampson—distinguished-looking in a three-piece banker's suit—stood up from his table crowded with UPC officers and offered a prayer for Chicago's homeless before the fifteen hungry mouths chewed into frenetic action. I heartily joined in. Red wine flowed and everybody seemed happy. Too good to last. Somehow I could see into the future.

After several minutes of gorging, I looked up from the feedbags to see who everybody was. The faces looked vaguely familiar, at least most of them, from my prior Chicago life. Others I had seen in the latest UPC propaganda, which I had read on the subway to Uptown. The Board consisted of a few community activists, a theologian or two from Evanston and Hyde Park, a Monsignor renowned for being a worker priest in the days of the Packinghouse Workers Union, three businessmen who were active in civil rights and interreligious coalitions, a principal of a catholic high school, and the head of the Baptists of America Convention, an association of black churches mostly in the Midwest. And then there were a few people I just couldn't place.

I sat next to one of those, a thirty-something blond, dressed in a crisp red business suit and purple scarf, with a fashionable haircut and newly renovated make-up. To my delight, I found out that she worked for a major futures trader at the Board of Trade, her specialty being pork bellies and soybeans. Her specialty seemed attractively incongruous with her corporate look.

Her UPC connection evolved from an internship that was part of her participation in Chicago's Civic Leadership of Tomorrow, what I called elite-ership, a philanthropic endeavor to groom a new generation of civic leaders in Chicago. The problem was that there were fewer and fewer homegrown leaders. And even the upcoming or wannabees knew little about Chicago because they lived in the suburbs or because their companies had only recently transferred them to town. I don't know if it accomplished the goal, but the program was usually a ticket to new and higher-paying jobs for lucky chosen ones.

Inspired by this resume-like conversation, I started in. "I hear that there always is a future in grain scams? What's this mean for the market?"

A lot of good my inquiry did. She shot a dismissive stare and turned to speak to the monsignor. I saw Sampson looking at me squeamishly, perhaps reevaluating whether he should withdraw my invitation. But what drowning man would let such doubts interfere. He wasn't dumb.

On my other side sat a long-time public housing advocate for the tenants at the Elizabeth Woods Garden Apartments on the near west side. Ella Peters was a tough grassroots leader and negotiator who had extracted as much as you could realistically squeeze from one of the most corrupt and ineffective public housing authorities in the country—one fueled on a deadly combination of segregation, corruption, politics, greed, and real estate.

"What are you doing here?" I asked Ella when she walked in halfway through the dinner, feigning surprise.

"Eat your dinner!" Ella commanded, bestowing on me her famous sideways glance that froze foes in their tracks. "Thank the Lord you've got something to eat. I'm on the Executive Committee, of course."

Of course.

Ella taught me a lesson in the 1970s when I was heading up the membership committee for the Chicago Housing Network, a coalition of community-based housing developers. I reported at one meeting that Ella's organization, as well as a few others, had not paid their annual organizational dues, a paltry sum of $50. Ella stood up enraged and responded.

"As a revolutionary black woman I demand membership on behalf of my people." I was left blushing as the board, including myself, unanimously and self-righteously affirmed her lifetime membership.

Sampson called the meeting to order at 8:30, yawns threatening to engulf the group as the feast continued with cannoli and coffee. Sampson's colorful Gauntlet story from the past elicited appreciative groans. Sampson then began the stupefying review of minutes, committee reports, and financial projections.

All was going well for Sampson until Ella Peters and a few other board members began asking pointed questions about the dramatic revenue shrinkage on the year-to-date income statements. Deficits were growing, as Omar Jutland had pointed out to Tom Woods, with no new source of money in sight. UPC was going broke fast. I admired the board members for speaking up. Non-profit boards are usually coerced by the charisma of leaders or worn out by endless meetings. Stepping up to the plate with concerns often means more meetings, a disincentive for blowing the whistle. But that was the job.

What surprised me, though, was how calm and collected Sampson was, not what I expected from a control freak who had been exuding anxiety on the phone. But comprehension slowly tickled my brainstem. This was a man with a rabbit in his hat. I hadn't noticed that Assistant Commissioner Gene Burke of the City's Department of Urban Development had slipped in and was straightening his nondescript tie and clearing his throat in preparation for speaking.

Sampson stood up and called for attention, an aura of grave concern infusing his bearing.

"I wouldn't be a very good executive director and leader if I hadn't foreseen this disconcerting fiscal pattern as well," he started, sounding the right level of seriousness. I was relieved that he hadn't gone biblical on us, but the night wasn't over.

"Unfortunately, as many of you old-timers know," he continued, "financial straits are not a new issue for UPC. Our mission and journey has not been an easy one." He paused, looking around the room, building anticipation as he nodded strategically to supporters on the board. A few nodded back.

"I have invited Assistant Commissioner Gene Burke here tonight," Sampson announced, unable to moderate the triumphal note in his voice, "to announce a special no-interest loan for non-profits that has been awarded to UPC for three years. It is made possible by the TDD program of the City of Chicago, Alderman Devereaux's Finance Committee, and by N&M Ltd, a Chicago firm that has successfully developed industrial real estate in many parts of the city.

"This loan will enable us to consolidate our debt and develop an effective financial plan for the future," Sampson said. His tone suggested that things really weren't as bad as them seemed a few minutes ago. The reverend, it appeared, was the kind of leader who could find redemption, even perched on a precipice of his own making.

"What's the collateral, Reverend?" Ella asked. "I know how these things work."

Mildly irritated at being asked about details and having the flow of his speech interrupted, Sampson snapped, "the building, of course.

"That old brick building is our lucky charm," he smiled, regaining his composure.

"Aren't we already mortgaged up?" Ella asked.

At that point, Assistant Commissioner Gene Burke stood up. He was above average in height and had once been in good physical shape. But a tire of fat from too many meetings and cocktail parties now hung around his bulging waist. His thinning black hair had not weathered time without the assistance of coloring. He looked worn out.

"Let me help out, Lee," Burke said, with a perfunctory smile. Not waiting for an answer, he plunged in, the professional public servant at work, in command of the technical details of City finances.

"This is not a loan in the conventional sense. It's what we call a balcony loan, meaning it's smaller and far from the real risk. The underwriting for balcony loans, for those of you who like details, is less stringent than that for private loans because of the larger social policy objective—in this case helping UPC. This is a way for TDD funds to benefit all Chicagoans. And N&M, as the owner of the Schoenhofen Brewery, which is in a TDD, has agreed to link a portion of its development fees to the TDD. You can't get a public-private partnership better than this. We're very proud. It's taken a lot of hard work."

Even though I was scheduled to speak later, I couldn't help jumping in feet first after this smooth, technically proficient lie. I knew too much about the prior financing of UPC and the Brewery. An unsettling feeling was growing in my gut that my report on Tom Woods and Omar Jutland might be tabled given all the good news. Panic rose in Sampson's thin face as I stood up and opened my mouth to speak.

"My name is Nick Spivak," I said, looking out at the table of faces that were both tired and expectant. "Many of you know me from my past neighborhood work in Chicago. I live in Baltimore now, but have been back in Chicago for a week trying to make sense of the death of Reverend Tom Woods, a member of the last Gauntlet class who was, as you know, murdered."

Sampson interjected, "Nick! You're out of order!"

"Let him speak," Ella Peters said with distinctive authority. "I want to hear about this murder. This is one of our students. We have a responsibility!" A hum of consent rose in the room. Sampson sat down reluctantly.

"Let me make things simple," I said, knowing they were far from simple but that I had only a brief reprieve. "Actually two members of the Gauntlet team were killed last week—Tom Woods and Omar Jutland, a friend of Reverend Sampson who was attending the training session under false pretenses."

"Hold on!" Sampson appealed.

"Two others," I bulled on, "Reverend Alphonius Jackson and Sister Mary O'Conner are in hiding, afraid for their lives because of what happened the night of the Gauntlet.

"The problem came to a head at the Brewery buildings at 16th and Canal Streets, owned by the same N&M Ltd, under the supervision of Assistant Commissioner Gene Burke. Developers and their political friends gerrymandered the Brewery into the TDD zone for the Casino Development District. You can guess why. It's about greed and grain from what I can tell!"

I began to describe the sordid details when Burke stood up again, hitting his water glass with a table knife so hard that it splintered, spraying water across the table.

In fragmented sentences, a pale Burke muttered. "Spivak is a troublemaker.... For many years...Not constructive." His words grew desperately incoherent and his breath grew labored. He suddenly grasped his chest and fell face forward on the table, his arms knocking over coffee pots, sugar bowls, and water glasses.

Pandemonium broke loose.

Last call at the Par-a-dice was 11 PM, a rule established by the white-haired and indefatigable couple who tended the place. The bar stayed open until midnight, so you had to nurse your drinks that last hour. The rule drove away the serious drinkers who, at that time of night, were just picking up steam. The Par-a-dice made its business on daytime drinkers, so the Beleckas had little sympathy for the forlorn pleas for one more Old Style.

The décor of the Par-a-dice hadn't changed since my last visit six days earlier, and wouldn't change for my next ten visits. There was no décor to speak of, except the cardboard paraphernalia that comes with serving American liquor in a saloon, and a faded black and white photograph of a family in a long, lost country.

The place was less full than usual when our party of four arrived at 10:30 PM, enough time to imbibe two drinks if we hurried.

"Burke's heart blow-out surprised everybody but his doctor," Seth explained.

I had called Seth minutes after Burke had tumbled; he had called Helen and they agreed to meet Ella and me at the Par-a-dice. She had told Alex that he would have to put up with some kinks in her work life, like me I suppose. It was a test of his love. Alex passed, to Helen's relief.

Ella and I had been detained at the Como Inn until nearly 10, first watching the Fire Department Emergency Squad rush Burke off in an ambulance, performing CPR as they wheeled him out. None other than Radachek, Pelegrino, and O'Malley, Chicago's traveling homicide dicks, questioned us for some time before they told us that Burke was dead meat.

"We heard you taunted Burke," O'Malley said.

"Not really," I replied. "I just stated the facts, like you guys do."

"Get out of here," O'Malley snarled. When had I heard this fond farewell before?

They threw us dirty looks as we walked away, but there was nothing more to be said that hadn't already been said three times.

Ella and I agreed that it was worth debriefing Sampson's latest lapse in integrity. UPC was still an important building block for the community movement, perhaps more as a symbol than anything else. But symbols were important because the Delaneys of the world could use their demise to declare the long-awaited death of community organizing.

"You were the last straw," Ella said. "I'm surprised Sampson didn't pop something as well."

"That's not quite what I intended," I replied, staring into my beer.

"What did Sampson do after Burke collapsed?" Helen asked.

"His last hurrah, I'm afraid," I replied. "Ella was there."

"Reverend Sampson is a smart man," Ella started, a natural orator finding her rhythm with slow deliberation. "He pressured that whiny chaplain from Hyde

Park to adjourn the meeting and move into executive session in another room on the first floor."

"Shouldn't they have called it quits out of respect for Burke?" Helen asked.

"You would think so," said Ella, "but Sampson was intent on completing business. He said it was very important that we act tonight.

"Didn't get him out of the mess, though," Ella laughed. "I'm on the Executive Committee and we unanimously agreed, after a short discussion, to suspend Sampson until we completed an outside financial audit and investigated Nick's charges. Too many unanswered questions. Sampson wasn't expecting us to take that kind of action because he completely broke down after being told of his suspension.

"'I've built UPC for fifteen years, weathered all sorts of crises, with meager help from the board of directors,' he said in tears. 'Now we are in deep financial trouble and all the help I receive is disciplinary action. You don't know what I've had to do to keep the UPC afloat. Well, I've had it. I resign. I won't tolerate this kind of treatment. You're fools!'"

Ella recounted how Sampson stood up shakily after his speech and walked to the door, trying with all his powers to execute a dramatic exit.

Ella said she called after him: "We're not done yet Reverend. What about Spivak's questions about Woods, Jutland, and that N&M outfit? Why did you start dealing under the table with Devereaux and Burke? Those guys are enemies of Chicago's low-income neighborhoods, not our friends. We trusted that you wouldn't sell us out. But that's just what you did Reverend!

"And then Sampson turned. His whole body was trembling and he said, 'Talk to my lawyer!'"

Tom Woods and I took only one road trip together, south to Asheville, North Carolina in the Blue Ridge Mountains, two years ago, for four days. His family owned a cabin that was part of a Presbyterian retreat and summer camp. Perched on the side of a craggy ridge, the cabin and its big screened-in porch looked down on a expanse of pine and oak. We sat on the porch for hours with our feet up, drinking coffee in the mornings and gin and tonics in the afternoons. We told stories.

One late afternoon, as the sky darkened and the temperature dropped, Tom told a story about a small town in Tennessee where residents banded together to fight the rampant pollution of the coal and power companies. Generations of families had tolerated the pollution because they had received something in exchange, something they valued. Jobs for sons, jobs for grandsons.

People weren't stupid. They knew something was wrong because many of them contracted black lung, cancer, or emphysema. Nobody escaped knowing someone with these afflictions. That was viewed, however, as another cost of having a good job that could support a family. After all, there were towns like this all over Tennessee and Kentucky with no jobs.

"I watched the town change overnight," Tom said. "I was doing a stint as an interim pastor at the church, along with two others in a fifty-mile radius. Everybody attended church and everybody told his or her stories. Usually it was women I met at the stores or when I made the rounds of the sick and dying. The men, as is often their way, pushed it down deep, and couldn't talk about it out loud without confronting their own inability to fight back.

"Well, I'll never forget how that changed. You see, what was smoldering below the surface was not the deaths of old men or even young men, however painful that was, but of children, the only innocence that kept the town alive, gave it precious moments that transcended the mines. The children were dying from cancer, leukemia, and birth defects.

"In the midst of all this dying and smoldering hatred, a young woman named Alice Baker took it upon herself to call the federal Environmental Protection Agency, not once buy every day, calling offices throughout the region and country. Her first child had died at birth, and another had a rare bone cancer. She knew it was the pollution from the mines that had caused it. She threw off the weight of decades, maybe centuries, of temerity, of adapting to the imperatives of the mine.

"The story didn't end pretty. Finally some Feds responded to Alice Baker, and a slew of community meetings, epidemiological studies, and groundwater tests ensued. Needless to say, the mine owners were furious and threatened to close down the mines, the only source of work in the town.

"That didn't stop Alice Baker or the meetings. Pressure mounted on the regional electric cooperative not to buy coal from the polluting mines. Then one night someone firebombed Alice Baker's house on the edge of town. The whole family died. Arson wasn't enough; they barricaded the doors and windows. There was no escape.

"The town exploded. A group of young men pulled the general manager of the mine company out of bed and would have lynched him if it weren't for my intervention. It was Saturday night and I was in town for Sunday service. They burnt down his home and office instead.

"The upshot is that the community won. The mine closed down. And now this little town is abandoned and empty except for a few old-timers who by some infinitesimal chance had avoided lung disease and qualified for pensions."

"So much for victory," I mused, looking at Tom and sipping my gin and tonic on that cold Appalachian afternoon.

"I dunno," Tom answered. "Fighting for your birthright always comes with costs, sometimes tragic costs. How many of us are willing to pay the price?"

CHAPTER 19

▼

I deserved a high-cholesterol breakfast after a late night and a restless sleep, full of colliding moral quandaries. Gene Burke's death was one. Sarah Larsen. Lee Sampson's abrupt resignation. And, of course, Tom Woods. Baltimore beckoned me enticingly.

The subterranean blues of El Torta, along with the eggs, soothed my soul. I was wiping up the last of my frijoles with a triangle of flour tortilla when Delaney arrived, a Chicago Bugle tucked under his arm. He wore a spiffy, neatly pressed tan raincoat over a blue blazer.

"Haven't you heard about the negative health effects of lard," he growled out of the side of his mouth, his mottled red face a tribute to showing decades of drinking.

"Hey, Mr. Bigshot," Jacinto objected from behind the counter and the six stools, his white chef's outfit speckled with chiles, beans, and who knows what else. "This is healthy food. My people have been eating it for centuries. Maybe you just eat too much or don't exercise your mind and body. That's what kills you"

"That's right Delaney," I added, sticking out my right paw just like Seth told me I should. Delaney ignored my olive branch and sat down.

"Okay, Spivak. Let's be straight at the outset. I'm doing this as a favor for Greenburg."

"That's fine by me," I said. "I'm not looking for a long-term relationship."

We looked at each other, warily, both of us wondering whether bolting for the glass door might be the most honorable and expedient course of action.

"Thanks for stopping by," I finally said. "I need to talk to someone who knows the ins and outs of the grain business and the Board of Trade. They're at the heart of something I'm working on."

"And what's that?" Delaney asked as if he doubted that I would really spill my guts to him.

I nodded to Jacinto for more decaf. My preference irritated him but he was willing to brew it for me if I was good. "Want some coffee?" I asked Delaney. "On me."

"You really are on good behavior, Spivak," Delaney said. "Sure, I'll match your decaf. No, better yet, make mine high octane."

We sat in silence for thirty seconds. It seemed like longer. The everyday life of El Torta and Wabash Avenue whirled around us. Orange and blue hair. Hookers taking time off from the convention hotels. Service workers slumped over coffee.

"I'll tell you the story if you tell me you have someone at the Bugle who can help me out," I said finally. I figured I didn't have any choice, as distasteful as it was.

"Yeah, that's the Spivak I know. A negotiator. Well, we've got an old-timer on the business bureau staff named Jed Hutchinson. He's covered the pits for years and has written a book or two about famous grain traders. He's your man, Spivak. He can meet with you tomorrow if I give him the word."

I entertained Delaney with the ten-minute version of the past seven days—the bodies, the rides and car chases, the Brewery, the bruises, and the connections to N&M Ltd and Devereaux. I didn't trust him, but he listened and took notes in a small spiral notebook that he liberated from the inside pocket of his blazer. I needed other people asking questions, the more obnoxious the better, if I was to refine my grain hypothesis. That's the scientific method. Delaney fit the bill unless he was spying 100 percent for the other side, whoever they were.

"You've sketched a plot that still has a few, no more than a few, holes," Delaney said when I had finished my summary of events. "Like who was running illegal workers through the Brewery? And what's the connection between N&M and Devereaux?"

"How about Gene Burke to answer your second question," I suggested, intrigued by Delaney's interest and cooperation.

Delaney rose from his chair, saying, "Times up, Spivak. One more tip for the road. Devereaux's more worried than I've ever seen him. Seth has got him nervous. He's called an emergency finance committee meeting for this afternoon to rebut your bullshit TDD allegations made at UPC's last supper, or maybe that's Burke's last supper. Or both."

"Sounds like he's scared."

"On top of his game," Delaney replied

"What will he do without Burke?"

"That's the question of the day," Delaney answered with a grin. "Want a job? I could put in a good word for you. It would be your ticket back to Chicago."

"I'll pass," I said.

"Oh, by the way," he said. "When Greenburg set up our date he gave me a head's up about your request for the name of somebody smart about the pits. I've already spoken to Jed Hutchinson. I told him that you would buy him lunch at Marshall Field's. He's very sentimental."

"Thanks, Delaney," I said, dismayed by the helpful outcome of this conversation.

There's good in everybody, right, I thought.

Every once in a while the usually elusive machinations of the powers-that-be become embarrassingly transparent, frightening everyone, which may be why we allow public and private corruption to flourish. It's as if the world would stop turning if we really acknowledged what transpires every day on our little green planet. At Devereaux's public hearing that afternoon the curtain was raised on how public largesse benefits real estate greed. And then, just as we were getting to the real story, the powers-that-be dropped the curtain. It wasn't pretty.

Media, community activists, real estate lobbyists, and good-government types packed the second floor hearing room at City Hall fifteen minutes before the meeting was scheduled to begin. Seth and I sat next to each other in the back of the room.

"How's the ankle," I asked when Seth sat down.

"I'll survive," he mumbled.

I updated him with the information from Sweeney and from my brunch with Delaney.

"See how being friendly is good for business," he laughed.

I nodded in resignation. There wasn't any thing else to say, for the moment.

Devereaux's chief of staff for the Finance Committee, Barry Greico, nervously stuck his head in the briefing room every few minutes, hoping he really wasn't seeing a mob ravenous for a public feast. He should have worried; pols like Devereaux regularly threw their staff members to the wolves when the going got tough. It was their right. Greico was unscathed so far. But the odds were against him staying that way. He was just a young guy in a suit with an inroad to Chicago patronage and the dreams of a political career. Poor sucker!

Delaney didn't show, a blow to my belief in the powers of reconciliation and free will. I wondered if his tip was compensation for bowing to the commercial wishes of the company that owned the Bugle, a four-star member of Chicago's growth machine, a loose, mostly invisible confederation of banks, utilities, building trade unions, and developers. They advocated growth, infrastructure, real estate development, and public subsidy—essentially for World's Fairs and casinos. And growth greased everybody's wheels, except if you were a working stiff or out of job. That was democracy Chicago-style.

At 2:15 PM the Finance Committee sheepishly filed in, Alderman Devereaux marching in last. Devereaux's silver mane and impeccable Armani suit suggested a Teflon capacity to withstand the most direct hits.

They took their seats. Greico handed Devereaux a prepared set of remarks roughed out on 3-by-5 note cards. Devereaux vigorously tapped his wooden gavel on the podium.

"I'm calling this hearing to order. I'm calling this hearing to order." The room grew quiet until only a few clusters of talkers could be heard, oblivious to what was happening around them as they chattered about the political gossip of the day.

"I'm calling this meeting to order," Devereaux repeated a third time, his voice now booming and annoyed. Two Chicago cops walked over to the flagrant violators and tapped their shoulders. Not surprisingly, the talkers stopped talking and turned their attention to the front of the hearing room, which was now overflowing into the outside hallway.

"The purpose of this special committee hearing," Devereaux began, "is to refute the irresponsible charges regarding TDD funds that have been made against the late Assistant Commissioner Gene Burke, who tragically died last night in service to this city. In particular, it has been alleged that our agreement with the Urban Pastors Convention was somehow mixed up with two deaths and other illegal activities. I want to unconditionally deny any wrongdoing by Gene Burke, this committee, or by our many private-sector partners.

"The TDD program has generated $3 billion of economic development in Chicago to date, leveraging $2 billion of private funds, creating $40 million in new local and state taxes, and the creation of and retention of 300,000 jobs. We have used $3 million of TDD funds to support worthy community projects that serve the homeless, promote adult literacy, and build grassroots leaders in our city. This is our future. Our staff will now distribute a report that documents in great detail our TDD projects, benefits, and linkage agreements."

"A preemptive strike," whispered Seth. "A good way to avoid our freedom of information request."

"He's the pro," I whispered back.

As staff handed out copies of the report, the room grew silent as in silent prayer. All of Chicago's most prominent developers were on the list, a massive feeding at the public trough. Nothing had been built in downtown Chicago in the past five years without an injection of public subsidy. I wanted to scream, "Just say no!" but I knew that the co-dependency of local politics and real estate was beyond therapeutic intervention.

For the next hour Devereaux paraded a predetermined set of witnesses, including business people, neighborhood leaders, recipients, and N&M's Affazzi. I was surprised Devereaux let Affazzi out in public after the previous night, but maybe he had a plan. Their stories had been carefully scripted to reveal very little except that their projects could never have happened but for TDD investments. These were the magic words that opened up the public coffers.

Finally, in between two developer teams who were a bit slow in shuffling on and off stage, Max Vargas of Street News, a homegrown, in-your-face paper sold by Chicago's homeless, grabbed the microphone and shouted, "What about trafficking in undocumented workers at the Brewery? What about using TDD funds to make political payoffs? We need affordable housing for the homeless."

The peanut gallery cheered, at least some of us.

The audience enthusiastically joined in the questions, having been shut up and ignored for too long. People lined up at the microphones. Catcalls and whistles greeted the committee members, including Devereaux, when they tried to respond to the outpouring of civic disbelief.

Jumping up and grabbing the microphone in the back of the room, I asked Devereaux whether Gene Burke actually worked for N&M?

In good Chicago fashion, the microphone suddenly went dead.

Alderman Devereaux said, "Thank you for your attention. This special committee meeting is now adjourned."

Seth and I walked down the marble stairs at City Hall, worn smooth by thousands of citizens, which led to LaSalle Street. I was about to launch into an update of my grain hypothesis when Affazzi rushed past us, dressed in a black cashmere overcoat and a brightly patterned silk scarf. He plunged two or three steps past us when I catcalled.

"How are those grain co-ops doing, Mr. Affazzi? I hear they're losing value. True non-profits!"

Seth played along. "Stop it, Spivak. Leave the man alone. He's just had his TDD balloon popped. He's got the public subsidy blues."

"Those walking blues?" I queried.

"Yes they are, indeed. You never get your fill. Those public subsidy blues."

Affazzi stopped and turned, staring at two aging and grinning yippies. His blank eyes showed no emotion or comprehension, just a predatory readiness.

Affazzi stepped towards us and said in a low voice, "You have far exceeded my patience and are now in danger of suffering my displeasure. You mean nothing to me and I doubt others would miss you, Mr. Spivak. I'm surprised by your stubborn lack of comprehension. I overestimated you"

"That's not nice," replied Seth.

"Yeah," was all I could manage.

"I've warned you," Affazzi said.

With those words he resumed his flight down the marble staircase and out of City Hall, rushing into a black limo waiting in a cordoned-off area reserved for the Mayor and other dignitaries. A cop slowed traffic for the limo. We caught a glimpse of Randy Blevins sheepishly looking out the rear window, fear apparent on his face. Someone abruptly drew the window shade and the limo jerked into traffic, turning left on Randolph Street with the help of the cop.

"Let's grab a cab and follow him," I yelled to Seth as we pushed through the revolving door, still energized by our performance on the stairs. "This is our chance to nail him"

"Your play, Spivak. Take it. I've got other business, including checking in with Al. And my ankle hurts. But watch your back. I think we just stirred up a hornet's nest or worse."

I paused.

"And what's with Blevins in the back seat?" Seth added. "He had the look of a rat caught in a trap. Somebody's got big trouble if the Sheik gets wind of someone taking his boy for a ride. Don't be stupid, Spivak. I know that's hard for you but you need to put this in perspective. Right?"

"Later," I responded, jumping into LaSalle Street to hail a cab against Seth's better judgment, as well as my own.

Affazzi was not difficult to follow once we left the Loop and headed south on Desplaines Avenue. There were no other shiny black limos in sight. My cab driver had plenty of time to give me his life story, an immigrant from Turkey who had migrated to Chicago ten years ago. He bragged about how many cab medallions he owned, and how he couldn't understand why poverty flourished in the United States when so much opportunity existed and there were twenty-four hours in the day.

I nodded, keeping my eye on Affazzi's limo.

Affazzi turned west on Roosevelt Road and then southwest on Blue Island Avenue, formerly known as the Black Road when McCormick Reaper workers marched northward on it in 1886 calling for the eight-hour day. It divided Pilsen, and was the main thoroughfare to Pilsen's first suburb, Little Village. I had a strange premonition about Affazzi's desitination. The back of my knees began to ache, no doubt a sympathetic reaction. Or maybe it was just age.

I was right. Affazzi's limo turned into a gas station that had been turned into a tortilla factory, the headquarters of Javier Centeno and the Latin Kings. I felt the bite of Centeno's shoe on my hand. Maybe Seth was right about me picking fights.

We drove past and my new Turkish friend parked. We waited, the cabbie growing nervous, no doubt wondering whether this escalating fare was jeopardizing his prospects for long and prosperous life—and wealth accumulation. I checked my wallet to make sure I could pay for this investigative extravagance.

Right across the Chicago River was the reported site of Father Marquette's roughhewn cabin in which he spent the winter of 1674–75 recovering from illness and internal hemorrhaging. A mahogany cross was raised on the spot in 1905 in commemoration of Marquette as the patron saint for the people of Chicago.

After fifteen minutes and three centuries of Chicago history, two burly men emerged from the tortilla factory carrying a rolled up length of carpet. They looked familiar.

Damned if a foot wasn't dangling from one end of the roll, a high-top shoe that reminded me of Blevins' footwear when I encountered him in Uptown. One of the men cleverly draped his dark coat over the end of the carpet and the foot. These guys were professionals. When they reached the limo one of them popped the trunk. They folded the rolled-up rug and dropped it in, bouncing the limo slightly. They slammed the trunk shut and they walked back to the building as Affazzi glided past them to the limo. Affazzi's driver gunned the limo and headed back towards Western Avenue. Where were they taking poor Blevins, I asked myself. Did I really care?

We followed as Affazzi's car turned on Western and performed a series of skillful turns and twists to arrive at an abandoned stone quarry on the northern edge of Bridgeport, home to Chicago mayors, machine politics, and the White Sox. There was no gate, fence, or other obstruction, just a mangled "No Trespassing" sign limply hanging from a weather-beaten wooden post. The limo drove half way down the makeshift access road for dumpsters and garbage trucks and stopped. The driver got out and dumbly looked around. We hung back, my increasingly nervous cabbie and me. The place was empty and he was ready to bail. After only a few moments the limo driver opened the trunk and struggled to extract the rug and its hidden cargo. Carrying it slung over his shoulder, he awkwardly dropped the bundle over the edge of the access road onto an enormous pyramid of garbage.

What looked for all the world like Blevins' leg jutted out of the rug.

As the limo pulled out of the quarry access road, we again followed, this time to a carwash at 35th and Emerald. I asked my Turkish cabbie to wait while I approached the carwash on foot, but he demanded to be paid. I relented. He was gone within seconds of my counting out bills.

I walked up to Affazzi's driver, an all-too-predictable punk whose excessive weight-lifting earned him a head and body that resembled a beer can. He was busily vacuuming the trunk. Nothing like cleaning up after a job.

"Where's Affazzi?" I asked. "I'm supposed to meet him."

"Yeah right! Who the hell are you?" the driver grunted. "Nobody here but me and my limo."

"So what did you drop off in the quarry back there? Planting a garden, maybe?"

He responded by grabbing the hose used to wash cars and blasting me full force in the chest. Anything after that was a blank.

When I came to, I was surprised that I had not been rolled up in a flea-bitten rug like Randy Blevins and stuffed into the trunk of the limo. Dead. Instead of relief, I felt sadness. I missed Dorothy and realized that I had expectations that distinguished me from Blevins and his dangling foot. Or at least I thought they did. I was alive, alive in the back seat with my hands tied behind my back and a piece of two-inch duct tape tightly stretched across my mouth. Sunlight hurt my eyes. My shirt was soaking wet from the hose that Affazzi's hulk had turned on my at the Bridgeport carwash.

As the grogginess lifted I more fully appreciated the peril of my current situation. I was not dead, nor wrapped in a rug. But surely I was on a death ride, maybe even back to the quarry. I was a real smart guy. I had said too much, too fast at the carwash out of sheer frustration. They would not allow me to live and report the sordid details to the likes of a Sergeant Radachek.

I was alone in the limo with the driver, Affazzi's hulk and rug man. There must have been someone else at the carwash, perhaps even Affazzi, who hit me on the back of the head with who knows what. I was collecting bumps like a pig with the hives. But I could see only the hulk in the limo. I pinched myself to avoid crying out hysterically about my doomed fate. Then I remembered my mouth was taped shut.

I needed to sort things out, calm down and check out my options. After all, that's what I was supposed to be good at. And that's what I did.

It began to dawn on me that the hulk was not operating on all cylinders. Too many steroids, I figured. He had tied my hands and put tape across my mouth. But my legs were completely free. I gleefully stretched my limbs. After all, I was free.

But what should I do with my free legs? Could I really turn them into weapons lethal enough to stop the hulk, and his limo? Or would a wrong move, perhaps with my legs becoming caught between seats, simply lead the hulk to tie me up more effectively? I could picture his fat grin as he tightened my death bonds.

There wasn't much time and I felt giddy. That worried me. The limo was traveling about forty miles per hour. I inched up the inside of the car door and took a quick look: Ashland Avenue, more or less.

The car phone buzzed.

"Yeah," the hulk answered. He was silent for a few moments as someone talked him through the thinking process.

"All tied up, boss. I'm taking him to the Stockyards. The old rendering plant. Yeah…fifteen minutes.

"Okay."

He reattached the phone to its plastic base in the car console.

"Hear that?" the hulk laughed, his blockhead swiveling back toward me.

Just the human target I needed. My right shoe crashed into the side of his face as he turned, making a soft crunching sound on impact. The car lurched to the right and then to the left, out of control.

The hulk muttered, making no sense.

He was stunned and bleeding as I deployed my free legs over the seat and around his neck. I didn't know I could be so agile. I squeezed his thick neck with all my strength, which wasn't much at the moment. I just hoped it was enough.

What followed for the longest thirty seconds in my life was a bronco ride on a human hulk struggling in his seatbelt in a black limo careening down Ashland Avenue. Luckily, the hulk took his foot off the accelerator so that the concrete viaduct we hit wasn't fatal, at least for me.

Seconds before impact he released his seatbelt so that he could escape my legs, only to have his head flung through the side window on impact. I glanced at his big skull dangling unnaturally from his neck.

The impact of hitting the viaduct jarred open the rear door. I used my legs to pull myself out of the wreck. I was dazed and my legs hurt. The car was smoking and gas soaked the area. I ran awkwardly with my arms tied behind my back to the side of the viaduct and launched myself into a drainage ditch five feet below.

Moments later I heard it. The black limo blew up, the hulk's head sticking our of the side window. Pieces of the limo, and no doubt the hulk, rained down on my body sprawled in three inches of filthy water. I wriggled my hands in an adrenaline-fueled rush to loosen the nylon cord around my wrists. Water did the trick, stretching the nylon enough to allow me to free my hands. I ripped the tape off my mouth, choking back a scream.

I crawled down the length of the ditch and out of harm's way, avoiding at the same time the gathering of rubberneckers, police cars, ambulances, and fire trucks. It wouldn't take long to track the limo back to Affazzi. The news wouldn't make him happy, especially the loss of such a good employee.

I figured a long walk was the only way to dry off, loosen my aching limbs and muscles, and reflect on the twin deaths I had just witnessed.

Affazzi was certainly a man of decisive action, unwilling to allow dissent or loose ends for long. I wondered whether that was the essence of the heroic entrepreneur, or simply the act of a psychotic needing to get his own way. Maybe Affazzi was both, a fatal combination that was probably becoming more common amidst disintegrating communist-bloc countries.

I made my way on a diagonal course through the factories, tenements, and rail yards on my way to the West Loop. I reached no conclusions, nor formulated any new hypotheses. One was enough. I kept walking. My clothes gradually dried and my adrenaline leveled off at the "just plain scared" plateau, a reasonable response given that Affazzi would be looking for me with even more intensity. My final thought as I opened the door to the Par-a-dice was whether I should phone Dorothy and call off her pilot visit. Chi-town was too dangerous.

I reached her office by phone from the bar, but Dorothy had already left, the receptionist told me. I half-heartedly left messages for her at the office and home, wondering whether I was drawing her into danger.

The early after-work crowd was beginning to populate the Par-a-dice. I ordered a draft beer at the bar and settled in for an hour of R&R away from the hectic life of a non-profit turnaround specialist. What a profession. But it wasn't my jobs that were the problem, I realized. It was my friendship with Tom Woods that had cast me into the inferno of Chicago muck and alligators like Affazzi and Devereaux. I gulped my beer and made faces in the mirror behind the bar. I was a serious guy with an attitude problem, of another era when good and evil were simple and obvious and guys like me were admired for their lonely pursuit of authenticity.

I was really laying it on thick. I needed to let up.

"A man with a face like Camus," I heard behind me. Snickering laughter followed those ironic words.

I liked Camus a lot.

I didn't recognize him at first when I turned to look at my tormentor. Mr. Beleckas eyed us in anticipation of breaking up one more fight before it got started.

I nodded to him and said, "No problem, Mr. Beleckas. A man's got the right to say what's on his mind." And then it struck me who was hassling me, although I couldn't remember his name. He was one of those footloose activists who had graced Chicago's soapboxes, coffee houses, and blues bars for four decades.

He looked the part and seemed about as frayed and weather-beaten as his ideology. He was tall and gaunt, with gray hair worn in a ponytail and a full mustache. He dressed in denim and wore a union baseball cap. A real collector's item. From my recollection, he survived by writing and part-time teaching at one of Chicago's community colleges. He was one of the last remaining links to the anti-Stalinist left of the 1930s, as if anybody had really heard of them. For them, the whole world was about betrayal; yet everything remained possible. This was hard to compute.

I didn't share their optimism or beliefs. Largely holding to humanistic interpretations of Karl Marx, they believed that they were freed of responsibility for death camps, prisons, and oppression of the communist bloc. Those folks just didn't do it right. They called me cynical for remaining skeptical but treated me as a fellow traveler gone astray.

"Heard you were back in town, Spivak," he said, somehow knowing my name. "Sorry for catching you in a private moment. You take things too personally."

Another round, I communicated non-verbally to Mr. Beleckas. 'Yeah, him too," I made clear by pointing a finger.

"I saw Greenburg at Andy's a few days ago," he said. "He told me you were back chasing sleazebags the likes of Devereaux and company. I had to laugh."

"Why's that?" I asked, preparing myself for the lesson of the day.

"Think of Chicago as a bird cage that has been dipped in soapy water," he began. I nearly choked on the image after my near-brush with a fat-rendering plant. "When you pull it out you've got one big bubble, or so it seems. What you really have is the structure of the birdcage and soapy film over the bars. That's the surface of things.

"You're always skating on the soapy stuff, Spivak, never going after the big things, what's underneath. No wonder you never make any progress."

"Aren't we all trapped in the birdcage with all the birdshit?" I countered.

"Well?" he frowned.

"I'll tell you something," I said. "I don't know if we can ever escape the cages we're in, called Chicago or whatever. But we certainly can breathe a lot better. The soapy film won't last for long with me, Greenburg, and the rest of our ilk mucking about. So, yeah, you're right. I'm skating on the soapy stuff."

I put a five-dollar bill on the bar and started to leave. Who needed this conversation after my escape from the hulk. I looked around suspiciously and whispered, "I've developed a grain hypothesis that gets beyond the soapy stuff in Chicago. It's a real sleeper. I'm about to get it confirmed by the *pitmaster*. I'll keep you posted."

His puzzled look told me that he didn't appreciate the good news. I patted his shoulder and walked out.

CHAPTER 20

▼

Jed Hutchinson—the *pitmaster*—almost choked laughing on a mouthful of his chicken potpie when I shared my grain hypothesis with him.

"Not likely, son," he gurgled after nearly asphyxiating himself at my theory's expense. His explosive merriment caused enough commotion that nearby diners looked around anxiously and the floor manager, hovering nearby, flexed his hands in nervous anticipation of performing the Heimlich maneuver.

Jed waved them all off with a fling of his right arm, clothed in a brown tweed sports coat. He must have been close to seventy and way over six feet tall. His long, thin fingers showed the yellow stains of an unsuccessful ex-smoker.

When I had arrived at the Walnut Room at 11:45 AM, the line for lunch was already twenty feet long and growing, including baby carriages, wheel chairs, walkers, and all the rest of us. I had dilly-dallied, in my grandmother's words, by cruising the escalators through six familiar yet still-enticing floors of Marshall Field's department store. I got lost in the seventh floor maze of wines, cheeses, and specialty olives on my way to the Walnut Room.

Luckily, Jed knew the ropes—inevitable lines, that is—and immediately asked to be seated after his arrival at 11:35, claiming that he had severe arthritis in his knees and that his son had just taken an emergency trip to the restroom because of a spastic colon and would be right back. The perfectly coiffed, white-haired hostess had taken pity.

The Walnut Room is a tradition from the bygone era of department stores and vibrant downtowns. This one still worked, serving up an immutable menu—founded on a chopped salad—that exuded comfort, old movies, and the good war.

"So what's with the Walnut Room?" I asked Jed after we had introduced ourselves and begun attacking the plate of assorted fresh breads and rolls. "Doesn't seem like a place a guy working the pits would habituate."

"My wife Jane," Jed replied, looking up from the menu he had been intently studying as if it was an antique document, "came here as a child from Evanston on the north shore with her grandmother during the holidays. They would always make a day of it. She talked fondly about the Walnut Room until the day she died three years ago this month.

"I'm sorry to hear that," I said. So you've probably been here many times?"

"First time," he answered to my surprise. "I didn't want to be seen with you anywhere near the pits," he laughed, his eyes dancing with delight. "Delaney told me you were a troublemaker. I still have to work my contacts. But he also said that you had a good story to tell."

We ordered chopped salad, chicken potpies and iced tea.

I waited until our potpies arrived before I presented my grain hypothesis. It took about ten minutes to tell the whole story. Hutchinson listened attentively, showing no reaction and asking no questions.

I was stunned and embarrassed by the old man's quick and unequivocal dismissal of the hypothesis a few moments after I stopped talking and took a few bites of chicken, peas, and carrots. What would Seth and Jackson think? They'd laugh, of course. Evidence pointed to a scam in the trading pits, somehow involving the strange activities of N&M, a sleazy outfit that bridged the worlds of grain, real estate, and public subsidies. And there had to be deep pockets to keep their array of scams in orbit. But none of that held water for Hutchinson, an old dog who had been sniffing around the excesses, intrigues, and spillovers of the pits for close to fifty years.

"You're hooked on the metaphor," he explained. "I'm surprised. You're not supposed to be a greenhorn. But you're like a young puppy in love. What you've told me sounds more like bread-and-butter prairie sleaze than a complicated scam related to grain futures, options, puts, or calls.

"Now in the old days, a hundred years ago or more, there were scams galore, everything from weighing and grading grain to cornering markets. It was legalized gambling, more and more abstract, hardly related to the material production, transport, and use of grain.

"The Board of Trade is just about all that's left of the swirl of grain supply and demand that built Chicago with the railroads, creating millionaires, losers, and towering grain elevators. All that's increased is the level of speculation. Three hundred million tons came through the port last year for global consumption. But nobody downtown bothers with that."

"But the Board of Trade has grown by leaps and bounds," I interjected.

"For sure, but it's more complicated than ever, hardly the stuff of Frank Norris and 'The Pit.' Everybody's an investor.

"It makes the market more rational, more predictable, more stable. Nobody corners the market anymore. That's not the game. Farmers are plugged in before they even plant, hedging their investments in five different ways."

"No scams?" I asked.

Hutchinson looked up from his plate, wiping one last dab of chicken gravy with a piece of white bread that he had methodically pulled into pieces. His eyes were circled with humor.

"Always scams, son."

"So why not now?"

"I didn't say, not now. Just not the players and the plot you're talking about. Today's scams are about information, split seconds, telecommunications, margins, and arbitrage."

"But wasn't information always the way to corner the market?"

"Sure, sure! But information hustlers don't hang out with the likes of N&M Ltd, Alderman Devereaux, and that ilk. These are cyber-folk who don't give a damn about the city, machine politics, or the clumsy antics of a bunch of muscle-heads."

"Okay, okay. I give up," I said. "I'm a sucker for prairie alligators. That's all."

"No crime in that," the old man said.

We ordered frango mint ice cream and Marshall Field's special brew of decaf. The Walnut Room bustled to its lunch-hour climax, the line winding fifty feet past the bank of elevators. The subtle and not so subtle pressures for us to move along mounted. Hutchinson was not about to be dislodged before he was ready. He launched into a meandering account of his journalistic feats while covering the pits. We had to ask for a second cup of coffee, an unheard of slip in service etiquette at the Walnut Room. We still refused to take the hint.

Hutchinson finally got around to telling me what he knew about N&M Ltd, which was more than I knew before but which still left gaps.

"N&M showed up on LaSalle Street about ten years ago, with a lot of cash and a penchant for speculation, real estate, and transportation. Sounds like a mafia laundering operation, or some new global, post-Cold War version of it. They never made a big killing as far as I know.

"Talk was that they had big backers from out of the country as well as a few local pols and real estate hounds.

"Affazzi took Chicago by storm. Everybody wanted to make a deal with him, but the rumors surfaced just as fast about deals dropped at the last minute and about Affazzi's negotiating style."

"What's that about?" I asked.

"He got real mean, real quick. Lots of brokers lose their tempers after hours of going back and forth. That's the business. But he was mean and personal. He left lots of casualties behind each deal. But nobody ever called him on it. The money was too good, or the other guys were chickenshit, or both.

"The play money is about gone, from what I hear," Hutchinson continued, taking a long slug of decaf. We were definitely soul mates.

"The pressure is on him to keep the money flowing and to make some pay-backs."

"What's the chance of doing that?"

"Not very big, I'd say. I think desperation is driving Affazzi now. That's why he's in all these small scams, too much out in the public for a real hustler. He's hurting."

Jed looked up and said, "He's a smart operator but somehow he's lost his soul. He's real cold. Watch out for him."

I paid with a credit card. This was a business lunch without anyone to expense but my own personal account for Tom Woods. And, of course, the IRS.

"So your advice is to go at Affazzi and Devereaux straight up. Nothing else I should know about what these guys are up to?"

"I'm sorry," Hutchinson said. "I know you wanted to bite Chicago on the ass. But that ain't Chicago anymore, not like the old days."

Hutchinson and I took the elevator down to the first floor on the Wabash Avenue side, the average age of our elevator mates being closer to Hutchinson's than to mine. I needed some wisdom and got it. Simple is better.

But simple isn't always better, especially when important stuff is left out. In this case that omitted something wasn't incidental small stuff; it was big time. How did Devereaux manage to float $1 billion in bonds for the Tax Development District that included funny money for N&M, UPC, and the rest of the gang?

I pondered big thoughts about sleazy things as I crossed the street to Seth's office on Wabash Avenue, a refreshing exposure to shadows, rumbling trains, and grit. I could almost feel the coal dust of a century ago settling upon me like an urban shroud.

Seth was in his usual pose, leaning precariously back in his captain's chair with wheels, his motorcycle boots propped up on the windowsill. He wore a vintage White Sox cap—the phone glued to his ear.

"So, have your grain hypothesis confirmed, doctor?" Seth gurgled, his bright blue-green eyes dancing. He slammed the phone down.

"Goddamn peckerwood!" he exclaimed. "Now what'd you say about grain?"

"Down the toilet. Straight shot to the Deep Tunnel," I murmured, referring to the one of the largest infrastructure projects of all time. It rivaled turning the Chicago River around to dump sewage on St. Louis. This time they built holding tunnels for runoff to protect Lake Michigan. Another good cause.

"Only cost me lunch at the Walnut Room and the eternal damnation of their staff. What's worse, now I can't trash Delaney anymore with a clear conscience."

"Painful, huh?" Seth said.

I grimaced.

"So what's Reverend Jackson have to say," I changed the subject. "He's surviving, I take it?"

"No problem," Seth answered, swiveling his chair at breakneck speed. This was a technique, Seth assured me, to fight the cigarette urge by invoking nausea.

"He's held up in another church on the south side, waiting for this mess to clear. Even though Centeno has backed off, the south side gangs have an appetite for mindless revenge."

"Find out anything?"

"He thinks he's identified one of the murderers of your pal Woods."

I held my breath.

"And who might that be?" I asked with mock interest, remembering Tom Woods and every bruise that this Chicago morass had inflicted upon me.

"Blevins! The Sheik's boy!" Seth said, his eyes sparking anger. Seth knew Blevins was responsible for Sarah's assault.

"Well, he's already taken his last limo ride," I said. "The one you passed up. Last I saw of him he was wrapped in rug and manhandled out of Affazzi's limo and thrown into the Bridgeport quarry. Affazzi was more than casual about the hit. Broad daylight."

"That reminds me," I said, "maybe I should pass along a tip about Blevins to Radachek."

"Why not?" offered Seth. "It's the right thing to do, even for a deadhead."

"Of course, the Sheik will go ballistic."

"Unless he's tired of fatherhood," I replied.

"That's hard, Spivak."

"Not hard enough for me," I said, remembering Sarah's bruised face.

"The Sheik knew Blevins was a jerk and a drug addict," Seth said. "But this is a personal insult to him. And by Affazzi. I don't get it."

"So why did Blevins kill Woods and Jutland?" I asked. "He seemed more like a frightened accomplice than a killer when I saw him on Tuesday night. And he didn't beat up Sarah. It was the Sheik."

"Who knows, but here's Al's guess. It really was a drug deal like Radachek said. Dish talked with a bunch of gangbangers and got the story, or a part of the story anyway. Blevins was in the middle of a cocaine deal when Jutland stumbled into the middle of things. Centeno's pushers thought the Canalport Boys were making a move on their territory. That's when things blew up."

"Why Blevins picked the Brewery is a testament to his dim wits. No wonder Affazzi took him out. He's not the kind of guy who can keep quiet about exciting things, or when he's fucked up and needs to cover his ass. And then stupider still, he dumps Jutland's body in the Brewery tunnel."

"Now you're being hard, Greenburg."

"Hmm. You got me, Spivak."

"You're welcome," I said. "But who was the other murderer?"

"Don't know."

Neither of us said anything.

"Only one other thing I still can't figure," I finally said. "How did Devereaux and his pals manage to sell $1 billion of TDD bonds? Wasn't anybody watching the store?"

"You talking about me?" Seth asked.

"You tell me," I replied

"This is really not such a big deal. It happens all the time," Seth said. "The downtown banks love it. Remember all those developers standing in line for Devereaux? Everybody's at the public trough. They don't care if a few million gets siphoned off for slush funds, pay-offs, office remodeling, or unspecified fees. All reasonable costs of doing business in Chicago. Remember, as the Alderman always says, the future of Chicago is at stake."

"Maybe it's time we pay Alderman Devereaux a visit," I suggested.

"Already on the schedule," Seth snickered, adjusting his cap with the bill pointing to the left. "McGinty's Funeral Home at Western and 112th Street at 6 tonight to pay our last respects to Assistant Commissioner Gene Burke. Join me if you can find your way and proper attire."

There was time to kill. Devereaux at 6 PM. Dorothy at 9. The recurring image of Tom Woods grew dimmer every day, less demanding. He was more at ease, acclimating to his newly deceased condition. What bullshit. He didn't want to die. I had to keep reminding myself.

As for me, only the thought of Dorothy kept me going. Would she really show up? I had my doubts. I felt like I was hip-deep in Chicago sleaze, nothing new, nothing spectacular like a scam at the Board of Trade, the genie of Chicago's tumultuous beginnings.

I found myself in the narrow corridor of phone booths in the LaSalle Bank building, home to N&M. There was no anxiety-ridden lady making furtive calls, just me. And somehow I had sleepwalked my way to the epicenter of Tom Woods' demise.

I called Radachek to fill him in on Blevins' magic carpet ride, in case he didn't already know. He didn't. We played cat and mouse about who, what, when, where, and how. I lost. He scoffed when I said Affazzi was in the limo. He tried to pawn me off to the top brass, Lieutenant O'Malley, but I politely declined, and then was mysteriously cut off.

Next I called Alex, Helen's beau, to ask whether First Federal Bank had bought any TDD bonds. Alex was surprised when I finally reached him after five transfers up and down the seventy-story bank building. My call would give him something to brag about with Helen.

He said that all the big Chicago money center banks had a piece of the TDD action as well as insurance companies and even a few wired foundation endowments. Syndicators put these investors together several times a year when project were coming on line. Usually with public development bonds of this kind there were preferred private offerings so that everybody in need of some risk-free civic brownie points could invest. And they were sweet deals. Good land backed by city tax revenues. Nobody turned down a piece of that action. "We're in for a $100 million or so," they'd say. And the bank regulators loved it.

"Who's the syndicator on this deal?" I asked.

"What? You chasing your tail, Spivak?" Alex said, giving me a tentative poke. All right, I deserved it.

"Your pals at N&M have made good money brokering TDD bonds," Alex continued, speaking quickly. "Affazzi has a corner on public development bonds in the Midwest. He's known for making generous political contributions to all parties, and crafting the right partnerships with minority investment banks and even a Bridgeport insurance company. It's all part of the family."

Maybe I was wrong about Alex. That made Helen a lucky girl.

My last call was to Sam.

"Can you take a few hours off tonight?" I asked after Sam's drawl flooded my earpiece. "Going down to the southwest side, your favorite part of town."

"Need me or my wheels?" Sam asked in a pouty voice—if that were imaginable.

"Both, and my lawyer too."

"Okay, since you know what's what. Be at the garage on 8th Street by 5:30."

I signed off with Sam and took a joy ride up to the seventh floor. Retracing my steps of several days earlier, I landed in front of the glass door that no longer held the gold lettering N&M Ltd, only the faint outlines of letters that had been scraped off.

The door stood ajar so I entered and found an office that was in the post-dismantling stage, a random mix of boxes, Styrofoam cups, and black plastic garbage bags. N&M had closed down quickly without leaving a forwarding address. Bad for business.

Looking back, I noticed a paper-sized official-looking document taped to the inside of the glass door. I pulled it off and saw that it was an eviction notice from the Cook County Court. N&M owed $75,000 in back rent. The walls had come tumbling down on this financial manipulator, and that was his good side.

Strolling to Affazzi's office in the rear of the suite, I heard the crumpling of paper—no doubt the ghosts of scams past. But I was wrong. Affazzi's girl Friday tried to whack me with a marble lamp base. I caught her arm on the down swing and twisted. The crunch of her shoulder socket immediately produced screams of agony. What shred of crazed loyalty had driven her to such a stupid act? Maybe she really needed the job.

The security guard at the desk in the lobby barely acknowledged me when I told him about the screams on the seventh floor. Then I left. One more stop before the funeral.

CHAPTER 21

▼

So far Affazzi and N&M Ltd were guilty of high-risk investing, bungled property management at the Brewery, cornering the TDD bond market, and—according to Dorothy and Jutland—manipulating business valuations of Midwest grain co-ops. And, of course, we couldn't forget gruesome murders. Several of them. This portfolio of greed blended white-collar crime, avarice, and public deception with brutality—the universal human trait.

With an hour left before I had to meet Sam I dropped by the office of the Civic Budget Commission, a watchdog group started by a small band of Republican fiscal reformers in the 1960s that provided up-to-date analyses of Chicago's twisted and arcane budget and financial quagmire. There weren't many Republicans in Chicago, and those that showed their faces, were closet Democrats. The point was that politicians kept the budget overly complex so that citizens could not understand it, in fact were intimidated by it. Even those who had time to wade through volumes of numbers stayed away out of fear of terminal boredom.

The Budget Commission was a different breed from Seth's Center for Neighborhood Options or my eclectic investigative work. They published highly regarded reports, held press conferences and dressed well. Everyone liked them, except the machine. Public education about financial shenanigans was as far as they went, not far enough in the eyes of neighborhood folk and Chicago cynics like myself.

I was lucky. Martin Kelly, the public finance expert for the Budget Commission, was alone in the office, the rest of the five-person shop having called it a day for Chicago muckraking. I had known Kelly for twenty years, since he had taught urban economics and finance at the Kellogg School. He left the school after not receiving tenure. Having been trained as a Jesuit from an early age, he felt that publishing useless academic papers for personal gain diminished his calling. The dean wasn't impressed. Kelly ended up at the Budget Commission, over the years developing an encyclopedic knowledge of the mysterious flows of Chicago tax dollars.

I found him in the front office trying to operate the fax machine. His signature clothing statement was elephant-ear collar shirts from the 1950s, usually pale gray or blue with small-stenciled sailboats, haystacks, or windmills. But he knew how to dress the role for those special public occasions. He looked pleadingly at me for help.

"Sorry. I'm an electronic illiterate myself."

He pressed a button that produced appropriate buzzing sounds; he turned towards me with a look of non-comprehension about what I was doing there.

"Do I know you?" he said.

"Nick Spivak, Martin. I don't know if you remember me but I took a course from you at Kellogg."

A moment passed.

He laughed. "I try not to remember that period of life. But I'm familiar with your reputation, Mr. Spivak. What can I do for you?" He gestured for me to follow him into the small conference room.

"You got twenty minutes?" I asked, taking a chair.

He looked at his watch. "How about fifteen? I have a train to catch."

"Okay. Let me be concise," I began. "I'm looking into the City's TDD program. I understand the mechanics of the program, more or less. Each year the City sells bonds. Most of the sales go to local banks in search of civic kudos and easy payback. N&M Ltd has brokered the financing, making a good penny on fees. The funds are released as developers close their deals and draw down financing. Not all deals go forward. And some portion of the TDD funds, after the City deducts administrative costs, are dedicated to a social linkage fund that supports community projects."

"You always were good at homework, I'm starting to remember," chuckled Kelly.

"I'm missing something, Martin," I said. "Something big enough to make murder worthwhile."

Kelly stared out of the window of his fifth floor office on State Street observing the failed pedestrian mall that had cut off the flow of traffic and people years before in a fit of copycat urban design run amok. Movement made for interaction and profits. Lack of motion meant boredom, crime, and low rents.

I couldn't tell if he was thinking, meditating, or indulging in a late afternoon fantasy about numbers. Kelly must have sensed my impatient scrutiny because he nodded his head toward me and sat at the conference table.

"Who holds the TDD money before the closings? I can't remember," he asked.

"I think it's spread out among bank depositories," I said, picking up the scent. "The linkage fund benefits from interest generated while the money is parked."

"Times up, Spivak. I think you know where to look. The City issues quarterly depository reports. Your pal Greenburg should sink his teeth into them. It's not our kind of research, but I will collect reports for him. Have him call me."

"Thanks," I said, picking up my coat and heading for the door. Kelly looked at his watch and walked back to his office.

"Remember. It's all in the float." He chuckled like the consummate nerd that he was.

I know that, I said to myself.

An Oldsmobile 98 is a very fine automobile if you are big, favor gas-guzzlers, crave comfort, and like the feel of leather. Sam treated his dark blue 1987 98 better than he treated me—a long-time customer, confidant and friend. I was hurt but not devastated.

I was becoming more and more comfortable knowing less than I thought I knew. We took the scenic route from downtown, down Archer Avenue and then south on Western, the site of battles between blacks and whites in the 1960s and 1970s. Now the neighborhoods were mostly Hispanic.

McGinty's funeral parlor was home for the politically connected on the southwest side, meaning the Irish. Its back rooms were stocked with cigars, whiskey, and telephones, and Mr. McGinty swept them daily for electronic bugs ever since the FBI's Operation Snow Shovel—a sting on aldermen arranging for City purchase of stolen rock salt—bugged one of the back rooms for incriminating conversations. A discreet metal detector at the front door identified unwanted weapons and other items of mischief. Bouncers in somber black attire took care of business, doing what bouncers do. If McGinty and his sons weren't part of Devereaux's biological family, they had certainly been adopted along the way.

In the old days Sam and I wouldn't have lasted ten minutes in this neighborhood before a gang of neo-Nazis or Aryan groupies would have pummeled our car with rocks and worse, even a 98, screaming, "Nigger go home."

Thankfully, times had changed, at least the surface of things had changed. I remembered my recent lesson about soapy surfaces. We both tensed as Sam

parked the Olds. We walked the half block to McGinty's. Police cars dou-
ble-parked everywhere. Was this really a good idea, I said to myself. Sam was in
the zone.

Political wakes combined the macabre and ridiculous in a unique Chicago
soap opera. The casket functioned as the centerpiece around which life, in this
case political gossip and deal making, swirled in new and mysterious eddies.
There was always the obligatory group of genuine mourners dressed mostly in
black who clustered near the casket, emitting sighs, groans, tearful gulps, and
fluttering handkerchiefs. Each newly arrived pol spent a few minutes shaking
hands and embracing the grief-stricken before retiring to the back rooms for a
few shots and a dose or two of political business, maybe even a deal.

This was a more mixed crowd than usual at McGinty's, indicating that Gene
Burke was ecumenical in his political and planning largess, and that he represented the modernizing wing of the machine, those who recognized kinship with
northside Poles, aging liberals, gays, and yuppies. Realpolitik. No more ideology.
Nothing wrong with making money. We all believe in reform, peace and quiet,
and no more homeless on the streets. New members of the machine wore pony-
tails and ate at northern Italian trattorias. Real estate and keeping the peace
bound the machine together.

Our perfunctory bows to Assistant Commissioner Gene Burke seemed to satisfy the mourners, allowing us to move quickly to the rear and refreshments.
Enveloped by a cloud of cigar smoke, we adjusted our eyes to the dim lights and
hazy atmosphere of the political back room. Above the haze, standing like an
Olympian was Alderman Ed Devereaux, his stately image communicating champion to all who cared to observe. And then were there were others, including Seth
Greenburg, hatless in a black three-piece suit, saved no doubt from his father's
funeral fifteen years earlier.

We caught a soliloquy by Ed Devereaux.

"Gene Burke and I have known each other for thirty years, since high school
at St. Michael's. We took the same classes, attended the same neighborhood
dances, and got chased by Negros, I mean African Americans, from our old
neighborhood.

"We both wanted to be priests when we were young. Each of us had cousins,
aunts, and uncles who had given their lives to the church. By the time we graduated high school, Vietnam was aflame as well as the streets of Chicago. Becoming
priests didn't seem so attractive.

"I went to DePaul all the way through law school. Gene went to Loyola and
earned an advanced degree in urban studies.

"We kept in touch as we both got jobs with the City. Our fathers were precinct captains. Gene worked in planning and development and I took a job in the Corporation Counsel's Office. Gene moved up the ranks in government and I ran for City Council. It's been a good life together. Gene Burke didn't abuse the public trust. He was a good man who loved his city."

Applause thundered in the backroom.

"What about the TDD deals, Alderman?" Seth asked, having to raise his voice above the camaraderie of the machine in mourning.

The room grew quiet and menacing, the team waiting at the ready.

Devereaux walked toward Seth, pointing his manicured finger at the bushy-bearded activist in a suit.

"I will not compromise this solemn moment by discussing TDD business," Devereaux lectured Greenburg. His gaggle of young-machine followers looked menacingly at Seth.

Why kick a hornet's nest, I mused. Did he realize this was the machine mothership? Maybe the cigar smoke had gotten to him. But I didn't believe that for a second. Seth had an uncanny sense of style and timing. He wouldn't pick a fight without a strategy, or at least a prayer of escaping through a hidden backdoor.

And then it was obvious. I was blind. The Sheik and Affazzi flanked Devereaux, a troika for public scamming the likes of which was rarely matched in Chicago's history. That a wanted man like Affazzi could stand up at the podium with public officials was a sick tribute to Chicago and its definition of tolerance. But this was a wake at McGinty's and anything was possible.

Fortunately, I knew something that the Sheik didn't know, which would rattle his cage and maybe more. Ignoring Seth's less than subtle hand gesture to follow his lead, I jumped into action.

"Mr. Sheik," I shouted. "I saw a couple of big guys wrap your sleazeball son, Randy Blevins, in a rug and dump him in the Bridgeport quarry. It wasn't pretty. For those of you who don't know Randy, he's the kind of guy who likes to beat up defenseless women."

If Seth had kicked a hornet's nest, I had walked into bear cave dripped in honey. The room had the silent feel of doom.

The Sheik turned toward me with an ugly gaze. Unlike his wasted son, he was still chiseled from granite, six feet tall and 200 pounds of muscle, even at his age somewhere past sixty. His creased face and dark eyes bristled. Devereax and Affazzi exchanged warning glances and signaled their guards to take care of us fast.

"Yeah, Mr. Affazzi's hulk performed the dump," I continued. "It was horrifying. Did you put a contract out on your own son, Mr. Sheik? Or was that your partner's idea? Some side business. It was Affazzi's limo that made the drop."

Affazzi was on the move before I finished my remarks, stumbling against the bar and sending whiskey bottles flying. What a shame. Devereaux carefully stepped back from the impending fracas and disappeared with his guards through a curtain that led to the rear door of McGinty's. But Affazzi could not outrun the Sheik's outstretched arms and iron grasp. The back room erupted into chaos as the lights went out and shots were fired. The upshot was a wild stampede of pols, lieutenants and hangers-on rushing for the front door. In their mad dash, they knocked over Assistant Commissioner Gene Burke and scattered the weeping mourners.

Sam and I hung with the neighborhood rubberneckers as police cars and fire trucks clogged the blocks that surrounded McGinty's. The place was a wreck and being consumed by a fire begun when the stampede knocked over novena candles on the casket. Before the fire could be brought under control, Assistant Commissioner Gene Burke, against his wishes and the rules of the church, had been cremated, his cherry-wood casket proving to be quite flammable under the right conditions. I couldn't imagine that this blasphemous exit would affect his one-way ticket to hell. In fact, it might prepare him for what was to come.

To our surprise it was the Sheik who came out on a stretcher in critical condition, bullet wounds to the chest and head, according to the EMT at his side. We moved in for a closer look. He was semi-conscious.

Somehow he raised himself on one elbow and mumbled in our direction, "I got a message."

"Too late," I replied.

The Sheik slumped on the gurney.

The Sheik's escort included none other than O'Malley, Radachek, and Pelegrino. They peeled off when they caught sight of Sam and me. The angry resolve on their faces told me we were in for trouble. Lucky I brought my lawyer.

No longer holding back waiting for the strategic moment, O'Malley took control immediately, limping right up into my face, froth gathering at the corners of his thin-lipped mouth. He needed a shave. I noticed he had nice teeth.

"Back off there, Mr. Lieutenant," Sam ordered. "I'm Mr. Spivak's lawyer, as you know. All three hundred pounds of me."

O'Malley started to laugh and then thought better of it as Sam moved closer, his bulk saying back off in a primordial male language that O'Malley knew well.

"Let's book them at the station," Radachek interjected, desperately trying to keep his eyes from bowing under O'Malley's gaze. "He's a material witness on the Blevins murder."

"Where's Affazzi?" I shouted before they could make up their collective mind, that is, the whim of Lieutenant O'Malley. "All this tough guy stuff by you guys should be aimed at him, not me. Or don't you get it yet?"

This sensible observation only made things worse. My trademark. O'Malley exploded.

"Your stupid mouth, Spivak, caused this tragedy. You had no business crashing this wake with your gorilla lawyer. This is a good neighborhood!"

"That sounds mighty racist, Mr. Lieutenant," Sam sneered, moving in close again. "I think we'll file with the Police Oversight Commission. I understand you've got an open file."

"Let's do it," I chimed in, with a big grin. "Let's take him down."

"You fucks don't know what you're getting into, even now," O'Malley shot back.

We moved in closer.

Radachek and Pelegrino uneasily edged between Sam and O'Malley. They didn't bother with me. The look on O'Malley's face said, I will personally break you unless you protect my ass. So much for team spirit.

"Bullshit!" I growled. "I found Randy Blevins, the murderer of Tom Woods, without your help. So much for random urban killings. And I watched Affazzi and his henchman make a fruit roll-up out of Blevins. Obviously, Devereaux and Affazzi didn't let the Sheik in on their disposal plan for his son. That's not my problem. If you goofs had done your job instead of running for cover maybe you could have prevented what happened tonight and maybe even Blevins' death. But I'm not really sure he was even worth saving. He beat up Sarah Larsen on orders from the big boys to give me a scare. Maybe the big boys got to you as well."

O'Malley stood frozen, his right hand on his service revolver. His eyebrows twitched. Everything hung in suspension for those few moments. The crowd of rubberneckers had stepped back ten paces to let the drama unfold.

The spell was broken by Seth Greenburg, who limped up from nowhere in his ill-fitting black suit, now torn in several places and speckled with smoky ash.

"Spivak, Sam! Devereaux wants a meet at his neighborhood office. Pronto!" Seth shouted. "You done with them, Lieutenant? We got to go!"

Radachek and Pelegrino grabbed O'Malley to keep him from doing something that he would regret as long as he kept his wits about him.

We headed for Sam's 98.

CHAPTER 22

▼

Devereaux's ward office was a hybrid of Hugh Hefner's mansion and Hitler's Berlin bunker. It sat on a prairie full of Chicago cottages built in the 1950s, taking up four lots and backing onto a railroad right-of-way. Surrounded by a ten-foot chain link fence and a fashionable concrete guard pillbox in the driveway, the aboveground habitat was a low-slung white ranch home that hugged the prairie flatland.

As we approached the bunker Seth assumed the role of expert commentator, leaning his head forward between Sam and me from the back seat. We could smell the recently departed remains of McGinty's Funeral Home on Seth's bushy wealth of hair and beard.

"All the action is underground," Seth stated with authority. "He keeps a wife upstairs for public consumption but rarely spends time up there. She's from a good Irish Catholic family that believes in perseverance and a stiff drink to make the veil of tears palatable."

"How do you know this stuff?" asked Sam, giving Seth a puzzled look. In his book, knowing about your enemies' dirty underwear was not cool.

"You wouldn't believe it. I met the wife's sister on a pub crawl with White Sox fans on Western Avenue. We struck up a relationship, one that included sticking it to her brother-in-law at every opportunity. She cares a lot about her sister and what she has to put up with."

"Why doesn't the wife leave?" I asked.

"Easier said than done," answered Seth as he pulled into the driveway.

The entrance guard checked the trunk and undercarriage of the Olds for assault weapons while his partner collected our IDs and talked to the chief of security up at the big house. We passed muster.

"Go up the drive to the right. The garage door will open automatically," the guard said in a voice reminiscent of a hit man I once knew.

We obeyed in our own way.

"What's the drill?" I asked Seth as Sam gunned the engine, leaving a provocative fuck-you patch of rubber, or whatever tires were made of these days. The guard ran after us waving his beefy arms for us to stop as we sped up the drive.

"Who knows, Spivak. It's the end game at this point. Devereaux will probably be figuring out how to escape the pile of shit that's hanging directly over his head."

"Only Affazzi's left to take the fall. But that could be a dangerous play," I said. Indeed, Affazzi was out there somewhere in Chicago, a sleazeball murderer backed into a corner. The question was whether he would run for it or stick around Chicago to exact revenge and liquidate assets.

That would be stupid. But I had no idea what made Affazzi tick. The death of his wife and son? Greed? Something bigger and stranger? Who knew?

The garage door opened as promised with flashing red lights and a series of loud beeps. We drove down a steep incline into the concrete compound two floors below ground level. Guards swarmed our doors before Sam had even cut off the big V-8.

Devereaux's endless supply of guards, no doubt loyal precinct workers, marched us into the anteroom to Devereaux's office and frisked us from head to foot. Sam balked, and the frisking came to a halt while the guards conferred. They finally relented and let us pass into Devereaux's inner sanctum. The room's décor combined pussycat pastels and security functionalism. We waited.

With an hour to spare before Dorothy's train arrived at Union Station, and a thirty-minute drive to the station, I prayed that Devereaux would be direct enough for us to understand the point of the meeting the first time around. That would be a first for a traditional Chicago politician, whose first instinct was to deliver an incomprehensible garble prefaced by a semi-religious, autobiographical preamble.

The sudden opening of Devereaux's office door brought us to attention. No silver mane. No professional tan. Instead lieutenant Barry Grieco in a gray pin-striped suit stepped into the room with an air of confidence that had just been inflated.

"Greenburg, Spivak, ahhh."

"Call me Sam," said Sam.

"...and Sam, then." We sat in chairs around the large polished oval meeting table. A picture of Devereaux and the Mayor in a gold frame graced the table, providing a focal point for all words and negotiations.

"The alderman asked me to meet with you first to discuss the parameters of our conversation," said Greico, dripping in sincerity. "I think this will make the best use of everybody's time."

"I've got thirty minutes tops, Greico, to talk about parameters," I said. "So let's cut to the chase."

"He's got a date," Seth laughed.

Greico frowned, losing a puff of his inflated composure. Underneath his professional veneer was one more street tough who got some political finishing at a local university.

"Consider the following," he began. "What if Alderman Devereaux were to hold a press conference tomorrow at City Hall, followed by editorial board meetings at the Bugle and Daily Times, at which he called for a full scale independent audit of the TDD program. He would say the deaths of Tom Woods and Omar Jutland, the conflict of interest of Assistant Commissioner Gene Burke, and the improprieties, if not illegalities of N&M Ltd, raise such serious questions that he feels compelled to take this action even though he still believes the TDD program is essential for Chicago's future."

"Improprieties!" I gasped. "Affazzi is a killer! Don't you get it yet!"

"So this is the high ground escape plan," Seth smiled. "What's he want from us? Safe passage? No public hits for ten days."

"Affazzi's a killer!" I repeated, but the conversation swerved around my anger.

"Very astute, Mr. Greenburg," Greico replied. "You'll get what you've wanted for six months. Full disclosure. Reform. And heads will roll. I can promise you that."

"But not Alderman Devereaux's," I said, finally attracting Greico's attention. "Will he share in the head rolling?"

"No," that's not part of the plan," Greico said. "The Alderman is as horrified by these eventualities as you are.

I interrupted, "Eventualities! Do you know the body count?"

"Calm down, Spivak. You're getting emotional," Seth chided. Sam whispered in my ear, "You'll get your shots." I leaned back in my chair and breathed deeply.

Greico continued, "Our lawyers assure us that he is on safe ground regarding the administration of the TDD program. Besides, to be frank, there are just too many developers, realtors, architects, and bankers who depend upon TDDs. And don't forget all your community friends who benefit from the social linkage fund. Alderman Devereaux is TDD's undisputed champion."

The point sank in.

"And what's the low road?" Seth asked just to make sure we knew our options.

"We are fully prepared to maintain business as usual and to argue that any malfeasance related to the TDD program has resulted from the misguided actions of Gene Burke and Affazzi. No more, no less. We have every confidence that this candid explanation will satisfy all but the most rabid critics."

"You mean us?" Sam asked.

"I hope not," Greico replied.

"What about the Alderman and Burke being old school buddies? That was quite a speech at McGinty's," I said.

Greico looked at me dumbly, knowing when to shut up before he dug a hole for himself.

"Why bother with the high road at all? That's not machine-style," Seth exclaimed. "No Chicago pol comes clean unless they have to, unless there is a percentage in it. You don't want to look weak and out of control."

At that moment the office door opened and Alderman Devereaux, along with the Reverend Lee Sampson and Jack Delaney, entered the room. Seth's question hung in the air and then fell flat. The room was getting crowded.

"Let me answer that, Barry," the Alderman intervened, commanding center stage at the front of the table. Sampson, Delaney, and Greico flanked him. The rest of us remained sitting.

For Sampson and Delaney to show up for this, and together, made me realize we had overturned a bigger rock than we thought.

Devereaux continued, "The simple answer is that I plan to run for mayor in two years and I want the TDD program to be the centerpiece of my campaign, 'Growth with Dignity.'"

Devereaux then broke into a stump speech. He couldn't help himself, even though talk of murder and corruption was in the air. You couldn't fault his confidence.

"Our city is a broken mosaic of neighborhoods, races, walks of life. My 'Growth with Dignity' platform is about healing, putting our mosaic back together to make Chicago a great world-class city for the 21st century.

"I come to this mission with extreme humility," he said, hanging his head slightly and wiping his tanned brow. "I have watched our city fragment, become engulfed in violence and intolerance. Today, I ask for forgiveness for waiting this long to tell you that there is another path for Chicagoans.

"Growth with Dignity..." his speech trailed off and Devereaux gave us his five-star smile, showing off his glistening capped teeth.

"You've got to be kidding," I muttered.

"Devereaux looked at me, a twinkle in his eye.

"This is what's called victory," Delaney jumped in. "Do I have to spell it out for you guys? You've won what you wanted. Now is the time, as Alinsky always said, to cut a deal, celebrate, and get on with life. Seth, you of all people have to understand. Spivak, well he'll be back in Baltimore in a few days with his grain hypothesis.

I grimaced.

Sampson sat silently, somehow everyone knowing that a word from him would kill any credibility or sympathy Devereaux might have mustered. He had gone over to the other side in a big way. Or maybe he had been there for a while and we had had our heads in the ground. He looked nervous.

"How about it, Greenburg?" Greico prompted like a cheerleader. "Can you live with 'Growth and Dignity?' Which road do you want us to take?"

All eyes turned on Seth.

"Tell you what," Seth said, in a voice so serious that I grew concerned. "You do what you have to do. This ain't about what I want."

Devereaux and Delaney looked stunned.

"Let's move it," I said. "I have a train to meet. Great digs, Alderman. Just the right touch for the apocalypse. Who's your decorator?"

"Could you send for our escorts, please?" Sam asked.

Devereaux's tan face turned beet red, an incredible transformation. He muttered to Delaney something incomprehensible that included the words "fuckin' assholes."

The guards ushered us back to Sam's 98 and opened up the garage. I had fifteen minutes to meet Dorothy's train.

No Dorothy. My adrenaline rush and the predictable tardiness of Amtrak enabled me to reach the Union Station waiting room as the Milwaukee passengers disembarked. Sam had dumped me on the corner of Canal and Jackson streets after a ride that deserved numerous traffic citations and verged on a near-death experience. Seth didn't notice. He remained quiet for half the ride and then unleashed a reservoir of invective that reached deep down. He usually didn't let things get to him.

"Those pricks!" he said. "They think I'll make deals, settle for something. Do they think I'm that desperate after all these years? Joining with them would be a death sentence for any credibility I might have with the neighborhoods."

"Our friend Delaney probably advised that your middle-aged self was ready for a life of compromise," I said.

"He's a prick, too," Seth replied. "I hate the expectation that growing old means that you're doomed to become a reasonable guy. For them, reasonable means accepting the inevitability of scumbags like Devereaux. I don't think so."

"You're just popular," I said.

"Leave 'em be," Sam chided. "Can't you see he's hurtin?"

"That's the point," I replied.

"Poor fucking Sampson," Seth said. "Imagine him sitting thirty minutes without pontificating. They must have him by the short hairs. A prominent and meaningless campaign position to keep him under wraps. What he doesn't know is that Devereaux will drop him in two seconds if anybody raises a stink about UPC."

"And nobody's going to keep Ella quiet," I said.

"That's right!"

"I've never known Sampson to be so quiet. Something's going on with the good Reverend."

"Like what?" I asked

"Time will tell," Seth replied as we pulled to the curb.

I told them not to wait for us at the station. I had other ideas: a late-night walk across the Loop, filled with spine-tingling commentary by me about the blood and guts of Chicago, charming Dorothy and recharging my battery.

This story was completed as far as I was concerned. I had found Tom Woods' killer, at least one of them, and the motives for his death. I would have preferred a judicial rendering but I wouldn't lose sleep over the outcome, Blevins buried in the quarry, or wherever Radachek had him taken. I felt strangely indifferent to the identity of the other killers. One was enough for this trip. Let Radachek and company clean up the rest. And I had a hand, however clumsy, in helping Seth and others shine a bit of light on the sleaze that underpins big-time real estate development in Chicago. No matter what road Devereaux chose, the TDD program would not operate at the same level of corruption and insider dealing, at least until things settled down. That was a victory. Delaney was right.

I asked the exiting Amtrak conductors if they had seen a tall brunette with short hair and green eyes. Nobody had. One old fart said he wished he had and winked; that hardly cheered me up. Maybe my doubts were well founded.

Maybe, after second thoughts, Dorothy decided to hide rather than consort with a known troublemaker who was chasing ghosts in Chicago. I admired her common sense even as I nursed my self-pity. The heartache gave way to fear. Affazzi and his henchmen could have prevented her from taking the train, or worse.

I waited another hour, making the rounds of all the nooks and crannies, bars, and hot dog stands in Union Station. No Dorothy. I called her home in Milwaukee only to reach her answering machine and a generic not at home message. No Dorothy. There was nothing else to do but return to the Balboa. Beat, I tried to charm myself with my late-night Loop walk, but the shadows scared me. I ran most of the way.

I headed straight for the elevator when I walked into the Balboa. Sam was off-duty and I didn't feel like making any new friends. A couple of lobby rats stared at me anxiously as if I might be their personal messenger of salvation or death. After all, it was the eleventh hour. Their old, colorless lips moved silently in supplication. I disappointed them by hurrying by and their heads dropped.

The weight of two weeks of mad rushing about was finally catching up with me. I needed to crash quick, but I also needed to clear my head about Dorothy and figure out what I should do. I managed to find my key and unlock the door, groping to undress as I stumbled across the transom.

Lights were on. Even my muddled brain registered that this pattern of light was all wrong. Affazzi's cold gaze flashed in my mind. I had no means of defense. I couldn't think. I wanted to run but there was no energy left to propel me out of harm's way, or even put on the shoes I had drop kicked off my feet as I walked in.

"Nick," I heard. "Nick baby. It's me, Dorothy. It's okay."

She came toward me in a satin purple robe with her arms outstretched. "I took an earlier train and conned my way into your room, saying I was a friend of Sam's. It worked. I thought you would be proud of me."

I fell into her arms.

After a few minutes—maybe more—I felt like an emotional squall had gathered us up and then tossed us on an island of calm. Dorothy helped me complete my manic undressing and led me to the shower. I watched her take off her purple skin, mesmerized by her softness and silhouette against the ancient, flowered wallpaper. She ignited an emotional and physical reserve that I didn't know I had. Under hot, steaming water, we gently folded our arms around each other, exploring bodies from head to toe. The hot water cleansed us of the sleaze and contempt for life that had surrounded us in the past two weeks. This was temporary, I knew, yet I felt myself falling inward into a safe place, one I hadn't felt for years. I made it back to the bed wrapped in an assortment of Balboa Arms towels, and fell into a deep sleep, almost before Dorothy lowered my head onto her lap.

CHAPTER 23

▼

Morning sun filtered into the Balboa Arms windows despite the mottled film of urban dust and grease that covered the glass, warming our bodies and promising blue sky. This was Chicago at its best, even as the temperature dropped and the hawk turned over. I awoke first, my body wrapped around Dorothy. I kissed her back and neck, my hands caressing the rise of her hips. She stretched and turned over to face me.

Later we sat together in El Torta, Jacinto bearing over us as if we were newlyweds. Apprehensive about whether Dorothy would appreciate El Torta for the culinary gem that it was, I ordered huevos rancheros, which seemed safe for both of us. Her smile told me that she approved of El Torta or that she was extremely tolerant of my aberrant taste in restaurants. I had never seen Jacinto beam so brightly. It was annoying.

Dorothy agreed to my walking tour of the Tom Woods case, from chopped-down homeless retreat on Van Buren Street to the sock man on Maxwell Street. And of course, we concluded our journey at the Brewery. Somehow this tour was both a resolution and goodbye to Chicago.

"Milwaukee's got a bunch of these," Dorothy commented when she saw the old red brick buildings of the brewery.

"At least your breweries still brew," I replied.

"Fewer every day."

We carefully stepped inside the Stables building where Sister Mary O'Conner had hidden and in which Helen Trent and I found the drainage tunnel that led us to the corpse of Omar Jutland. His death still puzzled me, although I knew that Randy Blevins was fully capable of killing Jutland without a good reason, as if there were ever good reasons to kill, just as he had killed Tom Woods over drugs. Still, what did Blevins have to do with the tunnel, undocumented workers, and river barges?

My question was answered sooner than I wanted. As we turned to leave the Stables building, thoughts of our cozy afternoon nap at the Balboa sparkling in our eyes, we confronted the madman glare of Affazzi, and the muzzle of his .45 automatic.

"How convenient," was all he said. Affazzi's crumbling mental state was evident by the sweat dripping down his forehead and his shaking hands. His dress clothes were rumpled and torn from his fiery escape from McGinty's the night before. Insanity, however, had not diminished the shrewd and violent killer behind the events of the past two weeks.

"This isn't smart, Affazzi," I said, trying to come off cool and collected. "Let us go! You've got nothing to gain, and you're bound to get caught."

"I don't think so," Affazzi replied. "You have ruined my business. Now it's time for me to repay you and your friend."

I kept him talking. I thought that was what I was supposed to do.

"Tell me, Affazzi," I said as Dorothy clasped my arm. "Who killed Jutland? Was that Blevins' work, too? That's the only piece of the puzzle missing for me."

"Fool! Just a fool!" Affazzi sputtered. "No control! Reverend Sampson told Jutland that someone at the Brewery would take him to a new hiding place. The point was to scare him, hide him, and then take him back to Milwaukee. We didn't expect your foolish friend Woods to follow, and I know nothing about the drug deal and the commotion that followed. That was Blevins' weakness. The Sheik convinced me to use him against my better instincts. And then he simply lost control along with his drugged-up pal. No, don't bother asking me for a name because I don't know. He made a mess of things, to say the least. I had to get rid of him. But he wasn't the one to kill Woods and Jutland. You've got that all wrong."

I was stunned to say the least. "So who killed them?"

"That's enough for now," Affazzi said with a disconcerted look on his face. Dorothy's grip grew tighter.

"Is it consoling to have your mystery cleared up? I hope so for your sake. Mr. Spivak's the only witness who could testify about how Blevins died, a mistake on our part. Getting rid of Ms. Edwards is an added bonus; now no one will know about my fun with the grain co-ops. Thank you both for making it so easy to clean up after Blevins and escape Chicago. I still have done quite well despite what you might think. Thank you very much."

Affazzi prodded us with his gun to retrace the steps Helen and I had taken several days earlier, down the elevator, across the basement and into the tool room, down the stairwell and into the tunnel to the Chicago River. No one had bothered to fix the locks or replace the manhole cover. Affazzi would never make it as a property manager unless he took building security more seriously.

There was no obvious, or even less than obvious, tactical maneuver, to overcome Affazzi. So we complied. That didn't stop my mind from racing. Dorothy was hanging in. The joy of new relationships.

At the end of the tunnel, on the right side of the steel doors where we had found Omar Jutland, a rusted ladder—attached to the concrete retaining wall with bolts—led to the top. Affazzi grabbed Dorothy and held the gun to the back of her head.

"Get up there, Spivak, and open the hatch. Any wrong moves and you lose a loved one. Understand?"

"Yeah. We're with you, Affazzi. Calm down!"

I opened the hatch and climbed back down. Dorothy climbed up with Affazzi still pointing his gun in her back. I followed. At the top, we stood on a broken concrete retaining wall on the west side of the South Branch of the Chicago River; all around us weeds, scrap, and railroad tracks carpeted derelict industrial land awaiting new uses. The 18th Street Bridge loomed above us but no one could see or hear us from their cars. Pedestrians avoided these empty, silent stretches of the city even though, strangely enough, they were the safest.

Affazzi's twelve-foot skiff was tied to a rusty steel post anchored in the concrete wall. It had a small outboard engine. The only explanation for Affazzi's preparation was that Dorothy and I had stumbled unknowingly upon his well-planned escape route. I was still doubtful.

He told us to get in the boat, revved the engine after two pulls of the starter cord, and steered us into the thick green waters of the Chicago River. The thick water imperceptibly moved south, a change of direction from its original trajectory into Lake Michigan. Chicago engineers changed all that in 1898, reversing the flow of the river in order to dump residential and industrial waste on urban competitors like St. Louis. It worked.

Affazzi didn't take us far. A barge full of processed scrap metal was anchored on the river no more than a half mile below the 18th Street Bridge, at the beginning of its voyage down the Mississippi and to any of a dozen countries to build somebody else's industrial and transportation infrastructure. Affazzi steered around to the front of the barge.

"Grab the ladder, Spivak, and pull us tight," he ordered. "Then get on the barge, and no funny business."

He pointed his gun with new resolve. The question was when he would kill us. Sooner or later? My guess was that he would wait until the barge started moving at nightfall. He would be cautious. But my ability to see into the future hadn't done us much good so far.

If, by chance I was right, we didn't have much time.

Affazzi grabbed the ladder after securing the skiff to the bow of the barge. He climbed on top of the scrap heap, the automatic revolver still pointing at our heads, and ordered us to move to the center of the barge. Was this the end? We stumbled as we crossed rusty, sharp-edged steel.

We arrived at a crude space dug out around irregular-shaped pieces of scrap. It was not visible beyond the barge and contained two duffel bags. Affazzi had given this escape and kidnapping plan a great deal of thought.

Dorothy and I held each other's eyes every few minutes as a way of keeping our morale afloat.

"Sit down next to each other," Affazzi said. He pulled out a pair of handcuffs from his coat pocket and snapped a cuff on each of our wrists.

"That should make you two happy. Quality time, I think you say. If you promise to keep your voices down I won't tape your mouths shut. Don't even try to scream or get away."

We complied.

"How did you find us?" I whispered.

"That's right," he said. "Pure coincidence. Don't you have a saying about great minds thinking alike," he laughed, his thin lips barely parting.

Dorothy pinched my arm.

It was mid-afternoon and growing colder. Sitting on cold steel, even scrap steel, made it worse. The cold quickly penetrated our bodies. Dorothy leaned against my shoulder and closed her eyes.

"Any ideas, big guy?"

I didn't know whether to laugh or cry.

"I love you, too!"

"Be more assertive," she replied

"I love you!"

We dozed off.

A sudden jolt of the barge slamming against the concrete retaining wall awakened us. It reminded me of ferries docking in Manhattan, ominous sounds that my child's mind associated with the end of the world. I managed to prevent Dorothy and me from becoming mincemeat—and acquiring a severe case of tetanus— from the rusty steel poking at us from all sides. Affazzi lost his footing and fell to one knee behind us. If I had been more alert I could have attacked him or at least knocked away the gun. The tug had arrived, and we began moving. It was sunset. The hawk bit our faces.

"Sit tight!" Affazzi said, regaining his composure and standing up. "And don't worry about anybody seeing me. I own the boat and my second cousin is the tug captain."

We sat tight.

Within minutes the tug and barge moved as one, and the repetitive sounds of water lapping and the drone of the engine were hypnotic and annoying at the same time. We moved through the remnants of industrial Chicago and its new persona. I caught a glimpse of invading boat marinas and condos as I crouched in our steel hole.

"You're cooked, Affazzi," I said. "You really think you'll escape?" I wanted him talking. Maybe the unexpected would save our asses. Some plan.

"Certainly," he smiled. "Why not? I have the money."

"But there's an all-points bulletin out for you. Everybody's looking for Blevins' killer," I lied, wondering if Radachek had gotten off his fat ass to check for the body before it was buried in more garbage.

"On the river?" he smirked. "I doubt it very much. The last place you Americans would look."

He was right. Nobody would be out here. No pleasure boats. No storm warning. I had to keep him talking. I decided to give my grain hypothesis one more try.

Affazzi laughed, but not quite so hard or dismissively as Jed Hutchinson.

"Mr. Spivak, you do have an imagination, one much like mine. Humility is uncomfortable for me but I'm forced to say that I had much bigger plans, along the lines that you suggest, but I never got that far. The TDD program took too much of my time. And then this fiasco."

"Were the grain co-ops a first step?" Dorothy asked.

"A small part. Rather, a warm-up game, as you say."

"How would you have done it?" I asked.

Affazzi was silent, engaged in some unknown mental calculation.

"Since both of you will not live much longer, I see no problem in telling you." He pointed his gun to show control and to underscore our fate. "Perhaps you could offer me some feedback on my plan, as you Americans say. I know I will use the plan in the future."

At the exact moment of Affazzi's revelation, a clatter erupted at the front of the barge. Affazzi cautiously turned to look, keeping the gun pointed at us. As he turned, a barrage of rocks the size of golf balls pummeled him in the face, head, and chest. Other rocks hit after ricocheting off of the scrap metal. He cried out in pain, loudly cursing in another language.

I jumped for his gun arm as he lifted his hands to protect his bloody face. Luckily, Dorothy was moving with me. I hit his gun hand with a downward blow and the .45 clattered down amongst the pieces of scrap metal. Unreachable. Affazzi looked at me, and for the first time, fear showed in his eyes. Rocks bombarded us from behind. Dorothy and I crawled for cover.

I looked back and saw Seth Greenburg, Alphonius Jackson, Dish, and a group of kids on the California Avenue Bridge throwing rocks, some of the kids handing from the steel structure underneath holding up the roadway. It was the same bridge I had stood on four years ago, with Sarah Larsen, and threw a pair of black dress shoes over the rail after being fired by the City.

Blood ran down Affazzi's face and he was on his hands and knees desperately crawling to the front of the barge. He was muttering. He fumbled a cell phone from his coat pocket and was frantically trying to call someone, perhaps his cousin the tug captain, as the rocks pounded him. He pulled himself up to escape the rocks, trying to jump over the jagged scrap piles. Mesmerized, we watched as his right foot caught under a twisted clump of scrap causing him to lurch forward with tremendous momentum. His left side landed hard, impaled on a long, triangular piece of steel. Affazzi's body shook violently and twisted like a fish caught on a hook.

Dorothy and I held onto each other.

Affazzi's second cousin must have seen the bloody impaling of his esteemed relative because he detached the tug from the barge, swung around it, and came alongside the barge. Affazzi somehow managed to crawl to the side of the barge, having yanked the pointed metal shaft out of his body with a jerk and a piercing scream. He lifted himself over the edge and tumbled onto the deck of the tug, after casting one last malevolent look at us. The tug pulled away from the barge and churned south. We could see Affazzi crawling toward the cabin.

We drifted for a long time, or so it seemed, the weight of the barge and its load pushing us toward St. Louis. That was the last place we wanted to go. Eventually, two police and fire tugs lassoed the barge and brought it to a crunching finale against the concrete retaining wall down near the big sewage plants.

Dorothy and I were cold and in shock. Our only defense had been to sing songs from our childhood, silly songs, great songs. I sang a solo version of the Wabash Cannonball that sent Dorothy into hysterics. We did our best to ignore the bloody steel that had impaled Affazzi.

Moments later appeared Radacheck, Pelegrino, and O'Malley, who stared grimly at our shivering bodies and merry, slightly insane faces. That didn't stop them from taking our statements together, separately, and repeatedly. Then they sent us to Cook County Hospital. I had been there only a few days earlier, I remembered, at the start of this quest to find Tom Woods' killer.

After a nurse took care of our minor abrasions, Seth and Jackson transported us back to the comforts of the Balboa Arms Hotel. They had called Sam who managed to prepare a repast of burritos and brandy that was waiting for us when we settled in our room with our saviors.

"How did you ever find us?" Dorothy asked, still astonished that we had escaped.

"That was Dish," said Jackson. "We were keeping an eye on the Brewery to protect ourselves from further retaliation. Maybe pick up some dirt we could bargain with. Centeno don't give up, no matter what the cops think. Dish saw you two enter that Stables building, as you call it, but not come out. And then Dish saw Affazzi and called me; the rest is history. A few of the boys joined us in some constructive recreation. I can't say I recommend stoning an evil man as the proper moral lesson. But that's what was called for, and that's what we did."

"No argument from us," I said with a smile. "Too bad you didn't wait a minute, though. Affazzi was about to tell me his plans for the grain scam. He believed me, didn't he, Dorothy?"

"Take this guy back to the barge," Dorothy exclaimed, throwing a pillow at me. "Remember Affazzi said the only reason he would tell us was because we were going to die, big guy!"

I started to say something and then realized there was nothing more to say.

We talked and drank brandy for another thirty minutes. It was good to be alive, warm, and slightly anesthetized.

Finally, I said, "Case closed. Thank you, and goodbye."

They filed out with no argument, leaving what was left of the brandy.

Dorothy and I embraced, not saying anything, but holding on as tightly as we could. We knew we were lucky, and lucky to have such friends.

Then we slept and slept.

CHAPTER 24

▼

"DEVEREAUX ANNOUNCES TDD INQUIRY." "FUGITIVE SPECULA-TOR ESCAPES."

The headlines greeted us when we opened the newspapers that Sam had sent up with a carafe of freshly brewed decaf. The hawk had risen during the night, rattling the loose wooden frames of the windows overlooking Balboa Street and the Hotel Continental. The cold mantle of Siberia settled on the city of big shoulders. It was time to get out of town.

"Can't we have real coffee?" Dorothy objected. "I need something to get me in the swing of things after our death cruise. Or is this what life with Spivak is really about? Half awake? Living dangerously on one percent?"

I grunted, my nose in the Bugle. Dorothy hissed, blew a kiss, and headed for the shower. Delaney's editorial congratulated Devereaux for his political courage in publicly acknowledging the deficiencies of the TDD program with which he was so closely associated. "Devereaux is a true Chicagoan." Yeah. Delaney, bless his two-faced heart, also congratulated the tenacity of Seth Greenburg and the Center for Neighborhood Options for their investigative vigilance about TDDs during the past year. I was sure that Seth would explode when he read this back-handed connection linking him to Devereaux's political charade.

Articles in both papers expended extra column inches on the disappearance of Affazzi, concluding that he was ultimately responsible for four deaths and the plague of TDD corruption that had settled in Chicago. N&M was discovered to be a front corporation with Affazzi being its only principal, with unknown but no doubt scurrilous backers providing the cash. The FBI launched a national man-hunt for Affazzi and the trail of money and influence.

Most of the quotes in the articles were from Lieutenant O'Malley and Barry Greico, as the spokesperson for Alderman Devereaux. They painted a picture of intrigue, underhanded dealings, and public deception—all reasons why so many smart, well-intentioned, committed Chicago leaders and public servants fell captive to N&M's machinations. Of course, this pervasive evil left everybody off the hook, except those who had been killed because of Affazzi.

There was no mention of Jackson, Sam, Dorothy, or me, or for that matter, the Reverend Lee Sampson and UPC.

"Well, we're clean," I said, slightly irritated.

"I'm clean," Dorothy countered, walking towards me from the shower in a towel. "You still smell like a rusty bolt."

"Right! I'll shower in a moment, dear. My point is that the papers left us alone."

"And that's it?" Dorothy asked.

"For now."

I must have sounded pouty because Dorothy teased, "Don't you like being a lone ranger? The man behind the scenes? The magic touch from Baltimore?"

"A few minutes more and I would have understood the grain scam," I complained, deciding to share my feelings, at least some of them. "That would have been worth the wait, don't you think?"

Dorothy grabbed the paper out of my hands and glared as she sat down, wrapped in an odd but provocative combination of towels.

"Nick, that is really stupid. Don't you get it yet how close we came to getting killed? Affazzi wasn't kidding. He was going to shoot us. I was more scared than I have ever been in my life, and so were you. So, why keep talking about grain scams?"

"Okay, you're right, I guess. But I'm always on to the next round, the loose ends."

"How about waiting a week?" Dorothy sighed. "Let's enjoy life."

I sensed that a moment of truth had arrived.

"What are we going to do, Nick? About us?"

"I don't know."

"Is that all?"

"You mean I have to figure it out?"

"No. But aren't you the detective?"

"Nobody in their right mind would trust me to chart a course for love, for life. Disaster!"

"Well, then we'll have to do it together."

"That's common practice."

"No lip," she said. "Not yet."

"What are the choices?" I asked. "No, that's the old Nick. Let me try again. Seriously, I love you and want to make something of this." The voice that didn't sound like mine.

"This?"

"Us."

"Me, too"

"The problems are time and place. Baltimore or Milwaukee? No Chicago for a time. Sooner or later? Formal or informal? Take your pick."

"I don't have a job anymore," Dorothy admitted. "I forgot to tell you, given all the fun and excitement.

"What happened?" I asked, guiltily happy that Dorothy had become jobless.

"Chalk one more up to the long arm of Mr. Affazzi. They will pay me to go away and keep my mouth shut."

"You ought to send them these headlines and ask for a better severance package."

"Is that the right thing to do?" Dorothy asked.

"No, I would spill the beans. Don't sign anything. It will only put you in the line of fire. Have a talk with Radachek and the FBI."

"So, you can see, there's not much left for me in Milwaukee. No job, no family, and then there's you," Dorothy smiled.

"So let's make it Baltimore, sooner, and together," I said, drawing her close.

"It's a deal" she hugged back.

"Wait," I said, pulling back and looking into her wonderful green eyes. "I'm all for impulsive acts, particularly with you, but they've been getting me in trouble the last few years—with women, gangbangers, and Chicago pols. Maybe we should have counseling, wait two days, or toss a coin? No, not a coin, I am sure of that!"

"Spivak, are you afraid?" Dorothy asked.

"Yes."

"Good. I am, too. That's the best way!"

Seth arose, slightly drunk, to make a speech. He tried to compose a serious face. He hit a water glass with his cigarette lighter and the room quieted.

"Spivak has again showed all Chicagoans that he is a big time guy," Seth slurred, beginning his speech.

There was laughter.

"Right down to the last piles of scrap metal. He's put himself and others—especially loved ones—in harm's way in pursuit of the truth," Seth said, looking at Dorothy. More laughs.

"It is therefore my honor to present Spivak with 'The Pit Award,' granted every so often to a mad soul in search of the genie that has driven Chicago's obsession with growth and expansion ever since the last campfire of Father Marquette."

He handed me a small box of cornflakes.

"May Mr. Spivak's grain hypothesis, as we have come to revere it, live for eternity." Now there was infectious laughter.

I blushed. Dorothy reached over and held my hand.

Clapping and laughter filled the 250 square feet of El Torta's super-compressed dining area, including the six counter stools. Jacinto had closed down El Torta to outside customers at 3 PM to host the private celebration and going-away party for Dorothy and me. He served all his specialties, with accompanying bottles of mescal and Negra Modelo. It was a small party in a small place. Most of the cast of characters showed up. Even Alex agreed to escort his fiancée Helen Trent. Sam played host.

Reverend Alphonius Jackson called in his regrets when I first arrived. SIA was launching an action on the public housing authority and he had to mobilize his congregations and prepare for his role in this community theatre. We thanked each other.

Seth threw himself into a chair at our table after the awards ceremony. He started to put his feet up on the table but then thought better of it as he caught a nasty look from Jacinto.

"Devereaux called," he said matter-of-factly.

"Offer you a job?" I teased. It caught Seth's attention.

"Watch it, Spivak. I can take back those cornflakes."

"So what did he want?"

"He asked me to sit on the Commission overseeing the TDD inquiry."

"Smart guy. Worried about being accused of a cover-up. That won't help his mayoral dreams. He needs to look crispy clean. So, what was your answer?"

Seth suddenly seemed quite sober.

"I made him an offer with three conditions. Drop Sampson from the campaign. Stay away from the Commission's hearings. And call off Delaney. No more media pressure."

"And?"

"He told me to go to hell. Said I'd missed a big chance to be relevant and change the world."

"Good for you."

"Then Delaney called, ranting and raving about how I was under the influence of outside agitators like Spivak who didn't give a shit about Chicago. He even called you an ideological hack."

"What's that?" Dorothy asked giggling.

"Somebody who talks too much," Seth replied.

"So did you defend my honor, my reputation in Chicago, my grain hypothesis?"

"No way. I agreed with him and said I didn't listen to half of your shit anyway, including the stuff about grain."

"I knew you were a disbeliever," I said.

"Me and the people," Seth replied, laughing.

We paused as Jacinto passed a plate of chile rellenos. I saw Sergeant Radachek knocking at the front door, thankfully without his two sidekicks. This was a pleasant surprise. Jacinto let him in, and Radachek walked up to our table and stuck out his paw.

"Spivak, I gotta hand it to ya. You stuck with it. And we got the bad guys, most of them anyway. Your friend Woods would be proud. You're a good friend."

We shook hands, tears in my eyes. Radachek was intimately involved in the Woods' case from day one, more so than anyone else.

"What about Affazzi?" Seth asked. "Any sightings?"

"Nothing so far," Radachek frowned.

"Have a drink, Sarge," I said. He took a glass of mescal and threw it back.

"Be careful with that," Seth counseled, an unusual moment of sensitivity from a committed drinker.

"Fuck O'Malley, etcetera, etcetera," Radachek replied, already slurring slightly. "He's got his ass in the screws again for letting the Woods case go to hell. That means letting you upstage the Chicago Police Department. I heard O'Malley's slated to head up the downtown foot patrol."

Radachek headed for the door. "Next time, Spivak."

Seth and I exchanged glances. "There's somebody who appreciates me."

"Yeah, after the fact. That's great."

"He supported you all along," Seth said. "Maybe you didn't see what he was doing."

"So, what's next," I asked Seth, steering back to our former conversation.

Seth opened his rumpled tan suede coat and pulled out the latest issue of *Street News* from his vest pocket, the paper written and distributed by Chicago's homeless. The front-page headline read, "***DEVEREAUX AND AFFAZZI LINKED***," by Seth Greenburg and Max Vargas, the editor, writer, printer, and distribution coordinator. The gist of the article was the story of N&M, the Sheik, Sampson, and Devereaux. No slimy detail was left unsaid. Seth had followed up with Martin Kelly of the Civic Budget Commission and learned about the discrepancy between TDD bonds sold and the dollars deposited. Seth's preliminary conclusion was the N&M was skimming a substantial amount of TDD dollars and investing them somewhere else. Maybe in the futures market, although Seth wouldn't go that far. Affazzi hoped to make a killing and return the money with interest. That was the optimistic story. It didn't work out so well, but it gave some legs to my grain hypothesis.

An editorial by Vargas called for Devereaux's resignation from everything having to do with the investment of public dollars, particularly in real estate development. No much left to do for the head of the City Council Finance Committee. It concluded by summarily declaring Devereaux's mayoral campaign dead before arrival. "There's no dignity in Devereaux," he signed off.

"Bravo," I toasted. "I hope someone is listening to the tinkle of penknives being drawn."

"Don't worry yourself, Spivak. We've got more than penknives," Seth replied. "I taped two TV interviews this morning. And I have a talk show after today's grand finale, when we declare Spivak, once again, a Chicagoan missing in action. MIA in Baltimore."

###

0-595-31476-7

Printed in the United States
24197LVS00005B/248